THE UNTAMED DUKE

The Secret Crusaders, Book 3

Melanie Rose Clarke

ARE YOU SIGNED UP FOR DRAGONBLADE'S BLOG?

You'll get the latest news and information on exclusive giveaways, exclusive excerpts, coming releases, sales, free books, cover reveals and more.

Check out our complete list of authors, too!

No spam, no junk. That's a promise!

Sign Up Here

www.dragonbladepublishing.com

Dearest Reader;

Thank you for your support of a small press. At Dragonblade Publishing, we strive to bring you the highest quality Historical Romance from some of the best authors in the business. Without your support, there is no 'us', so we sincerely hope you adore these stories and find some new favorite authors along the way.

Happy Reading!

CEO, Dragonblade Publishing

Additional Dragonblade books by Author Melanie Rose Clarke

The Secret Crusaders Series
Escaping the Duke (Book 1)
Captured by the Earl (Book 2)
The Untamed Duke (Book 3)

For my beautiful grandmother, Katie, and in loving memory of my grandparents Bea, Bunny, Larry and Elizabeth. I will forever remember the smiles, laughter and love. You are always in my heart.

CHAPTER ONE

The Private Diary of Sophia Hawkins

The Untamed Duke has returned. He slipped back into London last night, a predator present but unseen, lurking from afar. I anticipated his arrival with excitement, eschewing the fear others would expect. Fear would show weakness, vulnerability already assigned based on my gender. I am not defined by what others believe. The man who would harm my brother will face a challenge as he has never known.

I will claim victory.

"WHO IS HE?"

"Where did he come from?"

"He is extraordinary."

Yes, he was.

The questions came from every corner, whispered behind bejeweled fans, hissed under tightly clutched dance cards, glistening in fervent eyes. They were a tangle of debutante's whispers, matchmaking mama's hisses, eager swain's bemoans, each desperate to solve the night's grand mystery. The man's exact features were protected by a gleaming obsidian disguise, covered in onyx, sapphire and deception. Would midnight's strike solve the mystery, the identity behind emerald eyes? Perhaps. Yet for her, it was unnecessary.

She knew who he was.

Massive. Powerful. Muscular. Controlling. Dominant. But most of all...

Dangerous.

A hundred ladies watched him. A thousand voices whispered his praises. Assessing. Calculating. Desiring. Lady Sophia Hawkins, sister to the Duke of Bradenton, would admit to the first two, never the last, as she lifted the cut crystal goblet of fruit punch to her lips. It was cool and refreshing as it slid down her throat, a welcome foil to the sweltering warmth a perfect crush always inspired.

Despite its balminess, the Colesworth Masquerade was spectacular. Lit by hundreds of candles nestled in cascades of crystal, the ballroom was a storybook come to life, with whimsical paintings brushed on every gilded wall. The ceiling was high and domed, held by columns and curves reminiscent of an ancient temple. The refreshments were just a sampling of the evening's seven-course meal, yet the display dominated an entire corner, piles of steaming delicacies, interspersed with fruits painted by nature's hand.

Garbed in finery, crowned by decorated masks, the guests sparkled as brightly as their surroundings. They danced to a perfectly timed waltz, performed by masters of pitch and harmony. Gracious laughter and boisterous conversation punctuated every note, from the crowd watching the crowd watching the crowd. Yet there was no one the crowd watched more than the mysterious lord.

"He is the finest specimen of man I have ever seen. No mask could hide such handsome features." Lady Constance Welleby's hushed whisper reached far more than the half dozen debutantes who leaned their tightly corseted bodies forward. Dramatic perhaps, yet her assessment was not incorrect.

Coal black hair shimmered under the lights, dark and gleaming, so rich it invited a woman to run her hands through it, to ascertain if it was truly as thick as it appeared. He towered over almost everyone, his shoulders broad, his chest expansive, his power evident by the muscles that strained the crisp black suit. He was dominance defined, this man who took control.

The man who hunted her family.

Lady Constance fanned herself, gazing at the scribbles on the back of her dance card. "I am waiting to be introduced so he may reserve a dance."

"Do not raise your hopes." Lady Hannah let her own fan dangle limply on her wrist. "He has not danced a set all night, and he resists all attempts at conversation. Both lords and ladies have approached him, yet he grants few words."

"Yet not severely enough for the cut direct." Constance swatted her fan lightly towards Hannah, her bright smile belying any animosity. "Not all of us hide from our suitors. Although you weren't able to avoid them all, I see."

Hannah drew her dance card against her skirt, concealing the offending name. It was unnecessary. Everyone knew Michael Colborne, the Duke of Crawford, played unrelenting suitor to the reluctant debutante.

Such was not something Sophia would ever tolerate. "His identity will be well-known by the end of the night." His anonymity was not a purposeful secret, simply an artifact of his recent arrival, obscuring mask and distaste for words. Yet sooner or later, someone would whisper his name, then that whisper would crash over the guests like the waves of the ocean. Overexcited debutantes and eager mamas would battle to capture the ducal prize. Yet to her, he was an enemy.

And she didn't even know why.

"He's watching you."

Sophia twisted so quickly, the fruit punch sloshed in the glass, just missing her pale blush dress, before splashing onto the swirling marble table. A great save indeed, as her mother would have lamented the ruination of the gown that perfectly complemented her blond curls and sapphire eyes.

"I'm certain it just looks that way..." She pivoted and *froze*.

His gaze pierced her, raw scrutiny blazing with determination and purpose. It challenged her, dared her to stand against the warrior in gentleman's clothing. Motives remained unknown, yet his goal burned clear. Victory.

"He *is* looking at you." Hannah's voice was low, concerned. Unlike whimsical Constance, she would not imagine attention that didn't exist. "He hasn't moved."

No, he hasn't. Suddenly thirsty, Emma grasped her drink, tilted it to her lips.

His gaze tightened.

Sweetness soured her stomach. She shifted in deliberate slowness, replacing the glass on the table, and jutting up her chin. He thought he could intimidate her? She glared.

The corners of his mouth quirked up.

"My goodness." Constance fanned herself with the golden edged fan, her wrist flicking in a blur. "You've quite caught his eye."

Whatever his interest, it was not her appearance. She attracted her fair share of suitors, yet the ton was rife with lovely ladies, whom he had not afforded but a moment's glance. She was not his true target.

She'd waited weeks, and then months, for his return. Of course, Edmund had succinctly forbidden her from approaching, talking or otherwise communicating with the man, stopping only short of inhabiting the same planet as him. Of course she had nodded her agreement. Of course she had no intention of actually obeying.

She supposed she should consider herself lucky. Edmund had kept her two younger sisters in the country this season, with their aunt. Of course, her sisters would much rather be running among the trees, and truthfully, so would she.

Now was her chance. Usually Edmund watched her like a mama bear her cubs, yet he was off addressing a "situation." Clearly the matter was urgent, yet when she'd asked, Bradenton had not wanted to bother her with *gentlemen's* business. For once, his overprotective nature provided the perfect opportunity.

"He's moving." Constance's eyes grew wide. She pointed a trembling finger weighted with sapphires and diamonds.

"Towards us."

Light gasps punctuated excited chatter, as the ladies puffed, preened and pranced. Gowns were straightened, hair smoothed, lips plumped. That it would be inappropriate for them to converse without having been properly introduced no longer mattered, as their numbers and the sheer allure of the man swept aside any and all considerations.

Sophia stood frozen, even as he strode through the ballroom, his boots echoing against the hard floor in synchrony to the heart slamming against her chest. She sucked in a breath of heavily perfumed air, straightened as tall as her petite stature allowed. If he thought to challenge her, he would learn, she was far more powerful than any *man* believed.

The crowd hushed around them, as secretive glances transformed to blatant stares. The ladies stopped moving, yet through it all, his gaze never wavered. He stared directly at her, asserting his authority, seizing power over any who would dare defy him. Then he was right above her.

He. Was. Massive.

In her memory's eye, he hadn't been this large, this powerful, this determined. He stood a head above her, wearing the guise of an aristocrat, yet there was nothing domesticated about him. The scent of amber and bergamot tested her senses, enveloping, possessing, as he delved just a hairsbreadth from scandalous.

"Lady Sophia, so good to see you again." His voice was deep and strong, with a slight Scottish tilt that warmed her insides like a crackling hearth on a winter day.

Small gasps rose like breaking waves. She hadn't wanted to admit she knew this man, or that they had, in actuality, been properly introduced.

He reached for her. Like the rest of him, his hand was large and powerful, tanned from the sun. "Dance with me."

It was a command, not a request, an order, not a question. Inappropriate most definitely, scandalous, perhaps, for there was no semblance of an offer in the confident words. Had it not been the perfect opportunity to further her goals, she would have denied him in an instant, with a beautiful cut direct that would have stunned the ton. Yet she would not relinquish the opportunity to learn more about this man.

"I would be most honored." She slipped her hand into his warm one, and for a moment, it seemed she was offering more than mere minutes. Instinctively, she pulled her hand back, yet he did not relinquish his hold.

She was captured.

"Is this how you assume power?" she whispered, as he led her to a gleaming dance floor. It was a waltz, and his arms tightened all around her, stealing her senses and blocking her vision. "You command others to heed your wishes?"

"I have no need to command." His voice was low and dark, as he studied her with a thoroughness that defied every shield she dared erect. Suddenly her corset was way too tight, its knotted laces stealing her breath. "I take what is mine."

The musicians' melody pierced the air in an explosion of notes, and then they were in motion. His hold did not loosen, as she swirled and twirled, caught in the maelstrom of a single man. She fought for air in a tight throat. "Clearly you refer not to me, Your Grace, as we barely know each other."

"Indeed?" he murmured. "Yet you did not hesitate to dance with me just now. As usual, no one is watching you properly."

Red edged into her vision. "If you have not noticed, I am a grown woman."

His lips curved upward. "I noticed."

Her heart took a pause, then restarted at thrice normal speed. "As an adult, I do not need watching."

"I disagree." He edged closer, bringing his power, and his heat. It seeped under her clothing, dampening the skin underneath. "Were you under my care, I would not allow you to dance with strangers bearing covert plans."

Covert plans? His hatred of her brother was undisguised, yet his actions towards her were far more clandestine. "Your schemes have no bearing on me. I will dance with whomever I wish."

"Not anymore, you won't." His fingers tightened ever-so-slightly. "Your watchers have neglected you for too long. I plan to correct the situation."

How. Dare. He. "You have no power over me. I only agreed to this dance because of your threats. You will cease your hostility towards my family immediately."

"Careful, my dear," he whispered. "The ton is watching. We wouldn't want them seeing you upset."

For once, he was correct. The gossipmongers already had enough fodder with their unlikely dance. She could scarce afford more. "Most people think you are a suitable, if not enviable match. They believe you to be a gentleman."

"Are you insinuating I am not a gentleman?"

In official terms, he was indeed a gentleman, his title unarguably legitimate, his inheritance legally and properly conveyed. His father had been a duke, and he was the eldest son. Yet, underneath, he was anything but civilized. "A title does not make a gentleman."

He leaned just a little closer than proper. "You may be right."

She swallowed. Every challenge she flung, he rearranged to his benefit, before pitching it back with knifelike precision. With every note, she grew closer to the dance's conclusion, and with it, her opportunity to discover the truth. "Why not focus on the many debutantes vying for your attention? Most men enjoy the benefits granted by their position and..." She waved her hand. "Other attributes."

"Other attributes?"

She gestured once more towards his long, well-muscled body. "You know."

"I do not know." His astute expression belied every word. "Would you be so kind to explain?"

"Even you must be aware of your qualities." Specifically, he possessed the body of a Greek God. Not one of the minor ones, but the one who ruled everything, or perhaps the one who was the strongest of them all. Possibly the one who carried the world on his shoulders. In any case, he could not be ignorant of his attributes, or that every woman in London noticed.

No doubt he was being intentionally difficult. "If you wish for diversion, pursue the thousands of ladies eager to be the next Duchess of Foxworth."

"Thousands?" His gaze was unwavering. "There are scarcely that many in attendance."

"You have far more admirers than fit in these walls." It was true. The guests may not know his identity behind the mask, however the ton was well-aware of the new Duke of Foxworth. A handsome, wealthy duke was every debutante's dream, every matchmaking mama's fantasy. "Focus on your countless pursuers and leave my brother and me alone."

"I cannot do that." He pulled her closer, as heat flared, as iron muscles took control. "Once I commence a pursuit, I do not rest until I am victorious. I'm not nearly done with Bradenton–" He lowered his gaze. "Or you."

Her breath caught. What was he pursuing?

Or was it whom?

"You needn't worry about my romantic endeavors." He spun her closer. "I already have the perfect duchess in mind."

Another inexplicable burst of emotion electrified her. "That does not surprise me. No doubt you will be endlessly possessive and overprotective." Her brother was the same, although he'd softened somewhat since his match with Priscilla. This man, she imagined, would never waver.

"I'll admit I'm possessive." The dance picked up speed. "I care for what is mine."

Mine? He couldn't possibly believe– She stood taller, even as she reached only his chest. Clearly, he was trying to distract her. "Why do you hate my brother?"

A sliver of surprise shone, before it melted away. "What makes you believe I hate your brother?"

"Do not play coy with me," she hissed. "Your animosity is

clear for all to see. You tried to engage him months ago, before you were called to Scotland. Now you've returned, and your quarrel is just as strong. Why do you seek revenge against a man you don't even know?"

"I may not know the celebrated Duke of Bradenton, but I am well acquainted with his actions," he growled lowly. "My disagreement with your brother does not concern you."

"How can you say that?" She brushed against him, as he decreased their distance. "Why are you dancing with me?"

He hesitated, even as he spun her. When they exited the curve, he bent down. "I am dancing with you *despite* your brother. You cannot escape me, Lady Sophia." Fiery heat enveloped her. "Do not even try."

Around her, the world blurred, centering on the gentleman warrior who would dare assert control. It should have brought fury, terror and frustration, yet the previous two were succinctly absent. The third was present in copious amounts, yet other unbidden emotions overshadowed it: Exhilaration. Anticipation. *Excitement.*

"Not. Your. Choice." She flexed her fingers, as the musicians quickened their pace. Soon she would escape. "You have everything a man could ever want: a title, wealth, admiration. Already ladies are pursuing you, and the guests do not yet know you are a duke. Although I imagine that is changing rapidly." The audience now pointed at them, an ever-increasing number deciphering his identity. Soon all would know the mysterious man as Kenneth Macleod, the new Duke of Foxworth. Then the matchmaking frenzy would truly begin.

"They see the duke, not the man." For a mere sliver in time, he sounded ill at ease, before his control snapped back into place. "I am forever bound to a title I abhor."

How could he be anything but exuberant? A duke's life was filled with privilege, lived atop a golden pedestal by the sole virtue of a fortunate birth. "Most men would do anything for a title, yet you are the opposite. Of course, you are something all on your own." She clamped her mouth shut. She had not meant to share that.

"Indeed?" The slightest tint of amusement entered his voice. "What exactly is something?"

Uncivilized. Dangerous. Tempting.

She would never admit such traitorous thoughts. No doubt he would take every mistaken admission and use it for his own purposes. "Difficult, volatile and exasperating."

He shrugged. "That is a reasonable assessment."

What was wrong with him? Most men were aghast, angry even, when she showed her more spirited facets. It was a splendid strategy for discouraging unwanted suitors. "Aren't you incensed?"

"Why would I be? It is a fair calculation." Danger lurked in his eyes, hidden yet present. "Am I not responding the way you hoped?" Now he made no attempt to hide his amusement. "Your efforts to aggravate me are failing spectacularly."

Yes, they were. "Explain the grievance you have with my family."

He regarded her carefully. This was not a man who acted rashly, or without thought. It made him all the more dangerous. "Our family has a past that must be remedied. My interaction with you is a separate entity, and perhaps unwise, if one were to worry about unintended warnings to one's foes." His gaze sharpened. "Yet I find the reward quite worth the risk."

His words tangled in her mind. What role could he possibly see for her? "Of what past ills do you speak?"

"That, my lady, is between your brother and me."

"I think not." She forced her expression to remain neutral, on a dance floor as much a stage as any London theater. "Tell me, Your Grace, do you believe ladies should be protected from anything more dangerous than the prick of a sewing needle?"

"Absolutely not."

"Then why–"

"A sewing needle is far too dangerous for the fairer gender."

"I see." She scraped her fingers against the fine fabric of his suit. It was luxurious, supple and all-too-tempting, just like him. "If I didn't know better, Your Grace, I'd think you were trying to get a reaction from me."

"You are quite ravishing when angry. However, if you prefer I shall endeavor to arouse other emotions."

Heat flared, as he *aroused* other emotions.

Hard muscles rippled under her fingers. "I wish I could be more forthcoming, yet I must hold my secrets close if I am to accomplish my goals, at least until the path is set."

Her stomach lurched, even as his hold solidified, as if he recognized her unease and steadied her. Every iteration brought her closer to him. "I have two goals, which I previously thought conflicted. Now I realize they converge perfectly."

"I imagine I will not like either." She matched each step with one of her own. "What are these goals?"

"The first regards your brother."

"You admit it," she breathed. "You seek revenge against the wrong man. Edmund hadn't even met you before your recent arrival."

In an instant, his entire countenance changed. Unabashed fury lit his eyes, apparent even under the mask. It sparked unease and alarm, yet not for herself. Somehow instincts still insisted this man was no threat to her.

"You have no idea of the pain Bradenton wrought." His eyes darkened. "There will be retribution."

"How dare you threaten my family." She inhaled anger, exhaled courage, defying the urge to shout her fury. "Are you planning to call out my brother?"

For the briefest of moments his eyes widened. For once, her abruptness had surprised him.

"I considered it."

Her heart skipped a beat, as unease changed to raw fear. Her brother was an honorable man, and would let no challenge go unanswered. "I will not allow it."

"It is perilous to place yourself in two men's quarrel." A muscle ticked in his jaw. "Your habit of confronting danger stops now."

Who was this man who thought he commanded her? "Do you intend to challenge Edmund?"

He took a moment to answer, as they soared through the dance, in perfect synchrony. "No. As furious as I am, I am not a man who resorts to violence, unless no other choice exists. I know where such impulsiveness leads."

Relief loosened her muscles.

"Yet justice must be attained."

She missed another step. What was wrong with her? She was acting like a debutante on her first day of dance lessons, stumbling through steps she had known for years. "I shall thwart whatever you have planned."

His lips curved into a humorless smile. "You do not have the power to stop me."

He had no idea of the power *she* wielded. "You claim Edmund wronged your family, yet you reveal no details. You promise revenge, yet you refuse to share your mysterious retribution. You, sir, are trying to scare me."

"I have no desire to frighten you." His gaze didn't waver. "Bradenton took something irreplaceable from me. I plan to do the same to him."

"What could you possibly take–"

A commotion sounded from the corner of the room, and she turned. Edmund had entered, followed by Priscilla, and as usual, the crowd descended upon the golden couple. Her brother greeted people, even as he searched the room, no doubt looking for her.

It was obvious the moment he saw her. His eyes flashed, his lips etched a deep frown. Displeasure turned to anger, and anger to fury. He strode towards them.

Their time was nearly at an end, yet Foxworth paid no heed. "I shall steal one of his most precious possessions."

She followed his gaze back to her sister-in-law. Her breath caught in her throat. "You plan to harm Priscilla?"

"Of course not." His deep rumble was aghast. "I don't plan to harm anyone, and most certainly not her. I would never upset a woman in her condition."

"A woman in her condition?" Sophia blinked. "You don't mean—" She stopped, breathed. That she'd almost blurted out personal matters in the middle of Lord Colesworth's ballroom was proof of this man's tumultuous effect. "Even if it's true, how could you know something like that?"

"I notice things."

Conversation rumbled louder, as Edmund neared. She had only seconds before he arrived, and she hadn't garnered anything of use. "If Priscilla isn't your target, then who is?"

"Are you certain you want to know?"

She nodded.

"As you wish." He pulled her closer, capturing her nearly flush against his tall, powerful body. Heat flamed, as he whispered, "I plan to use his—"

"Sister." Edmund Hawkins, the Duke of Bradenton, sliced through the conversation, his voice sharpened with pure fury. He pierced Foxworth with the blade of his gaze, then reached for her. "I'm cutting in."

Sophia had no choice but to accept her brother's intrusion, releasing one powerful man for another. Behind the mask, Foxworth's eyes were a green wall, while her brother's were stiff and grim. Around them the conversation quieted, as the ton got a second act to their now three-person play.

Foxworth bowed. "Thank you for the dance, Lady Sophia. We shall finish it later." He turned towards the duke, and his eyes hardened into emerald shards. "We will speak soon, Bradenton."

"That is a certainty."

Edmund put his arm around her, launching a hushed lecture likely to last into the night and beyond, yet the words melted together. Foxworth stole her focus as he cut a path through the dance floor, even as the guests whispered his name. With his identity now known, the crowd savored their elucidation, yet a single question burned:

What had he planned?

"ARE YOU GOING to challenge Bradenton?"

Kenneth straightened his 6'3 frame, shifting in the too-small seat of the too-small carriage as it rolled over the too-small streets. He inhaled a deep breath of smoke the exclusive street couldn't quite hide, a taste of the world the ton pretended didn't exist. Most would adore the outrageously priced coach, as if it captured some measure of success, yet to him its value was measured in the good that money could have provided others. He would have much preferred ride on horse, anyways, limited only by the endless fields of Scotland and the stars above, than be ensconced in the coach like some pampered aristocrat. "That is the second time someone asked me that tonight."

Adam Edgewater, the Duke of Huntington and Kenneth's cousin, stretched his long legs in front of him. He wore a dark mask similar to Kenneth's and carried a large book in his hands, before tucking both into his coat. They shared a set of grandparents, yet were as different as the highlands of Scotland to the streets of London, both in appearance and temperament. With his fair hair and light blue eyes, Adam possessed an almost angelic appearance, calm and ever-poised, while Kenneth inherited his mother's dark features and the passion of the Scottish highlands.

Kenneth had not known Adam before his father's demise, yet he was grateful for the relation now. Adam was one of the few lords he respected, and more importantly, trusted.

"Do you have an answer?" For the briefest of instances, concern shone in his cousin's eyes, eliciting unexpected satisfaction.

Kenneth sobered. He could not afford to let his new position make him soft, not when he had a quest to complete. "Of course I am not going to call him out."

It shouldn't matter that so many people assumed he'd happily lodge a bullet in another man's chest. He'd only recently become *good ton*, a deceiving moniker indeed, yet he'd always considered himself honorable. Even if Bradenton's actions justified a duel, he would not deprive a lady of her brother, and another her husband.

"Glad to hear it." Adam sat back with a sigh. "In the ton, scandal is always a hairsbreadth away. Of course, any action affects the entire family."

Kenneth grimaced deeply, loosening the noose masquerading as a cravat. Wretched thing choked him all night. "I am all too aware of the consequences the family would endure should scandal arise. Such concerns temper my every action."

"Yet you wish for vengeance."

"Of course I wish for vengeance." He clenched his fists, looking away from his cousin. Outside the street was dark and dank, grimy with animal droppings and far worse. So different than the lush green expanses of his home land. "My family is forever changed because of his actions."

"You never met your father." Adam leaned forward. "You had no interest in the English side of your family."

"I knew nothing about him." Kenneth's fingernails dug into the buttery seat. "It does not mean I wished the man dead."

"Of course not." Adam's voice softened. "Yet you inherited a dukedom. Most would consider it the rarest and most splendid of luck. You are now wealthy beyond compare, endlessly lauded and inordinately powerful."

"I was already wealthy and powerful." It was no boast, but merely a telling of fact. His mother's family possessed vast lands and deep fortunes, ever-increasing due to his gift for management. They were powerful and well-respected, not only throughout Scotland, but also England, before he knew he was related to a duke.

Before he *was* a duke.

"Now you possess more power and wealth. Scores of ladies are vying for your attention, and everyone wants to celebrate the newly appointed Duke of Foxworth. Enjoy it."

He did not need people applauding a position and wealth he hadn't earned. "You are also a duke. Do you enjoy the marriage mart?"

Adam shrugged. "Not the matchmaking, naturally, but the choice of diamonds of the first water? I cannot say it is not an advantage."

"Yet you have not chosen."

Adam sat back on the luxurious seat. "In all due time, cousin. And you are one to talk. Unless you have made a decision without informing me."

The carriage tumbled over a dip in the road, yet Kenneth stayed perfectly still, silent to his cousin's inquiry. To be successful, one must take bumps stoically, turning them into advantages.

"Have you someone in mind already?" Adam's gaze turned curious. "All the more reason to discard your quest for revenge, lest it interfere with your pursuit. Tell me, who is the lucky lady who snagged the attention of the mysterious duke?"

Not for an instant did Kenneth consider revealing the truth. "You have my highest respect, cousin, for your kindness these past months, yet I will keep my secrets a little while longer." He lightened the words with a nod.

Kenneth's eyes took on a strange light. "It is a mystery, then. I hope you do not mind, but I shall continue to wonder. Solving mysteries is something of a hobby of mine."

Kenneth inclined his head. His cousin may try, yet he was unlikely to discover the truth.

Not before it rocked the entire ton.

CHAPTER TWO

Journal of the Duke of Foxworth:

The time has arrived.

Finally, I will realize vengeance over the man who shattered our lives. He will live every day with the same pain I endure, knowing something precious was stolen by the man he hates most. Of course, his loss shall be temporary, yet he will always remember I had her, if just for a little while.

I cannot wait.

"I HAVE WONDERFUL news."

Priscilla Livingston, the Duchess of Bradenton, did not look like she had good news. She quite resembled a cat who had bitten into a ripe orange only to discover it was a lemon in disguise. An extra-sour one. "If you read the *London Daily News*, you know the measure on orphans' rights passed. With your hard work, hundreds of children will see their lives improve. Congratulations."

The ladies smiled and clapped. And Priscilla?

Still the lemon.

This should have been a glorious day. Not only had they achieved the favorable vote for orphans' rights, but one of their own, Emma Sinclair, had just become betrothed to her earl. She'd actually already been unofficially betrothed, well, not really, yet that was a different story.

The sky burned a bright yellow outside the wide windows of the stylish mauve-colored drawing room. Little blue birds hopped on the sill, dancing on the cool breeze as they chirped the day's news. Orange cookies and banana tarts sweetened the world with their delicious scent, their savory taste evidenced by the rate at which the silver platter emptied.

Could Priscilla's grimness have anything to do with Foxworth? Of course, Edmund was furious with the duke's reemergence, chasing the record for the longest lecture ever uttered on planet Earth. Afterwards he forbade her from seeing him at least fifty-seven times.

Priscilla continued in a monotone tone, even as few noticed in the joyful post-vote atmosphere. "Our next effort is not a vote, yet it is just as critical. It is no secret that many women are mistreated, leaving emotional and–" She paused. "Physical scars."

Sophia sobered immediately.

"Even under the dubious protection of the law, few are able or willing to escape. We are opening a new sanctuary for women fleeing such situations." Priscilla held the ladies' attention like a soldier. "Of course, this is a problem that transcends class. I am certain you all know women in similar situations."

Gazes hardened and lips pursed, as some glanced at each other, while others studied the floor with ferocity. Priscilla's voice softened. "We shall endeavor to support all women in this situation, whether of the working class or ton, although, of course, our approach will be quite different. Obviously, no sanctuary exists for ladies, yet perhaps we can still help them escape their situations. The first step is convincing them to accept assistance."

"Excuse me, Your Grace?"

Priscilla turned to a petite young woman in the last seat of the last row. Betrothed to a baron, Lady Julia was timid, but lovely, with pale skin, midnight black hair and azure eyes. "Yes, Julia?"

The younger woman colored, averting her eyes. "I'm sorry for interrupting. It is nothing."

Priscilla opened her mouth, yet a series of loud bells chimed, signaling the hour's end. The ladies had numerous commitments, with a schedule rarely of their own making. "We will talk more of this at our next meeting. If you know any in this situation, speak to me in private, and we will do what we can to help."

Sophia rose from the chair, and smoothed her pale green dress, as the ladies slowly drifted out of the room. The moment the last member left, she wasted no time. "What is wrong?"

Priscilla held her gaze, then softly sighed. She rubbed her arms. "Was it that obvious?"

"I'm afraid so." Sophia grasped Priscilla's hand. They had become close these past months, and she considered the duchess another sister. "Is everything well?"

"Not at all." Sophia gazed at the ornate table in the middle of the room. Usually it held the journal where Priscilla recorded their efforts, yet today the wooden pedestal stood empty. "The journal was stolen."

Sophia gasped. The journal contained all the information from the *Distinguished Ladies of Purpose*. It detailed their covert missions, revealing the so-called sewing guild was actually a secret society to advance social action. "Did it contain our names?"

Priscilla hesitated. "Only the initials, but it would be enough."

Sophia exhaled. The ramifications were almost too much to bear. "Whoever took it could ruin us all." She rubbed her forehead, as a burst of pain exploded behind her temples. "Did someone break in the townhome?"

Priscilla shook her head. "I made the grievous error of bringing it to Lord Colesworth's masquerade. With the orphan's vote so close, I wanted to ensure we targeted the right lords. I only put it down for a moment." She clenched her skirts. "At first I thought it was a mistake, that the man who grabbed it didn't know what he took. Yet, by the way he fled, clearly he planned the theft."

Sophia exhaled lowly. "He targeted you."

"Without a doubt."

It meant someone suspected their group's deception, possibly realized the extent of their ruse. Now they possessed proof. "Who was it?"

"I cannot say."

Sophia's breath caught in her throat. Without the thief's identity, they could make no effort to retrieve the journal. "You didn't see him?"

"No. Yes. Sort of." Priscilla clasped her hands tightly. "It was a masquerade. He was wearing a nondescript suit and a full mask. I was across the room when I realized I'd forgotten the book, and before I could catch him, he slipped outside, jumped into his carriage and fled."

No wonder Priscilla had been so distraught. "Were there any clues, any indication who it could have been?"

Priscilla paused, but then slowly nodded. "I didn't get a good look at the man, but I believe I recognized the carriage. I'm not entirely certain, which is why I cannot outright accuse him."

Tempered relief lightened Sophia's chest. Perhaps there was a chance. "That's wonderful. Who was it?"

The name Priscilla whispered vanquished all relief.

"Foxworth."

"WHAT IS YOUR scheme?"

Kenneth relaxed, closing the book. He looked up and smiled.

"Oh goodness, a smile. Now I'm truly fearful."

"There's no need for dramatics." Kenneth stood and walked to the newcomer. He ruffled her curls. "I often smile around you."

The suspicion in his sister's gaze did not lessen as she strolled into the library. With a pale dress some shade of green, she was all feminine grace and delicate movements, so different than the boisterous imp who flitted from garden to garden in Scotland. England had changed her.

It had changed them both.

Clara looked as out of place in the stuffy room as he felt. The large space smelled of leather and wood, with a massive oak desk as a centerpiece and huge shelves with countless books, which he had only just began to peruse.

She circled the room, tracing her fingers along the spines of leather-bound books. "You have been more serious of late. Plotting your vengeance I assume?"

His jaw hardened. Rotten enough his cousin had sensed his plot, but his sister too? Would his grandmother be next to warn him of ill-begotten plans?

"You need not worry about such matters."

She turned. She was so petite, yet her eyes burned with an inner strength that made him proud. He adored her spirit, even as he worried for her safety in a perilous world. He would always protect her.

He had the urge to do the same with another woman.

"Both Bradenton and Priscilla have been kind to me. I will not see either of them harmed."

"I have no intention of harming Priscilla." He tempered his annoyance. "Do you actually think I could hurt a woman?"

"I don't mean physically, of course." Clara frowned as she wandered away from him. "Yet other wounds can be just as damaging. I know you are angry at Bradenton because of..." She took a shaky breath, and he had to stop himself from embracing her. She had chided him the last time he tried.

A moment later, she composed herself. "By circumstances. Yet I wonder if we truly have all the details. No matter the truth, I will not have you mistreating Priscilla, either directly or indirectly in your revenge against Bradenton."

"My revenge will not touch Priscilla," he promised.

"What about the rest of Bradenton's family?"

He paused just long enough to reveal the answer. Her eyes widened, yet before she could speak, he continued, "No one will be irreparably harmed. Lives may be altered, yet some for the better."

The distrust in her eyes deepened. "What could you possibly have plan–"

A discreet scratching rattled the door. "Enter," he boomed before she could interrogate further.

A servant opened the door, standing so straight it was as if the starch he employed on cravats had seeped into his very bones. "Lady Sophia is here to visit."

Emotions flared: Surprise. Suspicion. *Satisfaction*.

He showed none of it as Clara inclined her head. "Of course. Please direct her to the Emerald Room. I shall be there post haste."

"Lady Sophia?" He waited to speak until the servant departed, and they were once again alone. He even managed to keep his voice neutral. "I didn't know you had a visit planned."

"She sent a note this morning." She looked down her nose at him. "She is my friend, which means your nefarious mechanisms cannot include her."

"I would protect her with my life."

That was true.

"I certainly have no nefarious schemes that involve her."

That was only partly true.

His schemes very much involved her, yet they were not nefarious, at least not when it came to her.

Whether she would agree was up for contention.

"Would you like to see her?"

To an extraordinary amount. Yet he must restrain himself, at least for now. Her presence was a mystery, her motives unknown. His sister had mentioned Sophia regularly visited during his absence, yet it must be unusual to come on such short notice. Did she suspect his true plan?

Visiting with his sister would provide little insight into the clever woman's mechanisms, but watching from afar could illuminate the schemes she hid. Perhaps he could discover her secrets while she hunted his. A smile, as genuine as it was rare, curved his lips.

The predator was about to become the prey.

SOPHIA SHIFTED ON a settee as stiff as Lord Dryfus' fifth-favorite cravat. On the outside it was extraordinarily handsome, covered in rich brocade fabric and gleaming embellishments, yet underneath it was as hard and unyielding as iron.

Just like Foxworth.

She forcefully relaxed tight muscles. Focused on the crackling fire in the white marble fireplace, the scent of lilies from the massive display in a cut crystal vase. The room was decorated in shades of emerald, with rich tapestries of rolling Scottish hillsides, wingback chairs swathed in green jacquard and jade-enameled tables. A feast of tea cakes, miniature sandwiches and a full tea service sat in an artfully arranged display, bearing more food than some families saw in a day.

The change in the Drummond household was significant, undoubtedly a product of Clara's gentle touch. Darkness had dominated the abode ever since the dowager became a widow, yet now small portions of light pierced the gloom, in fresh and fragrant flowers, pastel artworks and colorful furniture amidst the somber renderings. Did Foxworth notice the change?

And just like that, the mysterious duke usurped her thoughts once more.

That he stole the journal was all but certain. He'd confessed his plot to exact revenge, and no one had more to lose by the guild's exposure than Edmund and Priscilla. He could reveal their identities and bring scandal upon them all, setting the ton afire. Of course it would cast dire consequences for all involved, including Clara. Could he truly hate Edmund that much?

Of course Foxworth could be one of those men who abhorred bluestockings so much he considered himself responsible, nay, a hero, for exposing their mechanisms. He'd made his overprotective nature quite clear.

Whatever he had planned, time was running out, which was why she already formulated several options to address the situation:

A. Calmly ask Foxworth to return the book. Advantages: easy

and peaceful. Disadvantages: Chances of success less likely than the patronesses of Almack's hiking up their skirts and dancing on the tables at White's.

B. Tell him if he didn't return the book she would plot her own revenge. Advantages: Showed she was a powerful woman who wouldn't back down. Disadvantages: Chances of success also less likely than the patronesses of Almack's hiking up their skirts and dancing on the tables at White's.

C. Throw a potted plant at him and reclaim the book before he realizes what is happening. Advantages: Enjoyable, could be effective. Disadvantages: Would harm a perfectly innocent potted plant. Also, against the law.

D. Visit his townhome, locate the book and steal it back. Advantages: The only option that didn't involve the patronesses of Almack's hiking up their skirts and dancing on the tables at White's or violence. Disadvantages: ~~Could get caught. Likely to get caught.~~ Almost certainly would get caught.

However unlikely, the last option was her only choice. She couldn't simply confess her suspicions to Clara. Her friend was considerate, kind and undoubtedly loyal to her brother. If Foxworth learned they were investigating him, he may take the journal beyond their reach. Too many lives were at stake to take that risk.

"I'm sorry to keep you waiting." Clara floated into the room, garbed in a sage green dress with tiny pearl roses. Her curls were fashioned into a simple knot, her eyes alight. "It's wonderful to see you again."

"And you, as well." Sophia rose and clasped hands with the debutante. "You look lovely."

Clara blushed lightly. So shy and sweet, she presented a stark difference from her brother.

"I've been admiring the changes you made to this room." Sophia traced the soft fabric of the sofa. "I would love to see the rest of the home, if you are inclined to give a tour."

"It would be my pleasure." Clara smiled wider.

They strolled to the room's exit. "I can't believe your grandmother allowed you to do all this," Sophia said honestly. Technically, the home belonged to Foxworth, yet he hadn't sent his grandmother to the dower house. It was a surprising kindness from the formidable duke.

"She was a little hesitant, but Kenneth has a way of convincing people. You could tell she was elated."

Sophia smiled. A wry grimace was the most elated she'd ever seen Lady Drummond.

"She nearly smiled." Clara chuckled. "Of course, she resisted at first, yet she finally capitulated, as everyone eventually does to Kenneth."

Not everyone.

"Kenneth is the one who insisted on changing the décor," Clara revealed. "He wanted a more jovial atmosphere, especially after…" She paused, as stormy clouds overtook her sunshine.

Sophia put her hand on her friend's arm. Clara didn't share much about her past, but the change from Scotland to England must have been tumultuous, as was the death that precipitated it. The old duke never talked about his children, and Clara never talked about him. Word was they'd been completely estranged. "I'm sorry. I know how difficult it has been."

Clara sniffed, then patted her nose with a delicate linen handkerchief, embroidered with the words *Cherished Sister*. "I don't know how I would have made it if not for Kenneth. He takes care of everything and everyone. Even grandmother is happy with the redecorating, or he never would have done it." Clara continued describing a Foxworth she had never met. To her family, he was a threat – untested, unknown and uncivilized – yet to his sister he was a hero.

"In the end, we are all better for the changes," Clara concluded with a firm nod. She stood tall, and a tenuous smile returned. "Where should we start? Perhaps the common rooms first, and then my quarters."

Sophia followed Clara down long corridors, filled with rich

paintings and light-colored adornments. The air cooled as they passed an open window. "What about Foxworth's domain?" She said the words mildly, as if an idle thought. "Did he make significant alterations?"

"Kenneth?" Clara cocked her head to the side. "I suppose he made some changes, as well."

"I would love to see that, too," Sophia replied earnestly. "If it's not an imposition."

"Of course not." Clara's smile widened. "I cannot show you his private quarters, of course, yet we can visit the common areas he frequents, such as the study, music room and library."

Sophia followed Clara to the dining room, which was indeed lovely. Gold patterned paper covered the walls, with matching carved molding. A sparkling crystal vase stood on a huge carved cherry wood table, flanked by damask-covered chairs. Sophia walked around the set, touching the cool wood. It was perfectly smooth, with deep grains in shades of red and maroon. "Your taste is impeccable."

"Actually Kenneth selected everything."

Sophia stared. Who was this man who cared so deeply for his family, while threatening all that she loved? "Tell me about your brother."

"Kenneth?" Clara's features softened. "What can I say? He's the most wonderful brother in the world. He's kind, gentle and sweet as a puppy."

Sophia parted her lips. "Do you have a second brother named Kenneth?"

Clara giggled. "I know he can seem daunting."

Like a wolf. "I was jesting, of course. Clearly he is kind, and I'm sorry, did you compare him to a puppy?"

Sophia laughed again. "Indeed, I did." Her eyes shined in the natural light. "Please don't tell him I said that. He can get quite growly when he realizes people see the real him. He may appear fierce and difficult, but underneath it all…" She sighed.

Sophia lifted her eyebrows. "Puppy?"

Clara nodded firmly. "That's right."

Sophia drew back. Foxworth possessed more facets than a cut diamond. Of course Clara's opinion didn't necessarily reflect his true character. Sisters often idolized their brothers.

"We've done quite a bit with the music room." Clara led her through a curved doorway to a cream and cobalt room with high ceilings and gleaming instruments. "Kenneth even paid for it with his own funds."

His own funds? She pushed aside tender feelings she couldn't afford. It didn't matter if he acted kindly to his family. He was still trying to shatter hers.

If he possessed the journal, he could destroy every woman in the guild.

Clara showed her a host of other rooms, each exquisitely renovated and skillfully decorated. She may have asked for the tour to investigate, yet it was an enjoyable diversion, tempered only by the absence of Pricilla's journal. "I would love to see where the duke conducts business."

Clara smiled, and another flash of guilt surged. She hated deceiving the kind woman. "My grandmother didn't want to alter my grandfather's office, so my brother had his desk installed in the library. He enjoys being surrounded by books."

"I love books, as well." The words emerged before Sophia could stop them. She cleared her throat. "Of course, many people love books. It's not uncommon."

"Actually, you and my brother are alike in many ways. Perhaps that's why he acts like he does around you." Before Sophia could ask what she meant, Clara led them down a long hallway. "I must warn you, Kenneth was in the library not long ago."

Sophia slowed her steps. "We shouldn't disturb him."

"He won't mind." Clara continued at a brisk pace, and Sophia hurried to catch up with her, as they arrived at a large double door. One side was ajar, revealing oversized furnishings, rows of books and a thankfully empty desk. "He always keeps the door closed when he is working," Clara frowned. "He must have been called away. If you'd like I can find him–"

"That won't be necessary." Sophia forced a smile. "I don't want to bother him."

Clara stepped towards the door, just as the housekeeper appeared from behind a screen. "So sorry for the interruption, but your grandmother wanted to consult about tonight's menu."

"Of course. Tell her I'll be there post haste." Clara smoothed down her skirt. "I'm sorry, Sophia, but Grandmother does not like to be kept waiting. Would you mind perusing the library while I see to her needs? It shall not take long."

What fortune. Clara's expression was apologetic, yet it was a gift, granting the opportunity to search the most likely location for the journal. "Take all the time you need. I daresay I will find something of interest." Like a stolen journal, with the power to precipitate a scandal the likes of which London had never seen.

"Thank you." With a quick nod, Clara hurried down the hallway. Sophia stood still, waiting for her to turn the corner before pivoting towards the library. Time to investigate.

The heavy door was soundless as it opened wider, a sign of a smoothly-run household. She padded over the threshold, her feet sinking into the thick wine-colored carpet as she closed the door behind her. It wouldn't do to have a servant notice her scouring Foxworth's belongings. She strode quickly through the cavernous room, straight towards the massive desk.

The Drummond library had always been impressive, but now it was extraordinary. Bookshelves soared three stories high, covering every wall, carved from a deep cherry wood. A huge fireplace crackled in the corner, its marble mantle holding ceramic bowls filled with roses. Dark red settees provided ample seating, while Foxworth's enormous desk and throne-like chair stood ready for their formidable master.

She slowed as she reached the colossal desk, set to the back-drop of so many precious volumes. The room seemed the most likely location for the journal, yet what if he secreted it among the thousands of books? Hidden in plain sight, she would never find it.

She moved forward. Imagining failure would only sabotage her efforts. If this didn't work, another strategy would.

The desk was cluttered with papers, envelopes and writing instruments, as if Foxworth had stopped working mid-task for some urgent matter. There was no time to ponder it, as she lifted papers off papers off papers. Numerous books littered the desk, yet all regarded the running of an estate, land management and other such harmless endeavors. Drawers revealed nothing more nefarious than quills and fresh ink pots. That was, until she reached the bottom drawer. She pulled its golden handle, but it only gave slightly, catching with a distinctive thud. It was locked.

Not for long. The first thing she did upon joining the *Distinguished Woman of Purpose* was convince Priscilla to teach her how to pick a lock. She pulled a long pin out of her hair and slid it into the latch. With a soft click, the lock opened. She slid open the drawer.

More books. The top few were accounting journals, and those she left alone. She examined and passed over several with listings of businesses and contacts. Yet below that, a set of slim brown leather books peeked out. They were identical, each with a heavy script embossed on the top: *Journal of the Duke of Foxworth.*

She lifted a thin volume, traced the raised letters with the pad of her finger. The cover was well-worn, the pages yellowed with age. It was slightly crumbled, with sweeping ink peeking through the thin sheets. Of course it would be beyond the pale to read it, completely inappropriate. She lowered it back to the drawer, and stopped.

Foxworth pledged revenge against her brother. Threatened them with unknown schemes. He had most likely stolen the journal, placing them all in danger. If there was any chance he'd written about his plans in these diaries, it was not just her right to read them, it was her duty.

She needed no further reasoning. She opened the book, choking as the heavy scent of spirits leapt from the long dried pages, strong enough to coat her tongue in its sour taste. Goodness, had the duke soaked them in gin? The pages were stained with it, and frightfully delicate, crackling with every turn. The script was surprising as well, not the heavy cursive she'd seen Foxworth use, but a wobbly penmanship proving the writer managed to ingest as much of the spirits as he spilled. She focused on the small print, and froze.

Bradenton.

It was the very first word, written in heavy ink, and darker, as if the writer traced it a hundred times. She read on.

He has taken everything that matters to me – my family, my money, my reputation. There is nothing left.

The rest of the page was blank. She turned the page to a passage nearly identical to the first, a retelling of the injustices doled by Bradenton. Another page, another accusation. Every page showed no more and no less, pure hatred and bitter obsession, until the last entry.

I can no longer stand idle as Bradenton shatters my life. Tomorrow, everything changes.

We meet at dawn.

The duke's story ended there.

No.

The journal slipped from her fingers, drifting to the desk. Foxworth was going to duel Bradenton? He'd claimed he wouldn't, and certainly she'd know if Bradenton challenged him. Yet the writing was clear.

Her heart thumped like the heavy footsteps of duelists walking their paces. There would be a death tomorrow. Bradenton. Or Foxworth.

Both possibilities were unbearable.

She breathed deeply, fighting for strength. The duel had not yet been fought, which meant it was not too late. She reached for the journal, and stopped.

The journals numbered half a dozen, and at first they appeared identical. Yet next to the title, a number had been lightly embossed, and those differed for each. They represented years, she realized.

Last year.

She breathed pure relief, her lungs expanding freely now, as the weight of two potential deaths lifted. The Duke of Foxworth had not written in this journal. Well, he had, but not the current Duke of Foxworth. The writer was Foxworth's father, whose hatred transcended words, time and even the death of the man himself.

What happened that fateful day? She'd heard of no duel, yet Edmund wouldn't have necessarily shared such an abhorrent event with his little sister. She'd hardly known Foxworth's father, as most of the ton avoided him, despite his title and wealth. His vices were many and frequent, his reputation for gambling, whoring and drinking well-known. His death had been a result of heart trouble, a common enough ailment, especially for a man known for overindulgence. Yet what if the story was a deception? What if Bradenton had been involved?

Was this why Foxworth wanted revenge?

She scanned the journals' covers. Four of them delved further into the past, and while they may elucidate the feud's origins, the future mattered far more. There was one final journal, the date of the current year. It was slimmer than the others, without the bulk of crinkled, well-used pages. She opened to the first page.

The difference in the script was immediately apparent. This was the writing she expected from the Duke of Foxworth, heavy and bold, the letters sweeping across the page in commanding strokes. With time growing ever-shorter, she swept to the last entry, dated this very morning.

Journal of the Duke of Foxworth:

The time has arrived.

Finally, I will realize vengeance over the man who shattered our lives. He will live every day with the same pain I endure, knowing something precious was stolen—

Heavy footsteps shattered the silence.

She slammed the book shut, shoving it into the desk and closing the drawer. Or rather she tried, but it caught on a thick volume half-hidden under the others, the same shape and size as Priscilla's journal. She was out of time, as the footsteps delved ever-closer, yet she couldn't lose her chance. She grasped the heavy tome, pulled it out. It was...

Not the journal.

Raw disappointment streaked through her. She'd been so close! Yet the book was not the right shape, and the cover was lighter. She shifted the books, pushing the drawer forward one last time, when the title seemingly leapt from the cover:

Real-life stories of successful abductions.

The air in the room vanished. She lifted the volume, read the title twice and then thrice. What did it mean? Was Foxworth planning to *abduct* Edmund?

"Find something that interests you?"

She gasped.

She. Was. Caught.

CHAPTER THREE

The Private Diary of Sophia Hawkins

What is his scheme?

Foxworth claimed he would not physically harm my brother, and somehow I believe him. Yet wounding Edmund is undoubtedly his goal, if more subtle than with sword or pistol. He indicated he would take something precious.

What sort of items does a man consider precious? With Edmund's wealth, Foxworth could not take enough money to dent his fortune. The townhome and estates are fully owned, and Edmund would not risk them in any sort of wager. My brother is not a materialistic person, and I cannot think of a single "thing" precious enough to fulfill the sort of revenge Foxworth touts. The question remains:

What is he planning to steal?

HEAT FLOODED HER.

Sophia gasped, clutching the book she once thought her target. The manuscript burned in her hands, as she pivoted to a man whose identity was obvious. She recognized that deep, dangerous voice, in a room risen by a thousand degrees, the tension as thick as the volume in her hands.

A pair of expensive Hessian boots came into view. They led to powerful legs, a long torso, an expansive chest. When she finally reached his face, her breath caught in her throat.

Beautiful.

It seemed a ridiculous sobriquet for a man, especially one so powerful, so dominant, yet no other word fit with such precision. He was fate's masterpiece, chiseled features of high cheekbones, emerald eyes and full lips. His powerful arms were folded across his chest, his biceps straining the thin fabric, as challenge blazed.

Did he know what she sought? She might not be able to feign innocence, yet she would not admit guilt. "I apologize for my forwardness. I was simply browsing."

"Browsing?" He stepped towards her, his boots echoing on the floor like the drum at a traitor's execution. Her heart pumped furiously. "In my *locked* desk drawer?"

Heat spread throughout her, although whether from fear, anger or something far more mysterious was unclear. She resisted the urge to flee her predator, and the even more ridiculous urge to delve closer. He was like fire, and she a hapless creature entranced by the allure of the beautiful, perilous flame.

"Was it locked?" she muttered.

"We both know it was. Were you looking for something?" Before she could answer, his gaze swept to the table, where the hairpin shone, tiny and yet gleaming like a miniature sword.

Oops.

His gaze hardened. "You picked the lock." His voice was like honeyed wine, low and smooth. "Is that why you came?"

Fury swept through her. Who was he to accuse her, when he fought a mysterious war against her family? She held up the book. "What is this?"

"My property."

"You don't care about property when it belongs to someone else," she snapped, then bit her tongue. She swallowed an oath.

For the briefest of moments confusion lit his eyes, yet the challenge returned a moment later. "I do plan on stealing something."

She just managed not to gasp. "You admit your crime."

The confusion returned for an instant, then quickly vanished. "Are you accusing me of something, Lady Sophia? I have done nothing."

She breathed out.

"*Yet.*"

She clutched the book so hard it bent in her fingers. She loosened her grip. "Why would you have a book about abductions? Are you planning one?"

He covered her hand. Heat streaked through her body, and she released the book, yet for a moment, he didn't release *her*. She tugged away, yet the momentum was too much. She fell...

Straight. Into. Him.

Heat sparked an inferno. Large hands splayed on her back, steadying at the same time they seized. She pressed against the wall of muscles, as he towered over her, fully in control.

"It's all right," he murmured. "I've got you."

"Never." She ducked under his arm, emerged to freedom and an inexplicable chill. She turned with a triumphant grin, yet it was quickly extinguished by the power in his eyes. He shifted the book in his hands, the title blazing like a surreptitious message. If he didn't allow it, could she ever escape?

"You still haven't explained the book."

He returned the volume to the drawer and locked it firmly. He straightened. "The title interested me. It's a fascinating subject."

The claim was as believable as a lion's vow to forsake hunting. "Shall I suggest it to my ladies' book club?"

"A splendid idea." His eyes glinted in the firelight. "Ladies do not read enough about crime. Once you've finished, I have an excellent book on arson, followed by an entire series on tyrants."

"You should be familiar with that," she retorted. She pursed her lips together. This man tested her like no other. "You still haven't explained why the book was in the locked drawer, along with your accounts."

His gaze sobered. "Were you looking through my accounts?"

"Of course not." She waved her hand. "I wouldn't invade your privacy."

His expression turned incredulous, as heat crept up her neck.

Ah yes, she had been rummaging through his drawers.

Which had been locked.

And he didn't even know about the journals.

Perhaps respecting privacy was one of her *lesser* accomplished qualities. "You keep a book on abductions in your locked drawer. Tell me the truth. Are you planning to abduct someone?"

"I'd rather not say."

Which meant the answer was...

The world turned dangerous. The duke was always intense, yet now the atmosphere burned with it. She needed to retreat. Not literally, but figuratively, from discussions of schemes, revenge and abductions. Forceful confrontations did not work with this man. He was simply too intelligent.

It called for a new strategy. Perhaps if she was amiable, he would relax enough to let his scheme slip. It would be one of the greatest challenges she ever faced:

She'd have to be cordial to Foxworth.

She attempted a smile.

He looked concerned.

"I'm sorry for looking through your drawer. Sometimes my curiosity gets the best of me."

Concern turned to suspicion. "Did you just say you were sorry?"

She nodded. And smiled again.

"I say, are you all right?"

"Of course. Why do you ask?"

"Your expression is strange, like you are choking on something."

She was choking on the urge to grab him and demand he reveal all.

He stepped towards her. With his massive size, he could never be anything but intense, yet his words emerged soft, gentle even. "You have fashioned yourself my foe, even though we are no such thing. You are careless with your safety, and now I catch you rifling through my desk."

"I was not rifling through your desk."

"Then what were you doing?"

"Not rifling through your desk."

His eyes sparkled. "Do you know what the term 'rifling through a desk' means?"

"Indeed. I simply want to apologize. For..." *Rifling through his desk.* "The misunderstanding."

He looked at her as if she had left her senses in the desk.

She needed to be more convincing. "I have a perfectly reasonable excuse for being here. I didn't break through any locks."

He folded his arms across his chest, dropped his gaze to the drawer.

Oh yes. The desk.

"I didn't break in anywhere else." She smiled sweetly. "I have a perfectly good excuse for being in the library. The décor."

"I'm sorry?"

"Apology accepted."

"No, I didn't mean–" He stopped, shook his head. "Lass, you're doing this on purpose, aren't you?"

"I don't know what you're talking about." Since charm didn't work, perhaps she could confound him. "I noticed the new décor and asked Clara to give me a tour."

"That sounds reasonable, but you're missing one thing."

"What's that?"

"Clara."

She gulped back a chuckle. "You noticed, did you? You truly have an extraordinary grasp of small details. And, um, many other things." Perhaps adding a little flattery wouldn't hurt.

His frown deepened. "You're not trying to be nice so I'll tell you what you want to know?"

"Would it work?"

"Most certainly not."

She ignored the retort, stepping away from him and his distracting presence. "We were touring the home together, when your grandmother summoned Clara. She should be back any moment." She strolled past a trio of bejeweled emerald vases holding golden feathered fans. "I like your redecorating."

"You didn't like the previous décor?" He raised an eyebrow. "It was quite popular among ghosts looking to holiday."

Sophia bit her lip to stop the smile. "Did the somber duke actually jest?"

His eyes crinkled at the sides, and for the briefest of moments, something not altogether unhappy passed between them. She cleared her throat. "I'm surprised you changed it. The prior decor seemed better suited to you. In fact I'm surprised you didn't bring a whole array of Medieval weapons."

"Actually, I did."

She just managed not to stumble.

And he was beside her in a second, steadying her. "Are you certain you were only interested in the décor?"

And just like that, the world once more turned dangerous. She tore her gaze away to the book titles, yet they blurred next to his commanding presence.

"Everywhere I go, I find something that interests me," he murmured. "Even when I expect the worst, I find a diamond. It is a beautiful and rare surprise, which I do not relinquish."

She tightened. "I do not understand your metaphors, Your Grace."

"I think you do." He took a step around her. "Clara said you fought to better the world."

He had discussed her with his sister? She trusted Clara, as did Priscilla, which is why she'd been invited to the *Distinguished Ladies of Purpose*. Yet Clara was also far less worldly than her brother. Had she unwittingly helped him in his plot against Edmund?

She showed none of her suspicion. "It is not an uncommon trait, even among women, despite what the ton believes."

"I know many strong women." Foxworth's tone was genuine. "Including my sister. Of course, I do not consider myself true ton."

She furrowed her brow. "Of course you are ton. Few rank higher than a duke."

"As I am all too aware." Disgust laced Foxworth's voice. "Those who previously disparaged me now ingratiate themselves at my feet. Those who speak poorly of my country – my true country – now praise it, while insulting it behind my back. It is all a façade, a mirror of perceived desires. I'd have people treat me as a fellow man, not as a duke."

How unexpected.

It was a moment of discomfort, vulnerability even, which she would never point out, and he would never admit. The unexpected inheritance of a dukedom was a cause of great celebration, a boon that changed the path of a life. Yet perhaps not all considered it such.

For just a moment, sympathy surfaced. Was his dissatisfaction with his new role related to his anger for Edmund? Was this the origin of his crusade? "You should be pleased for your new situation. Scores of women want nothing more than a moment with the handsome new duke."

She closed her eyes. *Where had that come from?*

She opened them to see a smile as wide as the Thames. "Actually, I never had a problem with the lasses."

The heat travelled from the top of her head to the toes pinched in her fashionably tiny slippers.

"As Clara said, I would do anything for my family."

"How did you know she said that?" Clara had uttered the words when they were *alone*. She gasped. "You were eavesdropping?"

There was no denial, excuse or apology. "Of course. I always watch over my domain, especially when ladies with unknown motives visit."

"You're the one with unknown motives." She glared. "And nefarious plans."

"You have plans of your own." he countered. "You asked my sister some rather interesting questions."

"How dare you." Sophia clutched her skirt and her anger. It was far safer than the camaraderie of earlier. "Do you realize how inappropriate that is?"

Once again she'd underestimated him. While she believed she was conducting a covert investigation, he'd been watching her the entire time. It was only fate or fortune she'd had a chance to search the library and find the information she did. "I will not allow you to seek revenge on my brother."

"You cannot stop me, lass." He stepped closer and closer still, until he was standing over her. "You are playing a dangerous game."

She stood tall. "I'm not scared of you."

"You should be."

She clenched her fists, digging sharp fingernails into her palms. "Your veiled threats have grown tiresome. Tell me what you have planned."

"Do not worry," he rumbled lowly. "You will not have to wait long."

Her heart lurched at the confirmation that whatever he had planned was imminent. How much time remained? "Then I will have to move quickly."

"Lass–" His voice held an unmistakable warning. "You need not be fearful of me, yet it is perilous to challenge men twice your size." He flexed his muscles. "Someone stronger and larger could take control."

Unspoken indications filled the space. Did he plan to take control?

"The point is–" His tone darkened. "You put yourself in danger by your actions, and I will not allow it."

"You have no say in what I say or do." She lifted her chin. "I can care for myself."

"By your penchant for danger, that is clearly untrue." His voice was even lower, his exasperation turned to ire. "If Bradenton cannot care for you, someone else will."

Every muscle clenched. In fury. In frustration. In an emotion that impossibly felt like excitement. And yet, despite it all, somehow not fear.

"That will never happen," she ground out. "I will overcome any plans you have for my family. You may be massive, but I am just as brave and smart as you. Shall I prove it to you?" She glanced around the room, stopped at the ladder leaning against the bookshelves. Edged on by determination, she strode to it.

"What are you about?" He followed right behind her.

"When one faces challenges, they simply lift themselves up." She hefted her skirt and placed a foot on the lowest rung. It wobbled slightly under her slippers, yet she clutched the sides and stepped higher, progressing steadily, even as it swayed. She ascended another rung, and then another. "As you can see, I am already taller than you. Cunning and intelligence triumph over strength and power every time."

"Get down," he commanded.

She climbed another step. "I rather enjoy the view from up here." It was frustratingly true, despite the emotions he inspired. How could he still seem so massive, when she was now higher than him? Yet perspectives had not changed viewpoints – he was still a veritable giant.

He growled, low, deep and incensed. His gaze set, and he stalked towards her.

Uh-oh.

The ladder started to tip.

How he moved so quickly, she would never know. As the ladder swayed one way and then the other, her foot slipped, and she fell forward...

Into his arms.

Her breath whooshed from her lungs, as she fell against a solid wall of muscle. Powerful arms snaked around her, claiming, grasping, securing as tightly as iron shackles. He turned her, even as his hold remained secure. He always seemed large, never-endingly powerful, yet now he was enormous, as he gazed from so far above. His eyes blazed, their fiery depths alight with shadowy emotion.

He was going to chastise her, reprimand her for a taking a risk that could have led to grievous injury. He would be arrogant, overbearing and domineering.

Yet he did none of that. Instead, he reached out, and ever-so-softly stroked her cheek. "Are you all right, lass?"

She could fight anger. She could fight arrogance. She could even fight threats. Gentle words and soft touches? *Impossible.*

She closed heavy eyes against unknown emotions. His touch begot a longing, a feeling of utter rightness that had her leaning into him. "I am well," she whispered.

"As I said, I will *always* be here to catch you."

It wasn't true, yet in this moment, it didn't matter. She should retreat, thank him and pretend it never happened. She should cease all conversation, flee into the hallway to wait for Clara. Yet instead she stayed frozen, save for her rapidly beating heart.

He held her in thrall.

She didn't try to escape, and he never offered to let go, holding her as if his place and his right. Of course, no breech in propriety existed for a gentleman saving a falling lady, yet now they delved far past any semblance of decorum.

"Why haven't you released me?" she whispered.

"I rather like holding you," he murmured.

Her breath caught. And she just managed not to share she rather liked him holding her, too. "Shouldn't you put me down now?"

It was a question, not a demand, an inquiry, not a request. And somehow no anger arose when instead of letting go, his muscles tightened. "Is that what you want?"

It was her opportunity, her chance to escape this untamed duke. That he would release her was not in doubt, yet she would have to show him, or tell him.

She could move back.

Tell him she didn't want this.

Ask for her release.

Instead…

She remained silent.

He waited a moment, and then another, providing the opportunity she couldn't accept. Then…

He took her lips.

From a calm sea into a raging tempest, from constrained tension to unrestrained passion, heat surrounded her, powerful, fervent and all-consuming. The world blazed fire as he caressed her lips, tasting and testing with firm strokes. Senses scrambled as bodies pressed flush, every movement casting tantalizing friction and ribbons of desire. She breathed in his scent. He breathed in hers.

Out of the corner of her eye, the door started to open…

Chapter Four

Journal of the Duke of Foxworth:

I have always prided myself on my control.

Control over my domain, my world, my behavior. Control over the emotions, needs and desires that would render me powerless against a foe. Yet now unforeseen circumstances threaten all.

I cannot change the past, yet I can alter the future. I will attain both my vengeance and that which I desire. By the time Bradenton realizes what is happening, it will be too late. For despite Sophia's attempts, she will play her part as long as I keep control.

No one has ever tested it like her.

"THIS IS A shock."

That was most certainly true.

"No, shocked is not the right word. Stunned. Astonished. Almost speechless."

Indeed.

Kenneth had kissed many women in his life, beautiful, passionate, experienced women.

It had never been like this.

They had almost been caught. One moment he was drowning in the magnificence that was Sophia; in the next the intruder threatened everything. It had taken every bit of strength to pull back, to somehow move across the room, to the opposite wall. He'd even grabbed a book, although its title was as much a mystery as his inexplicable actions.

Clara stepped forward, her eyes wide with wonder. "The two of you in the same room and not at swords. A cause for celebration, I'd say. Although..." Her eyes darted back and forth. "You should not be alone. You are lucky it was me who arrived, because I know nothing untoward happened.

"Of course not." Sophia placed her hand to her heart, her chest rising and falling with the remnants of *nothing untoward*. A few strands of those luscious locks had escaped the confines of the pins, and Kenneth resisted the urge to smooth the silky tresses, recapture the softness. Her cheeks were alight with pinkness, her eyes glittering like sapphires. Had Clara not been so innocent, she would have recognized Sophia as a woman who had been thoroughly kissed.

"You do seem a little flushed." His sister now frowned. "Were you arguing?"

Sophia choked lightly. "Not at all. I'm just a tad warm." She fanned herself with a slender hand. "I must have delved too close to the heat, I mean fire... er, fireplace." Her cheeks flamed.

"Really?" Clara inclined her head. "I've always thought the library rather drafty."

"We were actually discussing the décor." Kenneth stepped forward. "I was showing her my artistic *touch*."

Sophia turned as pink as an overripe strawberry. "We should let you get back to work." She edged towards the door, practically hugging the wall. Did she think he would leap out and continue their sensual duel?

It was tempting.

Clearly the kiss had unbalanced the spirited woman. He would need to do it again. *Soon.* "It's not a bother at all. Did you enjoy it?"

As Clara looked on in confusion, Sophia's fiery expression proved she knew exactly what he meant. "It was..." Her voice trailed off.

"Riveting? Fascinating? Enthralling?"

Sapphire eyes shuttered, yet her expression betrayed the truth. The kiss had been all those, and more.

"Unexpected."

The whispered word was barely audible, yet somehow it carried the message of a thousand emotions. His amusement faded, as memories of the kiss swirled. It had indeed been unexpected.

"That must have been quite the conversation." Clara studied them closer, with a slowly widening smile. She may be young, but she was highly intelligent.

Not good. Clara could not get involved in his plans. "I'm afraid I must return to work."

"Of course." Sophia's relief was apparent. "It was a pleasure to see you." Her eyes widened. "I mean it was entertaining, I mean delicious…" She sighed, practically lunging for the door. "I'm leaving now."

He didn't move, despite the inexplicable urge to step between her and the exit, to prevent her departure. She was but a facet of his plan, the means by which he would accomplish his goal.

Yet something in him whispered, *Could she be more?*

As the door clicked shut, he released a breath. The kiss may have undone Sophia, yet it affected him more than he'd ever admit. The connection they'd shared…

Stop.

He could not allow her to upend his emotions, threaten his control. He'd seen such sentiments shatter his mother, and he grew up without a father for it. He needed to focus on his plan and the thousands of responsibilities thrust upon him by his new role. He strode to his desk, sank on the plush chair. For now, he'd have to settle for attacking the mountain of letters awaiting his attention.

The first letter was from Travis, a man who'd conducted "business" with his father. From the message's not-so-subtle hints, the word business was a metaphor for unsavory activities. Despite Sophia's labeling his intentions as such, he believed in honor. From the little he'd discovered about his father, the same could not be claimed.

His father's absence was more pronounced than ever, and the more he learned, the sharper the blade. His mother had never revealed his father's title, just that he was an Englishman with a short temper and an even shorter attention span. She'd stayed with him just long enough for two children to be born, before fleeing to her family in Scotland, and they never heard from the dukedom again.

Until Adam arrived to bestow the inheritance he never wanted.

At first, he gave his cousin a resolute no. Why would he leave a fine life in Scotland, sweep his sister to an unfamiliar and often unfriendly country? Yet when Adam revealed the next heir was a wastrel and gambler, ironically similar to his father, Kenneth could not abandon the estate and those under its care. He hadn't a choice.

Thus he became Foxworth.

He tossed the letter into the fire. He'd already written multiple times to say the estate would no longer conduct business with them, no matter how lucrative. Kenneth reached for another letter, yet the papers blurred, replaced by the image of a woman.

What had Sophia sought in her investigation? Something to use against him, or perhaps proof of his plan? If a disagreement between servants hadn't prompted his delay in reaching the library, she never would have seen the locked drawer. Yet it didn't truly matter. Nothing would stop what he had begun.

"You wanted to see me?"

Kenneth looked up sharply. Sophia had so beguiled him, he hadn't even noticed his cousin's entrance. "Thank you for coming."

Adam strode into the room. "I saw Clara and Sophia leaving the library, the latter of whom appeared to be scouring the corners. Did she lose something?" The words were said lightly, yet the slightest edge lurked underneath.

Kenneth grasped the papers on his desk, stacking them into a pile. "She was admiring the new decorations. She likes to keep abreast of all happenings in the ton."

"Does she?" Adam stopped several feet from the desk. "What about the world outside it?"

"World outside it?" Kenneth straightened the quills. "What do you mean?"

"Your sister is in Lady Priscilla's sewing group, is she not?"

"The *Distinguished Ladies of Purpose*," Kenneth affirmed. "Clara is quite adept with a needle."

"That would be something unusual for that group."

Kenneth stiffened, looked up. "Pardon me?"

"Never mind." Adam stepped forward. "There is a guild member with flaxen hair and sapphire eyes, who is not of the ton, but leads some sort of sanctuary. Has Clara mentioned her?"

It was a peculiar question, for which he didn't have an answer. "I am not familiar with most of the ladies. Are you searching for someone?"

"I am simply assisting a friend." Before Kenneth could inquire further, he swiftly continued, "Your message said you had important information."

Kenneth hesitated. If something was afoot with the guild, he had to know, for his sister's safety. Yet surely Adam would tell him anything urgent, and right now other matters took preference. Once it was concluded, he would investigate himself. "I'm going away."

Adam rubbed his jaw. "You've only just returned. Have you been called back to Scotland?"

"Not exactly." Kenneth would only share the necessary details, so that if matters went awry, his cousin would not be held responsible. In truth, he wasn't entirely certain Adam wouldn't try to stop him.

Adam's eyes darkened. "Is this about your feud with Bradenton?"

He stayed stoic.

"I see."

Kenneth lowered his eyes to the drawer that held his father's journal. Remembered every word. *Straightened.* "I will only be gone a few days. Grandmother and Clara are going on holiday, so you needn't worry about them."

His grandmother had grumbled at the sudden trip during the height of the season, but he'd convinced her Clara needed a little escape from the chaos of the ton. It was not entirely untrue. His sister found London a trial, although matters had improved since she befriended Sophia.

"And where will you be during this sojourn?" Adam leaned against the desk. "How will I reach you in an emergency?"

Kenneth frowned. He'd planned to disappear completely, yet Adam brought up a valid point. What if his sister or grandmother needed him while he was away? Even when he visited Scotland, they knew how to contact him. He could not abandon them completely.

He grasped a quill. Dipping the tip into a fresh ink pot, he scribbled his destination on a paper. "I will be half a day's ride from here. Do not share my location, and only contact me in an emergency." He paused. "I will not be alone."

Adam's frown deepened. "Who will be with you?"

"Lady Sophia."

In an instant, suspicion turned to astonishment, doubt to anger. Adam stepped around the desk. "Now see here—"

"I plan nothing untoward." Kenneth stood, holding out his hand. "I do not intend to compromise her."

"You don't plan to compromise her?" Adam echoed. "This little trip will ruin her, even if you don't touch her."

What would Adam say if he knew he already kissed her? "I have no intention of allowing scandal to reach anyone, not even Bradenton."

Adam halted. "I don't understand."

It had taken a lot of time and effort to perfect his plan so that it punished the right person, while sparing all others. "This will be purely personal revenge. Bradenton will know I've taken her, yet everyone else will believe Sophia went on holiday."

"Why would they think that?"

"Because that's what Bradenton is going to tell them."

Adam stared. Kenneth took advantage of his surprise, pressing forward, "I will leave a letter for the duke, sharing I have taken his sister, and will return her unharmed in a few days. If he wishes to avoid scandal, he must do nothing while he awaits our return."

Adam opened his mouth, closed it. Asked in an incredulous tone, "Do you truly believe Sophia will go with you willingly?"

Not a chance. "I am certain I can convince her." *Convince may be another word for kidnap.* "She may even enjoy it." *There was at least a one in a thousand chance.*

"And if she refuses?"

"I will reason with her." *Which may or may not involve tossing her over his shoulder and disappearing into the night.*

Adam held his gaze. "Regardless of your intentions, your plan will shatter lives. Only that's what you want, isn't it? To destroy Bradenton?" He leaned closer. "This revenge is consuming you, Kenneth. You're a good man. I know about the people you've helped."

A frisson of discomfort surfaced. He looked away.

"I've seen the donations on the account books." Adam's sharp voice drew him back. "I know about your charitable work."

Kenneth frowned. He'd contributed far more than the books reflected, and he planned to do more after his campaign. "This isn't just about revenge. I'm ensuring Bradenton does not destroy another family."

"What could he have possibly done to deserve this?" Adam braced both hands against the desk. "What crime could be so great to convince you to seek vengeance?"

Kenneth's heart thundered, surging blood throughout his veins. He never planned to share his reasons with Adam, never intended to tell anyone. Yet a single word emerged, "Murder."

Adam froze. When he spoke again, his voice was low, deliberate. "Murder?"

Pure fury rose, his constant companion since the moment he left Scotland for a title he never wanted, to avenge a father he never knew. Bradenton hadn't just stolen his father. He'd taken his very life. "Bradenton murdered my father, but not before he destroyed him."

"I can't believe it." Adam pushed himself off the desk. "Bradenton would never murder a man. If it happened the other way..."

Kenneth tightened.

Adam held out his hand. "Forgive me. I shall not speak ill of the dead, yet you must be mistaken. Who made such claims?"

"My father."

Adam gaped.

"I can't explain, but it's true. There's no justice for men like Bradenton, unless someone is willing to fight."

Adam stared at him for a moment. "Have you confronted Bradenton? Demanded an explanation?"

"It would do no good." Kenneth walked around the desk, stopping directly in front of his cousin. "He would only deny it."

"It just doesn't seem possible." For a moment, Adam studied Kenneth, assessing, contemplating. "Yet I believe you have good reason for thinking it. Despite that, I implore you to reconsider. You risk scandal for both families."

"Which is why I sent Clara and Grandmother away," Kenneth admitted. "However, it's only a precaution. As I said, the chances of repercussions are low."

"You are underestimating the danger," Adam countered. "It is a dangerous plan. Bradenton is likely to call you out."

It was a distinct possibility, especially for a man who killed in a duel before. He couldn't let it sway him. "His sister will be ruined if he challenges me. The only way to avoid scandal is to accept what happened." He hardened his jaw. "Just as I had to do with my father. Bradenton will never harm another person again."

"I don't like it…" Adam grunted. "However, I will help if you answer one question. What happens if you are discovered? If the ton finds out you and Lady Sophia have been together, what will you do?"

A surge of unexpected satisfaction blazed within him, along with a single answer.

"I will marry her."

CHAPTER FIVE

The Private Diary of Sophia Hawkins

An abduction.

Would the Duke of Foxworth dare such a crime? Of course, his plan may still involve Priscilla's journal, yet I cannot discount a far more nefarious scheme. The offense fits his innuendos, and most certainly his personality. Yet who would he abduct? Not Priscilla, certainly. She has confirmed her delicate condition, and even Foxworth wouldn't dare abscond with a pregnant woman. With his formidable build, my brother would make a difficult target. Yet Foxworth is a giant of a man, tall, strong and powerful, giving him at least a chance of being successful.

I will stop whatever he has planned.

ANTICIPATION SIZZLED IN the air.

Excited chatter, glittering guests and glowing torches accentuated the masterpiece that was the Stanton ball, in an evening filed with mystery and expectation. It was one of the premier events of the season, in a massive ballroom decorated in silver, gold and dozens of crystal chandeliers. Gemstones adorned luxurious furnishings, curved bannisters and, of course, the exquisitely garbed ton.

The festivities spilled into an enchanting garden of roses, lilies and other exotic blossoms. They were a tour de force of color and artistry, prize-winning blooms the Stanton ladies nurtured into greatness. The sky was a breathtaking twilight blue, the air cool and temperate, carrying the scent of roses and the melodic strum of the orchestra playing under a towering oak.

Sophia fashioned a serene smile, as she smoothed down her silky dress. It shone silver in the moonlight, with tiny sewn-in jewels sparkling like the stars above. For most, the anticipation was about the event, yet for her it was about something, or rather someone, else.

Foxworth.

"Take care, tonight," Bradenton whispered in her ear. "As you know, your typical chaperones are away."

She waved her hand, not mentioning their absence was fate's fortune. Her mother and aunt had taken holiday at Bath, leaving her without their watchful surveillance. They had invited her, yet her negative response had been all but a formality. She would not leave Bradenton alone to face Foxworth's wrath. "I shall."

"And I will be watching, of course. Stay away from Foxworth."

She made no attempt to hide her smile. "Of course." Yet Edmund's focus would be divided between his wife and the endless attention his popularity ensured. Leaving her to completely ignore his order.

How else was a sister to protect her brother?

Foxworth was planning to abduct Edmund. The more she considered the evidence, the more probable, or certain, it seemed. Likely, he just wanted to scare him, yet it was not impossible more sinister aims motivated him. She'd considered telling Edmund, yet she had no proof. If he discovered she'd been alone with Foxworth, he'd relegate her to her chambers for the rest of the season, possibly her life.

Unacceptable. Tonight she would stop Foxworth's revenge, once and for all. "I'd like to greet a few friends. I shall see you later."

His lips tightened, but he nodded. "Be careful."

"I've already promised it." She tapped his shoulder with her silvery fan. "I'm not going in immediate search of Foxworth."

His eyes narrowed ever-so-slightly, but he gave another nod. Of course she wasn't searching for Foxworth immediately. First, she would fetch some refreshing fruit punch.

Then she would find Foxworth.

She greeted numerous friends as she made her way to the refreshment table, threading past ladies in ethereal gowns, men in formal suits. Heavy perfumes tangled, casting notes of fruits, wood, leather and spirits, as their wearers conversed, drank and laughed in the complex social scene. Although she was of age, she had not officially come out, and she treasured these precious months free from the clutches of the marriage mart. While she must eventually wed, no man had yet inspired a trip to the altar.

For just a moment, the image of an untamed duke rose.

The punch was cool and delicious, poignant with the taste of crisp apples, sweet strawberries and just a kick of something stronger. The hair on the back of her neck stood.

He'd found her.

Even from across the garden, his gaze pierced her. It was a physical force, a challenge. All around him, people engaged in conversation, their eyes alight with interest. Did they not see his divided focus?

She swallowed.

Then she straightened. He was trying to intimidate her. He wouldn't approach her now, with her brother staring daggers across the crowd, but Edmund couldn't watch her all night. When business snagged her brother, she would confront Foxworth and convince him to give up his scheme.

Time to hunt the hunter.

THE NIGHT WAS perfect.

For an abduction, that was.

Better circumstances could not have been planned. Sophia's mother and aunt had left on holiday, a fortunate circumstance. While he wished to aggrieve Bradenton, he had no desire to cause her mother and aunt undeserved worry. By the time they returned, his retaliation should be complete.

Everything was set. He would lure Sophia deep into the gardens, to the carriage in which they would flee. He'd arranged the letter to reach Bradenton an hour after they departed. By the time the duke realized Sophia was gone, she would be well out of reach.

It took all his control to appear unaffected, to greet the countless lords and ladies who approached. The title of duke was a powerful magnet, and he remained aloof, yet not unkind. Like it or not, this was the society he must now navigate, and despite his misgivings, not everyone was bad. Once he was finished with Bradenton, he would master the ton, and fulfill his duty, including taking a wife.

Yet as always, a single lady invaded his mind.

Somehow he made it through conversation, and then dinner, where he was seated next to an effervescent and eager young debutante. She was lovely and sweet, perfectly poised for the role of duchess, yet his attention kept wandering to a certain golden-haired beauty who sent a thousand surreptitious glances.

Finally, it was time.

The event was no less boisterous with dinner concluded. Their bellies full, their senses invigorated by copious amounts of alcohol, the guests talked louder, laughed harder, danced poorer. No one noticed as he slipped into the gardens, embarking on a final sojourn to confirm the carriage's readiness. Then he would return…

And seize her.

Kenneth strode through the lantern-lit gardens, nodding at various well-wishers, stopping for none. The crowd thinned as he delved further from the townhome, the deep scent of oak replacing perfumes, starlight replacing candlewick, as the edge of the garden neared. A light thumping sounded behind him, different than the occasional rustling of night creatures, and he stiffened.

He was being followed.

Subtly, he shifted his body, searching the shadows with his peripheral vision. Someone was there, someone petite, lithe and absolutely lovely. He allowed a slow, predatory smile.

Sophia.

Clearly fate approved of his journey. His huntress was alone, picking her way next to the brush, trying to blend into the foliage. Yet her efforts were in vain, as she stood out against the wood like a diamond among sand. What was her game? Did she think to confront him, demand he cease his plan? If so, she was about to be surprised.

Sophia was aiding in her own capture.

Following a lord through a deserted garden was:

A. Surprisingly exciting

B. Liable to get her unwittingly betrothed

C. Foolhardy, dangerous and generally a bad idea

D. All of the above

All through the night, Edmund had watched her, even es-chewing cards to lord over her. It was enough to drive a sister mad, yet she couldn't demand he leave so she may confront his enemy. Finally, she informed him she required the ladies' retiring room, the one place he absolutely could not follow. He'd muttered something about blasted retiring rooms, yet could scarce forbid her from attending to the necessaries. He would be furious if he knew of her duplicity, but she hadn't a choice. Foxworth could commence his plan any moment.

Now she slipped through the nighttime garden, delving as close to her quarry as she dared. Majestic trees soared above her, their leaves rustling in the shadowscape. An owl hooted in the distance, startling her, as the wind blew cooler. She wrapped her arms around herself, looked down for just a moment.

It was enough.

"This is convenient."

She gasped, pivoted to a man towering over her. How had

Foxworth moved so quickly? Now he stood before her, larger than life, crossing muscle-ridden arms across his chest. He seemed more massive than normal, cunning, calculating, domineering. His midnight clothing blended into the darkened world, he a part of its dangerous power.

He edged nearer. "You saved me a great deal of time and effort."

Her breath caught in her throat. She pushed forward, side-stepping him. "How have I done that?"

"You'll learn soon enough." He moved in step with her, not allowing her to increase the distance between them. His voice was low, yet held all the power he never relinquished. "First we will talk of your behavior. Once again, you have risked yourself."

"Perhaps, yet you are the only threat." She stood tall. "Am I in danger from you, Your Grace?"

"It depends." His voice was low, powerful. "Are you speaking of physical danger?"

It seemed the most likely, out here in the deserted garden, with only the night creatures as chaperones. Yet while an objective viewer may interpret physical peril, instincts clamored otherwise. "I do not believe you pose me physical harm."

He nodded immediate confirmation. "I would never harm a lady."

"Yet you would use one to gain revenge."

He did not deny it. "Which makes your presence all the more appalling. Were it any other lady, I would add surprising. Yet you are equal parts brave and reckless, a dangerous combination."

She would take it as a compliment. "We never finished our conversation in the library. I know your book was not mere leisure reading, just as I know you stole the journal."

A flash of confusion passed through his eyes. "I know of no journal."

His response almost put his culpability in doubt. *Almost.* "I refer to Priscilla's journal, and I do not think you've taken it; I am certain."

"You are mistaken."

Impossible. "Your denials are meaningless. Will you also attempt to convince me you don't plan on abducting my brother?"

He shrugged mildly. "I have no plans to kidnap the duke."

"Admit it," she hissed. The distance she fought for no longer mattered, as she advanced on him. "You're planning something, and I want to know what it is."

"Very well."

Surprise froze her. She swallowed a breath of cool night air. "You will finally share your plans for revenge?"

"What I meant—" He leaned in. "Is that I am indeed planning something."

A cool wind blew, causing her to shiver. She rubbed her bare arms. "Does it have to do with the journal?"

"As I said, I have no journal." He lowered his head. "I have never lied to you."

She parted her lips. He was a creature of the night, blending in perfectly with the shadows. Yet although he hid secrets, to her knowledge he had never uttered an outright lie, seemingly more content to conceal information rather than provide false oaths. Could he be telling the truth?

"Why is this missing book so important?"

She brushed by a sea of emerald leaves, their velvety surface tickling her skin. A hidden thorn pricked her, and she drew back. Such was this duke, smooth on the outside, concealed danger within. If he was telling the truth, she would not provide information. "Even if you don't have the journal, you are planning something. Do you swear it is not an abduction?"

A mysterious light flashed in his eyes. "Who said I wasn't planning an abduction?" He gave a slow, dark smile. "In fact, I'd say it's already begun."

That was the moment all became clear.

She was his target.

How had she not realized the truth? She stepped back, even as he moved forward. Why would he take her brother when someone far easier to abduct had all but offered herself? Foxworth said he would take something *away* from Edmund.

She had walked right into her own kidnapping.

Yet if he thought he could steal her, he would face a fight as he'd never seen. Somehow her voice emerged calm, with only the slightest waver betraying the unease of being a party to one's own kidnapping. "Why?"

"For revenge, of course." His eyes blazed. "To take away what he loves most."

"Take away?" she breathed. "What do you plan to do with me?"

He did not respond with words.

Instead he *leapt*.

She gasped and dashed back, but he was too quick. He captured her wrist, brought her into the scent of amber and bergamot. Danger surrounded her, locking her in the shadow of the mountain of a man, subject to his heat, the control he stole. Fury boiled her blood, tangling with other inexplicable emotions. "Let go!"

"I cannot do that, at least not yet." Yet a gleam in his eyes belied the words, a moment of uncertainty. Was he unsure of when he was going to release her?

If he was going to release her?

"I'm not going to hurt you."

"Let go, or I'll scream," she hissed. "Someone will rescue me."

"Perhaps. But you're not going to scream."

She was too stunned to resist, even as he pulled her forward, as she brushed against solid muscles. A night bird squawked in the distance, covering the sound of their movement. If she wanted to call for help, she would have to do it soon, as the edge of the property came into view. Once she delved beyond the guests' hearing, she would be well and truly abducted. "Why wouldn't I scream?"

With firm movements, he kept her moving, away from the

party, away from safety. She tried to dig her heels into the ground, yet her feet slipped on the dewy grass, and she had to step to avoid falling. With each inch, her chances of freedom dwindled, like the haunting final whispers of a melody. "If you scream, the guests will come running. They will know you were alone in the garden with me."

Blazes! What had she been thinking? If she wanted to avoid a betrothal, she would have to remain silent. "You won't get away with this."

"I already have." He grasped her closer. "Don't worry, lass. I meant it when I said no harm would come to you. We'll simply disappear for a few days, and then return. Think of it as a vacation."

"A vacation is a choice," she hissed. "I am a prisoner." She yanked back on her arm, but he didn't let go. "You think Edmund is going to let this go? He'll come for me. You'll be lucky if he doesn't call you out."

"He isn't going to call me out for the same reason you aren't screaming now. If he does, everyone will know what happened. Once you are safely returned, he will not risk scandal."

"He would risk it to save me," she countered. "When he finds me missing, he will tear London apart."

"Then it is fortunate we will not be in London."

Her breath hitched. Where was he taking her?

"I left Bradenton a note, to be delivered shortly. I explain that I am taking you for a brief sojourn, and will return you unharmed. I strongly suggested he tell the world you are visiting a relative, which, with your mother on holiday, no one is likely to question. In a few days you will return, and life will go back to normal, with one exception. Bradenton will forever know he failed you."

"What happens if we are discovered?" she snapped. "I will be ruined, cast with inescapable scandal. Does your quarrel with my brother include me?"

For the first time, he hesitated. "It does not."

"Yet I am the one most punished by your mechanisms. If we are found, my prospects will be forever lost."

"That's not true." Firmly back in control, his voice deepened. "On the contrary, you will find yourself with a most advantageous match."

A spark of foreboding flared. She glared at him, even as he ushered her closer to catastrophe. "How can you say that? Most lords would dismiss me out of hand if they discover the truth."

"You will not need another lord. Despite what you believe, I am a gentleman. If I create scandal, I will rectify it."

She paused for a heartbeat. "How will you do that?"

"Isn't it obvious?" He lifted a single eyebrow, even as he continued forward. The moonlight threaded through the trees, dappled shadows foreshadowing inescapable danger.

"You will be mine."

She stumbled on a log, but before she could fall, he reached out with impossible speed, bracing her. Now he was entirely too close, propelling her forward, steadying at the same time he secured. The sounds of the street came closer and closer.

"I will never be yours," she hissed. "No amount of scandal could convince me to accept a suit from you."

"If we are discovered, you won't have a choice." His eyes blazed in the moonlight. "If we are not discovered…" His voice trailed off.

She narrowed her eyes at the unfinished sentence. "Edmund would never force me to marry against my will."

"If word got out, the scandal wouldn't just affect you. It would damage your family, even threaten Bradenton's work in Parliament."

She would happily accept scandal for her freedom, yet he was not mistaken about the unforgiving ton. Could she truly sacrifice her family to save herself?

"Don't worry. My plan does not include scandal, only the illusion of it. You will be perfectly safe in my care."

Sophia tightened. "I am not in your care."

His resolve was a veritable force. "Do you truly believe that?"
Not even a little.

Ahead, the lush green paths gave way to dark roads, blackened stretches with barely visible street lights. She continued to
resist, yet did not scream. Had she truly felt her life in danger, she
would have howled for the world to hear, yet a few days
adventure was preferable to a lifetime trapped under iron control.
"Aren't you afraid of your own consequences, should your
actions be discovered?"

She could feel his shrug. "As a duke, the danger is appallingly
low. The ton allows lords shocking transgressions, so long as
wrongdoings are corrected."

"By forcing me to marry you?"

He smiled wickedly. "Precisely."

The street came closer, the carriages louder, wheels rolling
and horses trotting joining the melody of the night creatures. Her
heart sped like a runaway horse. If – when – they disappeared into
the night, no one would find them.

There would be no escape.

CHAPTER SIX

Journal of the Duke of Foxworth:

Unexpected events.

They can destroy even the best-crafted plans, leaving destruction and uncertainty in their wake. Hopefully the plot will work to perfection, with Bradenton thoroughly punished and Sophia unharmed, yet what if matters do not proceed as intended?

If the truth emerged, I would not leave Sophia to ruin's clutches. I would have no choice but to give her the protection of my title, wealth and name.

Like it or not, she would become mine.

E VERYTHING WAS PERFECT.

Perhaps too perfect, as if fate had dealt a hand of four aces. If Sophia's mother's absence and Bradenton's ignorance weren't fortune enough, Sophia had followed him straight into her own kidnapping, already beyond reach of any who might save her. She chose not to scream and summon the world, although that solicited the slightest sliver of disappointment, which he would not explore.

Indeed, all was perfect.

Until a royal flush conquered his hand.

Something was wrong. Every sense sharpened as he slowed his steps, every instinct whispering a warning. Far from the festivities, the music was no longer audible, the only sounds the leaves crunching under his boots and the rolling of distant vehicles. The world was gloom and darkness, away from the grandiose blooms of the ton's gardens.

Suddenly, three men appeared in the shadows, confirming instincts' warnings. They flanked his carriage, waiting, observing, watching. A gun peeked out behind a coat.

Kenneth slowed. Likely he could take them, yet not with Sophia next to him. She was innocent, and even if she weren't, he would never endanger a woman's life. At all costs, she must stay safe.

Even if it cost him his revenge.

"The plan has changed." He kept his voice low, glancing back at the men. "You must leave."

She stared at him in shock. "What?"

"Quiet." The rogues hadn't seen them yet, and it was vital it remain that way. "Several men are standing by my coach. I fear they have devious intentions."

"Devious intentions?" She put her free hand on her hip. "You are currently kidnapping me."

"Yes, but I would never harm you. I cannot say the same for them."

In the distance, the men bristled. They shouldn't be able to hear, yet clearly they grew restless. She had to leave now. "Return to the party immediately."

He released her. The feeling of loss was unexpected, a cold chill replacing the lushness of warm woman. She rubbed her arms, yet made no effort to flee like a reasonable person with an unexpected reprieve from a kidnapping would. "What do they want with us?"

"With me," he corrected. "There is no time for questions. You must go."

The woman who had spent the last five minutes demanding her freedom now stood up tall, stuck her pert little nose in the air and announced, "I refuse to leave you to get murdered."

"You cannot be serious." He gaped. "Are you afraid I'll haunt you from beyond?"

"I would not put it past you," she sniffed.

He stared at her. "Have you lost your mind? There are men out there, dangerous men, and you need to get away. This was not part of the plan."

"I told you your plan wouldn't work."

"My plan was working perfectly. I didn't know the criminals would show up."

"Next time you need to plan for contingencies."

"Perhaps next time you can plan your own kidnapping."

"Perhaps I will!"

What was happening? Did she wish to be kidnapped? More likely, she sought to save her big brother by giving herself up as the proverbial sacrificial lamb. A woman who would risk herself to save her family...

Now that was a diamond of the first water.

She shrugged. "Perhaps fate is punishing you for trying to kidnap me."

"It's not fate," he ground out. "It's bad fortune. And you'll be safe as long as you go back to the ball where your brother can *attempt* to watch you. I will address the situation, then I will be happy to resume your kidnapping."

"That is unacceptable." The jaunty chin went higher. "You will return with me."

He opened his mouth. "Did you just invite me to escort you back to the party? After I kidnapped you?"

"*Almost* kidnapped." she corrected. "I'm just trying to be polite. It's not at all fashionable to leave a lord to be killed."

For once, he was speechless. The fairer sex was as much a mystery to him as to any man, yet this was beyond the pale. He searched her eyes, amidst her calm expression. And suddenly, the mystery vanished.

She was frightened. She may hide it well, but she could not mask the distress sparking in her eyes, or the fear in her clenched features. Was she so worried about him, she would stay to convince him to leave? "You are the most unusual woman I have ever met," he murmured. And the bravest and kindest. "Whoever wins the right to care for you will be fortunate indeed."

For just a moment, something roared at the notion of someone else taking the position.

She. Was. His.

She scoffed. "Even if I am annoyed about the attempted kidnapping, I do not want you harmed. Return to the party with me. We will enter separately, and no one will know we were together. Later we will discuss your antagonism towards my brother, which I believe can be resolved without another kidnapping, attempted or otherwise."

At any other time her bravery would have impressed him, yet now his only objective was protecting her. As the men paced dangerously near, unease churned, as close to fear as he'd felt in forever. "I will take care of them. Your kidnapping is officially postponed."

"Postponed?" Even in the darkness, her pinkness was visible. "You cannot do that."

"I'm rescheduling," he explained. "To a more convenient time."

She stomped her foot. "You cannot reschedule a kidnapping."

"Why not? Flexibility is important in any abduction." He grasped her shoulder, propelled her in the direction of the party. "How does next Tuesday sound to you? If that doesn't work, we'll plan for Thursday after next. The point is, you are leaving."

Once more she dug in her heels, this time to stop herself from being released.

He would never understand the mystery that was Lady Sophia.

"I do not want to see you killed," she ground out.

It shouldn't matter that she cared whether he lived or died, or that she was risking herself to safeguard him, yet somehow it did. He fought the urge to toss her over his shoulder and march back to the party, where he would stake his claim once and for all. "If you do not return now, I will carry you back."

She gasped. "You wouldn't dare."

"Indeed I would." Out of the corner of his eyes, the men moved faster, their agitation clear. How soon before they saw them both? "I will make you a deal. If you leave, I will allow you to speak your mind about your brother before I commence my revenge."

She breathed out. "You will listen to what I have to say?"

He nodded.

She hesitated, her brow furrowing into a little wrinkle. Then she gave a quick nod, clutched her skirts and pivoted. He did not expect the intensity of the relief as she fled into the night.

He stood to his full height. His steps were heavy now, as he tramped toward the men who dared interrupt his plan. "I know you are there. Reveal yourselves."

The men emerged, large, hostile and armed far heavier than first apparent. They were not ton, not even close, yet powerful in their own right, hailing from the underworld of London. They were the sort of men his father associated with.

He stiffened. Likely, they *were* the men his father associated with, his so-called colleagues. When he hadn't accepted their written demands, they'd sought him out. He had underestimated them.

The man in the center was bald, with numerous tattoos and a long scar running along his cheek. He gave a humorless smile. "I am Travis, your father's business associate. I assume you haven't received our missives."

"I received them." Kenneth smoothed down his coat, confirming the comforting presence of both gun and knife. "Which you must know since I replied multiple times. Our business is concluded."

"That is unfortunate." Travis' eyes were as soulless as ice. "Because my associates and I don't want it concluded. We can help each other."

"I know how you help people." Kenneth had researched their business when they'd first contacted him. Indeed lucrative, it was not even close to being legal. The damage in its wake was *significant.* "I am not my father."

"That is apparent." Travis sighed, yet the relaxed pose was a ruse, as every instinct insisted he was poised to attack. "I suppose we'll just have to convince you."

They were quick...

But he was quicker.

Three men attacked at once. That Kenneth was expecting it gave him an advantage, perhaps a life-saving one as a massive brute lunged with a serrated knife. Whether his aim was murder or persuasion was unclear, as Kenneth sidestepped just in time, and gave a huge punch to the gut. One down, yet another attacked just as swiftly. Another solid punch, another fallen criminal. Kenneth stalked Travis, the last man standing.

Yet the rogue merely gave a wicked smile. "Do you remember how many of us signed the letters?"

"There were fou–"

The world went black.

SHE SHOULD BE dancing.

A nice Cotillion, perhaps, or a scotch reel, with one of her young suitors. If not dancing, she could be enjoying a refreshing glass of fruit punch, or sharing light gossip with her friends. There were many entertaining activities suitable for a young lady of her age and position.

None of them included hiding in the bushes, holding her breath as four dangerous men attacked Foxworth.

Unbelievably, he'd almost had them, despite their advantage in number and weapons. Yet the fourth had surprised him, lunging from the bushes like a rabid coyote. Sophia's blood had turned cold when he smashed the pistol down on Foxworth's head, inflicting a knot visible even from afar. It was a lesser form of danger than inserting a bullet into his brain, yet she'd seen what head injuries could bestow.

One didn't always wake up.

She had to do something. Foxworth may have wicked plans for her brother and definitely planned to kidnap her, yet the thought of him injured and alone was simply unacceptable. He'd shown glimpses of goodness, and the journal proved his grievous misconceptions about Edmund. If he truly believed her brother murdered his father, his thirst for revenge could even be justified.

She could only tell him if he lived.

A shard of fear pierced her stomach, as the men dragged Foxworth into the carriage, his head smashing into each step with a sickening crack. A thousand options flashed, all rife with danger and little chance of success. The smartest action would be to return to the party, seek help. The fact that it would elicit questions, and the inevitable assumption she'd been alone with him, didn't matter, not if it meant his life. Yet he may already be dead by the time she returned.

She had to do something, and she had to do it now. Only what? Even she wasn't foolhardy enough to confront four hardened criminals alone. They would laugh off her attempt, and she'd quickly find herself trussed up like Foxworth or *worse*.

The brutes strode to the horses, preparing to leave. She glanced around, but no one was within sight. If only she wasn't alone…

She stopped. They didn't know she was alone.

The plan was dangerous. It was foolhardy. It could backfire spectacularly.

It was her only chance.

"Gentlemen, come quick! They took Foxworth. Bring all the men you can find!"

The criminals looked up sharply at her voice, as they spun around, frantically searching the darkness. She pressed behind the giant oak, hoping she was far enough the guests wouldn't hear. If anyone saw her, criminal or guest, the consequences would be dire.

One of rogues stepped in her direction. "It's too dangerous." The self-identified leader stopped him with a growl. "If we're caught, it will be the gallows. We'll finish this later." Then, all four men turned and fled.

Sophia released a breath of relief, yet she quickly tensed again. The danger was not over. Just because the criminals said they were leaving did not mean they actually would. They could be setting a trap, waiting for her to emerge. The safest option was still to return to the party.

She was never one to take the safe option.

She waited a minute, and then a minute more, yet the night remained quiet. Finally she could delay no longer. She stepped from behind the tree, picking her way across fallen branches, hopping over damp leaves. That no one sprang to capture her was a relief, and a bit of a surprise. Ahead of her the carriage lurched, and she jumped, even as relief flooded her. Foxworth was alive.

The horses whinnied as she reached the black coach. She touched the gleaming side and grasped the door handle. With a deep breath, she pulled it open.

He lunged.

That no one actually touched her was almost an afterthought as she almost fell from the carriage, before she grasped the door. Sharp metal sliced her palms as she hung backwards, gravity pushing her to the rocky ground. With all her might, she pulled up, and gained a foothold. She stumbled into the darkness.

Had the criminals returned? She whipped her head about, searching the darkness. "Foxworth?"

"Sophia?" The duke's familiar shape separated from the shadows. He appeared lucid, his voice crisp and strong, if a little astounded. His stance was straight, and he didn't wobble or tremble. Yet just because he was conscious, and even well, did not mean he was out of danger. Head injuries could seem mild at first, even as they ultimately took a man.

Shock burned in his eyes, replaced by fury a moment later. "Why did you return? Leave at once!"

"They attacked you." She ignored his command as she delved

further into the blackness, wincing at the metallic scent of blood. A dull red spot matted his hair, yet not as bad as she feared. Something brown and dull glinted in the moonlight, and she gasped. Thick ropes encircled his wrists and legs.

She reached out. "Are you all right? Shall I fetch a doctor?"

"Do not call anyone. If they find us together, nothing will prevent the consequences."

"But you're trapped!"

She couldn't leave a man to die...

Not even if it meant she would become the property of that man.

"You would sacrifice yourself?" He regarded her intensely, shook his head and winced. Her heart lurched. He must be in terrible pain. "It's my own fault for not staying vigilant. Where are the men?"

"Gone." Her gaze wandered down his arms. The rope bands encircling his wrists were solid, with jagged edges. "I tricked them into thinking a group of men followed me. They won't return."

"You don't know that." He tried to move forward, but the ropes held him. "If they realize you're alone, they'll capture you, too. You must go now. I can take care of myself."

"Let me help." She pushed herself further into the carriage. He tried to stop her, yet the binding held firm. His wrists were raw from the rope and his efforts to dislodge them.

He pulled back. "I should be able to get free in a few minutes." He yanked again, and amazingly, the rope started to unbind. He strained against the restraints. "You have no idea of the danger you are in."

She notched up her chin. "I'm not scared of them."

"You should be." He tightened his muscles, straining the rope. "Once again, you have put yourself in danger. When I am free, I will ensure you never do anything like this again."

Her heart beat rapidly, yet she showed no trepidation. She was not afraid of him... much. "Perhaps I will leave you like this. At least until I convince you of the futility of your revenge."

"My revenge will be continuing shortly. It seems I won't have to postpone your kidnapping after all."

She gaped. "Are you seriously threatening to kidnap me while I am rescuing you?"

He ignored her question. "While I appreciate your efforts, you won't be able to help me unless you brought something sharp." He stopped, grimaced.

All anger fled, as concern swooped in. "Are you well? Do not despair. I shall free you post haste, and then we shall seek a doctor."

"I do not need a doctor, although they must have hit me harder than I imagined. How could I forget my knife?"

"You brought a knife to a ball?"

"I carry several." He lifted his foot. "The easiest to reach is the knife strapped to my ankle. You should be able to cut through the rope with it."

She bent down, and her shoulder brushed his knee. His legs were thick with muscle, his entire body coiled strength. She grasped the crisp fabric of his pants, then pulled up, holding her breath as she revealed strong ankles, tanned calves and the *knife*. Yet before she grasped it, something completely unexpected, wholly scandalous and altogether inappropriate emerged:

Desire.

"Are you all right?"

She bit back a gasp, fought for focus. She had halted her movement, with her hand resting on his calf. "Of course."

Gripping the handle with two hands, she lifted it. Gleaming metal emerged, sharp as the edge of fear. She tightened her hands as they shook.

"All is well lass," he murmured. "Just move slowly."

She nodded, and focused on the knife. Even a slight slip could slice right into his leg. Finally, the blade was free, its side curved and wicked, its engraved letters gleaming. She edged back, holding it away from her.

Foxworth exhaled. "Excellent." He lifted his hands, holding

the rope taut between them. "Now just slice through the rope, and I'll be free."

She nodded and raised the knife. It was all a matter of control, and she had a steady hand. She could do this.

She froze.

Should she do this?

He had been kidnapping her when they were interrupted. If she set him free, what was to stop him from continuing?

Absolutely nothing.

His eyes turned guarded the moment she lowered the knife. She moved back, out of his reach. "What are you doing?"

What was she doing? She wanted him to abandon his revenge. He wouldn't listen unless he was a captive audience.

What if she kidnapped him?

She wouldn't hold him for long – several minutes, an hour at the most. She could force him to listen, explain the journal and its implications. Of course, she couldn't stay here, where the kidnappers could return any moment. Her brother had taught her to drive a carriage...

She blinked. The thought was preposterous, crazy even. She couldn't kidnap a duke, for so many reasons:

A. *Kidnapping a lord was generally considered bad ton.*

B. *Kidnapping a lord was technically against the law.*

C. *If he escaped, he could very well kidnap her instead.*

Of course, this was for a good cause, for both her family and his, and certainly that overrode any objections. She could dispute his misconceptions, make him realize Edmund had not murdered his father. The feud would end, the kidnapping cut short. They would return with a gentleman's promise that her family was safe.

Yet what if he escaped before she convinced him?

The rope had twisted and frayed as he struggled. She may not have time to make her argument before he broke free. The brigands had left more rope...

Could she really do this?

She allowed a slow smile.

Yes, she could.

His eyes turned suspicious as she edged toward the rope. "What are you doing lass?"

"I'm afraid I can't release you, at least not yet." With a deep breath, she moved forward. He moved at the same time, and her breasts brushed against his chest.

Her breath hitched.

She pressed closer, ignoring every doubt whispering a warning. It didn't matter that he was restrained. It didn't matter that she was free, or held a powerful weapon. He never relinquished control.

"Isn't it obvious?" She lifted her chin. "I'm kidnapping you."

CHAPTER SEVEN

The Private Diary of Sophia Hawkins

*My brother has often chastised me for not considering the reper-
cussions of my actions. Yet if one were to list every possible
thing that could go wrong, undoubtedly one would never leave
home, for fear of something dreadful happening. Of course in
that case, something equally dreadful would happen in the
home, and then one would incur consequences without ever
enjoying rewards. Life is meant to be lived, and consequences
are part of that. Yet just because I risk them does not mean I am
not aware.*

What will be the consequences of challenging Foxworth?

T HE BLOW MUST have been harder than he realized.
Must have addled his senses, torn his perception of
reality. Yet even though it still felt like someone was stabbing his
brain with a dagger, his vision was clear, with no tell-tale nausea
that signaled a serious affliction. Still, he couldn't have heard
correctly.

Sophia could not possibly be kidnapping him.

Of course, he also never believed she would return. Seeing
her had been more than a shock, yet admiration for her bravery
had been tempered by concern for her safety. Didn't she realize
what could've happened, what could still happen? Fortunately,
with every passing second, the chances of the brigands' return
lessened.

He didn't know their exact plans, yet if they had wanted to

kill him, he wouldn't be breathing now. Likely they thought they could convince him to resume their business. As soon as he returned, he would make clear their relations were over in no uncertain terms.

He brought his attention back to the woman who never truly left it.

Could Sophia actually be concerned for him? It seemed unlikely, yet what other possible motive could there be? Behind her tough exterior, she had shown a kindness and caring so rare in the ton. It was apparent in her misguided yet fervent defense of Bradenton, her willingness to leap into danger to defend her family. Of course, he would be putting a stop to such reckless behavior immediately.

"What are you doing?" He annunciated each word, as she grazed him with hesitant fingers. Awareness flooded him, the unmistakable urge to pull her close, to take control.

She did not answer as she wrapped the rope around his wrists. She pulled tightly, yet he barely felt it. She bent down to his legs, practically laying herself in his lap. Her breasts brushed his thighs.

He felt that.

It was pure torture. Not that she hurt him, or even threatened his freedom, as she tied knots he could easily defeat. Yet he couldn't touch back.

"You are playing a dangerous game, if you think to challenge me." He flexed his muscles. "I always emerge victorious."

He would get what he wanted: Retribution. Revenge. *Her.*

Most ladies would be fearful, yet not his spirited lass. "Not. This. Time."

Did she realize her activities were about to be curtailed? "How many times must I forbid you from danger?"

"Until you realize I'm not listening." She pulled another useless knot. "You're allowed to kidnap me, yet I can't kidnap you?"

He gave his fiercest gaze, the one that intimidated Scottish warriors, powerful leaders and the most influential men in the ton.

She stuck up that sassy little nose and smiled.

"Untie me now," he demanded. "And I will get us out of danger."

"You're not doing a very good job of it."

He bristled. "Excuse me?"

"Well, I am kidnapping you."

Actually...

Why couldn't she accept she was the one being kidnapped?

This was going too far. Yet before he ended her fledgling career as a kidnapper and commenced his, he would discover her plans. "Is there any particular reason you're kidnapping me?"

"For the same reason you tried to kidnap me: ending the feud between you and my brother." She pulled hard on the rope, yet the knot loosened after her first try. She didn't correct it. "Don't worry. I don't plan to kidnap you for very long. Unlike your nefarious plan, it'll just last a few hours, until I convince you to abandon your vendetta."

He tightened, all humor vanished. The feud wouldn't end until he had a measure of retribution, and assurance Bradenton would never hurt anyone ever again. "I have no intention of forgoing my plan."

Her eyes blazed. "That's a bold statement, considering I'm the one in control."

No. She. Wasn't. "Are you so certain about that, lass?"

For just a moment, uncertainty flashed. Despite her daring statements, she recognized the predator in him, as he lured his prey. His plan may not be progressing as intended, yet nothing had changed. She was his for the foreseeable future... perhaps far longer.

Pinkness tinged her cheeks, as if she knew her future was being debated and decided without her agreement. "You no longer have power over me."

She did not understand how a predator stalked his prey. She didn't know he could release himself within minutes, quick enough to prevent her escape. He'd catch her before she ever made it back to the party. "You wield certain power," he murmured. "Yet you could never triumph against me."

She delved nearer. The scent of violets surrounded him, as desire swirled, untold attraction for this luscious creature. By her dilated eyes, it captured her, too. "Do you feel in control now?" she murmured.

"Entirely." He sat as tall as his bindings allowed. "Nothing you do can threaten my control."

Her eyes flashed, as she edged closer. "Are you so certain of that?"

Absolutely."

"Let's put that to a test, shall we?"

Then *she* took his lips.

She was sweeter than the wildflowers that grew in the Scottish highlands, softer than their dewy petals. Her lips were tender and supple, her breath warm and fragrant, as she pushed into him with an intoxicating mixture of innocence and boldness, ingenuousness and brazenness. Slender arms wrapped around him, testing him as never before. It took all his effort to stop from fighting the ropes, so he may properly secure her. Yet patience would be rewarded later, when he seized control.

Sweet surrender was in every sigh, capitulation in every gentle touch. She edged closer, pressing her small frame to his, as his ancestors' legacy to conquer surged. She was feminine glory, unbridled passion and strength. Yet it was not enough. He wanted more, and not just physically.

He gloried in the surrender she didn't realize she gave.

This must stop. The gentleman in him commanded it once, then many more times, as he fought a battle within himself. He couldn't continue now, where the brigands could return, when he couldn't protect her as the warrior in him demanded. Kissing required neither effort nor strength. Pulling back required all.

He withdrew, even as she stayed still, her lashes fluttering against creamy cheeks. Her lips were plump from his attention, her cheeks brushed with passion's rouge. For a moment, her eyelashes quivered up and down, like the wings of a butterfly, before her eyes widened. Awareness edged into her gaze, then shock and confusion. "What are you doing?" she whispered.

Their eyes locked.

"What am I doing?" Her voice grew louder.

He sat up tall, hovering over her. "I believe you were just explaining who was in control."

The hitch in her breath was audible, as she moved back so swiftly, she almost fell off the seat. The knife slipped from her gasp, falling to the floor with a clang. She held herself up. "There is much to discuss, and I need to return as soon as possible." She stepped toward the exit, halted. "I better take this." She picked up the knife, far too close to the blade.

"Careful, lass," he warned. "You could hurt yourself."

Once free, relieving her of it would be his first order of business. His next?

Her kidnapping.

As if she heard his wayward thoughts, her eyes flashed. She glanced around the carriage, stopping at the coat he planned to use as a disguise. "Mind if I borrow this?"

She didn't wait for an answer before donning it. The coat fell far past her knees, engulfing her like a child in her father's belongings. And despite everything, the urge to smile was almost irresistible.

Just like her.

Clearly she recognized his amusement. "Would you prefer I drive the carriage in only my gown?"

His smile froze. He'd assumed she was going to hold him captive here, so she could offer her argument.

"You are taking me somewhere?"

"Of course." She lifted a hand. "A seasoned kidnapper such as yourself should understand the meaning of the term kidnapping."

"I know what it means," he said through clenched teeth. "I just didn't realize you planned on leaving."

"Of course. We are far too close to the ball." Her eyes darted to the window and the shadows beyond. "A short ride will provide a safe place to talk. We shall not be gone long."

"We shouldn't be gone at all." Despite what she believed, he had no desire to cause scandal. Unfortunately, the stubborn tilt of her nose proved he would gain no quarter, and arguing would waste precious time. Best allow her freedom, for *now*. "Do not stray from the safe areas of London."

"I'm in charge of this kidnapping." She put her hands on her hips, as only an elite daughter of the ton could do, while conducting illegal activities. "I do as I wish."

"You will heed me." He would allow her to continue the charade as long as it was safe, yet unseen dangers lurked in the underworld of London. It may find her before he could free himself. "If I see you venturing into a dangerous area, you will not like the consequences."

"Have you confused our roles?" She glared at him. "I am the kidnapper."

Not. For. Long. "I am serious."

In a huff, she turned towards the door. She halted, softened just the slightest. "We will not go far, just enough to ensure our safety. Then you and I will discuss matters. I'm sure we can come to a solution that is amenable to both of us."

That would depend. Did she consider him abducting her amenable?

She said no more as she departed, the carriage shaking slightly as she ascended to the top. He didn't wait for the door to click shut before attacking the ropes. The ones she'd added were dispatched with swift ease, yet the brigands' efforts presented more of a challenge. Still, he loosened the first as the carriage lurched into motion, relieving the pressure on his wrists. He rubbed raw skin as his circulation returned, welcoming the pain. The kidnapping had begun.

Hers.

THE ALLEY WAS desolate and deserted, filled with smoke, waste and the other unappetizing odors the ton couldn't quite hide. Yet they remained in a respectable area, if not slightly towards the fashionable area, not because Foxworth demanded it, but because it was logical and safe. Despite what he believed, she did not run into danger at every opportunity.

Even if a dash of it did make life exciting.

Now the lower risk of being seen was tempered by the consequences if the wrong sort of person caught her. She would not risk danger, not to herself or her captive, as she urged the horses just a tad further, finally settling on a quiet alley with closed shops and sparse light. Hopefully no one would notice the coach for however long it took to convince Foxworth to abandon his quest.

She climbed down from the seat, pulling the rough coat around her. She could do this. She would show strength, logic and reasoning, and demand he release her brother from his vengeance.

She turned the handle and opened the door.

Foxworth was exactly where she left him, sitting in a relaxed pose with the rope still looped around his wrists and legs. She half expected him to lunge, with nothing and no one to save her, yet he remained still.

"You stayed in the safe areas. That's my lass."

His arrogant words extinguished her uncertainty. "I'm not your lass, and I didn't do it because you commanded me. I make my own decisions."

He shrugged lightly. How could a restrained man look so smug? "A wise decision, in any case. Now that you have me here, what do you plan to do to me?"

The images came without conscious thought:
Kiss him.
Then kiss him again.
And again.
Probably again after that.
Again, again, again and again.

She. Was. In. Trouble.

She cleared her throat.

He smiled wickedly. "I like what you're thinking."

She parted her lips. "You have no idea what I'm thinking."

"I don't?" His eyes shined. "Would you like to come closer so I can show you what you're not thinking?"

Yes, please.

"Of course not," she snapped. Lust may have infiltrated her traitorous mind, but her resolve was strong. She would ignore the spell he so effortlessly cast.

He flexed his muscles.

Her throat dried.

All right, so she couldn't ignore the paragon of masculinity. Yet she could focus on her mission. "I want to explore with you." She gasped. "I mean I want to explore you." Heat burned every inch of her skin. She whipped off the coat and placed it on the bench, even as his piercing gaze skewered her.

"We should indeed explore matters," he rumbled, eliciting a thousand images of her exploring his powerful body.

And even more of him exploring her.

This was ridiculous. Even bound, he usurped her control. She wouldn't have it. "The only matter to explore is this feud. You will cease your vengeance against my brother."

Now his gaze hardened, even as the heat soared halfway to the sun. "My feud is not settled until I exact retribution, which was interrupted. Next time, matters will progress far smoother."

"There will be no next time." She held herself up. "You are quite bold for a restrained man."

A mysterious gleam entered his eyes, gone in an instant. "I am bold, even while *bound*." He annunciated the last word, shifting slightly. Her eyes lingered on the ropes, but they appeared as before, secure around his wrists and ankles.

She gazed into eyes that shared no secrets. "This is not proper behavior for someone who's been kidnapped."

"Indeed?" His amusement deepened. "I'm sorry if my behavior is lacking. This is my first time being abducted, after all."

"I was just abducted for the first time as well." She plucked at her skirt. "And the proper action is to concede to your captor."

"You didn't concede to me," he pointed out, shifting forward. For a moment, it seemed as if he would go straight through the ropes, yet he halted a moment later. The rope was still against him, but was it as taut as before? "You argued with me the entire time. With another captor, it could have been dangerous." His eyes narrowed. "Fortunately, no one else will be kidnapping you, ever."

"What was I supposed to do?" she retorted. "Thank you for kidnapping me?"

"It would have been the polite thing to do."

"Are you trying to make me angry on purpose?"

"You are lovely when excited."

Her fingernails dug into her palms, leaving little crescent-shaped marks. Was she seriously having a conversation about the proper etiquette for kidnapping?

"Perhaps we should consult the ladies of Almack's." Clearly he was enjoying himself. "They are experts on propriety, after all."

She closed her eyes, opened them. "I know why you are furious with my brother."

He tightened, as golden fire blazed in his eyes. "How would you know that?"

A thousand and one responses flitted through her mind, truths, untruths, half-truths. Yet if she wanted to convince him, she had to be honest. "I read your father's journal."

All amusement fled from his expression. "Did you now?" His voice was deceptively soft. "You said you didn't go through the journals."

She braced her hands against the hard sides of the carriage. "I meant I didn't read your accounting journals. I read the diaries, but only because you gave me no choice."

His gaze turned incredulous. "I gave you no choice but to

read my father's private musings?"

"In my defense I believed them to be yours, but yes." She held out her hands. "What would you have me do? If an unknown enemy threatened your family, wouldn't you do everything in your power to save it?"

"That's different."

"Because you're a man?" His silence revealed the answer. "I will not stand by while you threaten my family. I hoped the journals would provide some insight into your motivations, and indeed they have. Most importantly, I believe they hold the key to resolving them."

"How?" He edged towards her, stopped when the rope stretched taut. Although it seemed a little longer than before. "If you read the journals, you know what your brother did to my father." His voice lowered. "Bradenton is a murderer."

"Untrue!" she hissed. "Edmund is a good man. He would never murder a man."

"Yet the journal proves otherwise." Foxworth's hard stare belied any skepticism. "A man's behavior towards his sister is not indicative of his true nature. Did you read the last entry?"

She paused, nodded. "Just because they planned a duel doesn't mean it was fought. Everyone knows your father passed of a heart ailment."

"An easy enough excuse," Foxworth rebutted. "Which can be neither confirmed nor denied."

"Surely it was obvious at the time." She softened her voice. "Someone would have seen him."

"Only no one did." Foxworth reached up, stopped himself before the ropes snapped. "The burial and services were done swiftly and in secret, by a man who is not associated with my father. I was informed weeks after it occurred, and by the time I found the journals, it was too late."

She frowned. That was strange, yet it didn't mean her brother was involved. "It appears neither of us knows the entire truth. I'm certain if you ask Edmund, he'll—"

"Lie." Foxworth's voice was as sharp as a shard of glass. "Which is what men like him do. All throughout the journal, my father documented your brother's transgressions. Bradenton set out to destroy my father, and he did. If the estate hadn't been so well-protected, my father would have lost everything."

"My brother would never destroy another person," she responded forcefully. "You must have heard of his charities, the causes he fights for every day, the people he helped. He's the most selfless man I know."

"And what of my father?"

She may not have known the former duke personally, yet tales of his indiscretions were rife within the ton. Despite Foxworth's assertions, the former duke had lived his life, quite to the excess. "What do you know of your father?" she asked carefully.

Unease entered his expression, yet no actual animosity. "I know he wasn't a saint," he admitted. "My mother's tales alone elucidated this, as did his absence. I do not claim he was a great man, or even a good one. Yet he suffered greatly at your brother's hands. Perhaps if Bradenton hadn't pursued his vitriolic campaign, matters may have been different."

Blazes. Not only did Foxworth blame Edmund for the murder of his father, but for his ruin, and even their estrangement. It was a heavy accusation, and, she was certain, an unwarranted one.

"I'm sorry for your loss." Truly, she was. No one should have to lose both their father and their entire way of life. "Yet just because he wrote those things doesn't make them true. You know of your father's struggles. A man influenced by the bottle does not always view the world with clarity."

He stared at her, and for a single moment, doubt entered his eyes. The next moment it was gone. "There is simply too much evidence. Even if the journal didn't exist, I have confirmation from an additional source."

Shock momentarily paralyzed her. "You do?"

"My father's man of business confirmed the journal's accounts. He believes your brother was responsible for my father's death."

"That's impossible." No evidence could convince her Edmund murdered a man. Yet why would the man of business substantiate a false tale? "I shall like to talk with him immediately."

He lowered his eyebrows. "Absolutely not."

She sucked in a breath of air, scented with amber and bergamot. She pushed aside all trepidation, wanted and unwanted desire. "My brother deserves the chance to defend himself. Obviously there's been some sort of misunderstanding—"

"There's no misunderstanding," he snapped, "and no explanation beyond common sense. For unknown reasons, your brother hated my father. He tormented him again and again, using his vast power and endless wealth to destroy him. My father never had a chance against Bradenton, yet he murdered him anyways."

"That can't be true. If you'd only ask him—"

"There's no point in asking a murderer for an explanation."

"You don't know Edmund," she hissed. "As you did not know your father. I am genuinely sorry for your loss, yet it does not justify your malicious campaign, especially without a comprehensive search for the truth."

"I know what happened." He flexed his muscles. "You admire your brother too much to see it."

"And you're too angry to investigate." She took a deep breath, fighting for calm. "If you truly knew Edmund, you'd know he is no more capable of such nefarious business than me."

"You kidnapped me."

"You kidnapped me first!"

She clutched her silky dress. The man wouldn't listen to reason. "Talk to Edmund, please. Find a solution together."

"I have a solution." He leaned forward. "For days he will worry over your absence, a burden he cannot show for fear of scandal. When we return, he will forever know he couldn't protect you. It will haunt him, just as my inability to protect my father tortures me."

Underneath his anger, something deeper lurked: pain, sorrow, vulnerability. She ran her hands through her hair. Pins fell out, but it didn't matter. The chances of her escaping unscathed dwindled with every moment.

He shifted, drawing her eyes to his muscular arms. "You made your case. While I appreciate your efforts, I have not changed my mind. Thus, the original plan will proceed."

Her heart took a brief sojourn, thumped loudly in her chest upon its return. "What are you about?"

"I am resuming your kidnapping."

She looked down at the ropes, back at him. His jaw was set, his expression determined. "If you didn't notice, you are restrained."

"Actually, that's not quite true." He moved forward and forward and forward some more. The ropes, once tight, loosened, as he pushed through them like lightly wrapped twine. "I only wanted you to believe I was bound. In actuality, I've been free this entire time. And you–" His eyes flashed. "Never were."

He gave no warning. No sign as he transformed into the predator she always knew he was. He lunged forward, a warrior poised to attack. She pivoted to the door, reaching for a handle a mile away. The cool metal bit into her hand as she turned it.

Too late.

He captured her from behind, heavy hands on her arms. The lever snapped back, the door still securely shut. With a firm yet painless grip, he pulled her back into the carriage, into the plush seat. She opened her mouth to scream.

"Do you want to be discovered?"

She swallowed her cry, as he loomed over her. He was intense, massive and *in control*. "What are you doing?" she whispered.

"I thought that was obvious." His power enveloped her. "I am kidnapping you."

CHAPTER EIGHT

Journal of the Duke of Foxworth:

One of man's most important roles is protecting the females in his care. Sisters, daughters, wards, and, of course, his wife. It is vital to protect those who are vulnerable, whether or not they wish for such protection. This is especially true for high-spirited ladies who delve into danger at every opportunity, taking no care for their own safety. Even when one is not officially respon-sible, a true gentleman will still protect her with his life.

After all, she may very well become his.

"CEASE YOUR KNAVERY immediately!" The bundle of glorious femininity struggled in his grip, and it was all he could do to keep his movements measured, to only touch her as necessary to secure her.

The need to possess battled with the need to comfort, as he maneuvered her so she wouldn't scratch her delicate skin. "I told you I was going to kidnap you."

"You said you were going to *attempt* to kidnap me!" she cried. "You were tied up at the time."

"I always get what I want." Right now, he wanted her. For retribution, of course.

Only that wasn't quite true.

Focus! He wouldn't have her at all if they didn't leave London post haste. Already Bradenton could be launching a search of the streets. No doubt the man would use every resource available to retrieve the precious woman. "As I said, there was always a kidnapping." He leaned into the scent of violets and sweetness. "But it was yours."

"Oh!" She tried to move past him, yet he held her carefully. "You can't do this!"

"I believe we've already established what I can and will do." He allowed a slow, curved smile. "Perhaps it will do you good. Teach you not to take chances with yourself."

"You don't teach me anything." She ground her teeth." I will get out of here the moment you leave."

"The carriage will be locked from the outside." He sabotaged her plan in an instant.

"You'll hurt yourself if you try to escape."

"You won't get away with this." She glowered. "Are you planning to keep me locked in the carriage the entire time?"

"Of course not." He rubbed his raw wrists. "As soon as we reach the estate, you will have the run of the manor. Consider it a vacation. In a few days, I will return you safely home."

She hesitated, bit that plump lower lip. When she spoke, there was an uncharacteristic catch to her voice. "You do not plan to compromise me?"

He drew back. The thought of forcing a woman sickened him like little else. "I am a gentleman. You will not be ravished."

The sides of her lips turned down ever-so-slightly.

He tightened. This woman may not be as physically strong as him, yet she held far more power than she realized. "That is, unless you wish for it."

"I have no intention of allowing you to compromise me," she snapped. Then she sat up primly, as if in a ton drawing room, and not in a carriage about to be spirited away. "I do not enjoy such activities with you."

"Really?" He lowered his voice. "Are you certain?"

She grew pink. And pinker. And pinker.

"Tell me, my lady," he murmured. "Are you planning to initiate something?"

Even in the dim light, he could see her stiffen. "Most certainly not. If you try something, I will make my feelings perfectly clear."

"Will you?" He raised an eyebrow. "Just like with the kiss?"

Now she turned as red as a theater actress' lips. "I did not kiss you." She held his gaze, then looked away. "Fine, I did kiss you, but only because the strain of the night affected my sensibilities."

"You could have pulled back any time." He kept his gaze steady. "Why didn't you?"

She hesitated, her eyes liquid and unblinking. Suddenly, her control wavered, as she whispered in a barely audible voice, "I don't know."

Neither did he.

He dropped his hand. "I will always stop if you wish."

Her eyes darted back and forth, as she nodded.

The distinct clopping of hooves emerged from outside. Tension thickened the air, as they locked eyes. By its quiet cadence, it was a well-appointed conveyance, expensive, luxurious, characteristic of the nobility. Hushed voices sounded, their words ever-louder as the vibrations increased. Then an unmistakable utterance: "We'll find her."

Who else would they be searching for, so soon after the abduction, so close to its source?

Had they already been discovered?

Sophia flushed. "One scream, and they'll know I'm here."

The assertion was undoubtedly correct. One scream and she would be his *permanently.*

He should remind her of the consequences, the inevitable outcome should they be discovered: a match, whether she liked it or not.

Instead, he said nothing.

The horses' rhythm slowed. Voices grew louder and louder. No names were uttered, yet every word made increasingly clear their target's identity. The horses moved slower still, the voices louder. Slower and louder, slower and louder. Sophia leaned forward, her lips parted. The hooves stopped...

Then picked up again.

He released a breath, even as she traversed from the redness of earlier to the paleness of the moon above. Her breathing had shallowed, and he had to stop himself from reaching for her. Emotions swirled, yet whether relief or disappointment was not clear. Perhaps both.

An owl hooted, and in the distance, another carriage. They were still in a populated area of London, and discovery was not only possible, but likely, the longer they lingered. "Time to depart."

She said nothing.

"The journey is only half a day. If you need anything, knock on the roof. I will hear you."

She glared at him. "What's to stop me from following you out of the carriage?"

He gave a wicked smile. "Do I need to restrain you?"

She gasped, scooted back. "Don't. You. Dare."

"Then I suppose I shall employ a different strategy."

"What—"

He kissed her.

This time there was no slow opening, no tender beginning. The kiss was an onslaught of passion, an expression of the hunger she denied. Of course, if she pulled back or showed any resistance, he would have ended it immediately.

Instead she pressed into the kiss.

That was his lass. The instinctual thought drifted into his mind as he caressed her lips, probing the intoxicating allure that was Lady Sophia Hawkins. The kiss started as a diversion, yet it captured him in thrall. She was perfection and promise, luscious curves and irresistible softness.

Sophia moaned softly, the small sound as powerful as any queen's command. Strength infused him, and a feeling of utter rightness. He accepted her surrender, demanding more, yet she demanded as well, pressing her small body into his. The need to take control, to possess, enveloped him.

Yet he couldn't claim her. Not yet.

Even as desire surged anew, he pulled back. He couldn't take her now, in a wobbly carriage parked in a backstreet alley. Even if he would do the right thing in the end, that was not the man he was.

The kiss had been for a reason. More than one, if he was honest with himself, but first to distract her, to allow the kidnapping. It was time. With one last press of his lips, he broke away. For a moment, she stayed motionless, her eyes still closed, her lips plump, swollen and pink, and so very tempting. He leapt to the door, exiting the carriage before she even opened her eyes.

He slammed the door with a loud thump, then slid the lock into place. Satisfaction surged, as he never expected, even as a loud crash shook the entire carriage. It was too late. The lock held fast.

"Open the door this instant!" The hiss was loud, yet measured, signaling she still remembered the dangers of being caught. Not that anyone was likely to hear in the desolate alley, with the carriage of earlier out of sight. Soon, they would be far from danger.

He pulled his coat around him. "Just relax, my lady. The journey is not long. If you become hungry or cold, the basket on the floor contains a blanket and refreshments."

"You'll regret this." The banging came again, yet lower this time, an acknowledgement of its futility, perhaps. He climbed into the seat and took hold of the reins. With low snorts, the horses stepped forward to the main road, leading to the edge of London and beyond.

The minutes passed in a leisurely manner, far from the evening's frenzied events. The night was cool and calm, the sky cloudless above. A few times Sophia demanded her release, but when he didn't answer, she eventually quieted down. Soon, they left the populated areas behind, embarking onto the quieter, darker countryside. They passed few carriages, and fortunately none stopped.

Sophia's argument had been compelling, and for the briefest

of moments, doubt surfaced. Could there be any truth to her claim that Bradenton hadn't committed the crimes his father accused? The duke was highly respected among the ton, known for his fervent support of social action and numerous charitable activities.

However, the evidence was just too great. His father had written the accusations in his private journal, with him as the only audience. He had died the day of the duel, with a mysterious burial conducted under even more mysterious circumstances. Yet despite that, a sliver of doubt could have existed if not for his father's man of business, who had confirmed the duel in explicit detail. When his father had fallen on the field, unable to lift even his gun, Bradenton had shot him point blank.

A man like that deserved retribution.

The carriage rocked, and he frowned. He had locked Sophia in for her own safety, to avoid her leaping from the moving carriage and injuring herself. As the coach wobbled once more, he pulled back on the reins, yet before he could stop, a few muffled oaths came from inside, filled with anger, but not fear or pain, including a very creative description of what she planned to do with his overbearing, domineering, ridiculously tight–

He chuckled. His lass was feisty indeed.

He'd told Sophia his plan was solely about revenge, yet perhaps more motivated him. Now he had days to explore the mystery that was this beautiful lady.

Ways she should have responded to Foxworth's kiss:
1. *Demanded he immediately stop.*
2. *Pinched his nose so he would he immediately stop.*
3. *Overpowered him until he stopped and used the opportunity to escape.*

All right, three was never going to happen, mainly because he was twice her size and as powerful as a mountain. However the other two were distinct possibilities. Unfortunately, what she actually did was far different:

1. *Sighed, moaned and made other assorted noises.*
2. *Curled her toes, while other parts of her body did interesting things.*
3. *Kissed him for all she was worth.*

What was wrong with her? She had literally just explained how his previous kiss(es) didn't affect her. Then he kissed her, the world turned all topsy-turvy and she just sat by while he locked her in the carriage. Likely he could have driven to the moon before she tried to escape.

Now it was too late. The carriage had been ambling for hours, first over the roads of London, then through the telltale rumbles of country roads. The sounds of civilization were far behind, replaced by the rustling of night creatures.

Like it or not, she was Foxworth's prisoner.

She tried to stay focused, making a list of all the ways she could – would – exact revenge. If Priscilla were here, she would recommend bopping him on the head with a vase, and Emma would suggest the use of an alligator. So far her best plan involved his overbearing, domineering, ridiculously tight–

Minutes and then hours passed, and she started to drift, repeatedly jerking herself awake. She loathed accepting anything from Foxworth, yet she had missed dinner and her throat was parched. She reached into the large wicker basket, retrieving a crusty loaf of bread and a platter of savory pastries. There was also a casket of wine, cheeses and even some sweets. As she bit into a sweet apple tart that had clearly been baked that day, she softened just a little.

No.

A thoughtful kidnapper was still a kidnapper.

Once full, the lure of slumber grew harder to resist. The sun still hadn't risen, and her eyes drifted lower and lower, until she finally surrendered to sleep. Yet if she'd hoped for a reprieve from the untamed duke, it was not to be granted. Foxworth appeared in her dreams, with his wicked smile, clever eyes and command-ing presence. He took her lips again and again, eliciting her surrender a thousand and one times.

Somewhere in the back of her mind, the cadence of the car-riage rolling to a stop broke through. Yet slumber was recalcitrant, clutching her, even as she shifted on the narrow seat. Then the man from her dreams returned, bringing warmth, comfort, and strength. She burrowed into the source of heat, more comfortable than she ever remembered, as she was in motion once more.

The seconds blurred together, as new sensations emerged: the scent of the outside air, not like London but fresh and sweet, and the beautiful melody of night birds. When a chill stung, a warm presence vanquished it. Suddenly she was being lowered onto a feathery surface, sinking into a cool, plush cloud. She gave a tiny mewl of protest as the source of warmth left, settled as his presence hovered again. Then the dream slipped away and darkness captured her.

KENNETH GAZED AT the woman sleeping on the massive four poster bed. Her lithe form lay sprawled under rose-colored sheets, creamy perfection among shimmery silk. The dress molded to generous curves, outlining tempting rises and alluring falls. Her cheeks were tinged pink, her lips parted as charcoal eyelashes fluttered.

The trip had been blissfully uneventful, with no brigands and no sword-toting dukes arriving to avenge their sisters. He travelled straight through, without leaving his charge for even a moment. No doubt Bradenton would launch a discreet manhunt, yet he was unlikely to find them. The estate was owned by his mother's family, with no relation to the dukedom. His scheme had worked, at least for now.

When he opened the coach to find Sophia curled into a tiny ball, he'd been unable to stop an unexpected tenderness. He should have woken her, yet instead he'd grasped her, held her safe and close as he carried her inside. When he placed her in the bed, it took every bit of strength not to stay. It wasn't about desire or physical attraction, but the inescapable urge to protect her from any and all harm, to shield her from the danger she endlessly courted, to simply be with her.

Less scandalous than intimacy, it was far more dangerous.

If only they met without the context of revenge, the specter of her brother. If they had been strangers, the path would have been theirs to forge.

This trip would provide the perfect opportunity to further his goals. That she would try to escape was without a doubt, yet he would not allow her to leave until he was ready...

If he ever was.

CHAPTER NINE

The Private Diary of Sophia Hawkins (in a temporary new journal)

Ways to escape an untamed duke:

1. *Hide all his clothes while he is sleeping and run. Problem: Likely he'll chase you anyways. Unexpected Benefit: The view will be interesting.*
2. *Sneak out while he is in the bath. Problem: Likely he'll chase you anyways, only wet and naked. Unexpected Benefit: The view will be even more interesting.*
3. *Tie him to something, and then escape. Problem: Tried before to a spectacular failure. Unexpected Benefit: If done while he is naked, will be the most interesting view of all. New problem: May stay to watch instead of escaping.*

S HE WAS GOING to escape.

It didn't matter that she had no idea where he spirited her, or that she couldn't contact her family. It didn't matter that she risked inescapable scandal. It didn't even matter that the only form of transportation could be her own two feet. Somehow, she would find a way.

She had awoken in an enormous bed, upon a feather soft mattress and tucked under a plush blanket. That Foxworth had carried her into his domain sent a shiver through her, yet true to his word, he did nothing untoward. Every bit of clothing was properly secured, laces tied and untouched.

The room was gorgeous, reeking of old wealth and raw luxury. Masterful tapestries lined cream-colored walls, next to ornate tables with curved edges and clawed feet. A massive marble fireplace stood in the corner, opposite a sitting area with two oversized chairs and a settee of deep mauve. A floor to ceiling window graced an entire wall, showcasing a breathtaking natural landscape.

Despite the situation, the view calmed her. Vast swaths of green stretched for miles, punctuated by towering trees and glimmering lakes. Above the lush land, the sky was a brilliant blue, the sun already high in its cloudless domain as it shined on a wide river that extended as far as one could see. A single road led from the estate, over a bridge that crossed the river, guarded by a tall and sturdy gate. She narrowed her eyes.

If Foxworth thought a gate would stop a member of the *Distinguished Ladies of Purpose*, he was in for a most startling surprise.

She toured the room, stopping at a note propped on the table. It directed her to a wardrobe with half a dozen dresses, all in her size, as well as directions to the dining room, where she would proceed after dressing. She took her time perusing the exquisite gowns, which were all in season and excellent condition. Who owned them? As quickly as the thought arose, she pushed it aside. It didn't matter who Foxworth brought to his estate. All that mattered was getting off it.

She donned a light blue day dress with wispy puff sleeves, a lace overlay and pearl embellishments. Afterwards, she plaited her long hair into a thick braid and slid her feet into the slippers she'd worn last night. She'd awoken to find them removed and placed neatly at the foot of the bed. The simple gesture shouldn't have mattered, yet somehow it did, showing intimacy, familiarity and, even more disconcerting, thoughtfulness.

Half-expecting the room to be locked despite the letter, she was almost relieved when the heavy wooden door opened, leading to a red-carpeted hallway flanked by brilliant tapestries.

Gilded vases stood like soldiers as she travelled through the corridor and down a curved stairway. She followed her nose through one cavernous hallway after the next, stepping to the sound of dishes chiming and pots clinging. Her feet echoed on the gleaming floor, as she entered a bright dining room.

As the sister of a duke, Sophia was accustomed to luxury, yet the room was impressive nevertheless. Two stories tall, with a long, white table flanked by throne-like chairs, it gleamed in the natural light from tall domed windows. Crystal candleholders cast fiery rainbows upon pristine white settees, painting a masterpiece of light. On the table, two golden place settings had been arranged, with a closeness that begot intimacy far beyond abductor and abductee.

Sophia padded to the sideboard, stepping into the delicious aromas of a dozen overfilling platters. The selection included steaming biscuits slathered with creamy butter, fluffy eggs cooked to golden perfection and a variety of cakes topped by hot fruit preserves. Fresh juices and creamy hot chocolate accompanied the fare.

"Do you approve?"

She gasped and pivoted.

How very unfair. A man that devious should be weak of body as well, or at least possess some major flaw. Yet Foxworth was chiseled perfection, pure masculine beauty as he strode into the room with the grace of a tiger. Freshly shaven, he wore a white shirt and black pants that molded to his muscular form. His hair was brushed, his eyes alight.

"Thank you for such a lovely feast," she said automatically.

She pursed her lips. Had she actually just thanked the man who kidnapped her? "What I mean is it is lovely, yet I would much prefer to be free."

Had she seriously just complimented him again?

His shining eyes proved the affirmative. "I'm glad the food meets your approval."

This wouldn't do. She needed to defy him, demand her release. Perhaps something truly shocking would sway him. "It is a shame I shall not be eating it."

His gaze didn't waver, as he folded his arms across his chest. The fabric splayed taut against his chest, straining against sculpted muscles. "Why do you *believe* you won't be eating?"

Annoyance brought heat to her cheeks. "I will not be eating because I'm not staying. Indeed, I shall not eat until you take me home." Her stomach chose that moment to growl in protest, yet surely it wouldn't have to wait long. He wouldn't dare allow her to starve.

The steaming food beckoned. Perhaps she could take some eggs for the trip. And a few of those butter cakes with strawberry preserves. The tarts looked delici–

"We shall return in a few days, but until then you will enjoy my hospitality. I made it just for you."

"You cooked this?" She glanced around the massive dining room. It was spotless, yet there wasn't a single servant to take credit, not a maid, butler, housekeeper or steward. Manors of this size usually maintained a small crew to prepare for the master's return. Were they truly, utterly alone?

Foxworth strode to the sideboard and grasped two plates, serving generous portions onto each with a golden spoon. "I employ caretakers while I am not here, which is why the estate is in good form, but I sent them away. I didn't want anyone to see you."

Relief and dismay rose in equal amounts. There would be no one to spread gossip, and no one to help. "Or aid in my escape."

He inclined his head, distributing a selection of miniature cakes, each with a dollop of cream. He finished filling the platters, then returned to the table, placing one at each setting. He strode towards her.

She backed up, stopped and straightened. She would not be intimidated. "Don't you dar–"

He captured her.

She gasped as her feet left the ground, as he took control,

pressing her against a body she knew so well. One hand gripped her back, the other under her legs, as heat engulfed her. She pried at his hands, yet he didn't appear to *notice*. "Let me go!"

He didn't obey and he didn't respond, instead striding back to the table with his prize. He stopped when they reached the chairs, but made no move to release her. "You will eat."

She scowled. "You can't force me to eat."

"Perhaps not." His voice lowered, "However, you can't force me to put you down."

Why, that little– or rather excessively large–

"How dare you!" she hissed. "You refuse to put me down unless I agree to eat?"

"That is correct."

"You can't do that!"

"I'm already doing it." He shifted her closer, splaying his hand across her back. He touched nowhere intimate, yet heat blazed everywhere. "I will not allow you to neglect your health."

"You don't allow me to do anything," she ground out. "Do not worry about me."

"I find I quite enjoy worrying about you," he mused. "The thought of letting you go becomes more disagreeable by the minute."

What?

She fought for strength. "You, sir, are untamed."

He showed none of the affronted indignity of a reasonable member of the ton would, and displayed no regret. Instead his eyes glowed with power and purpose. "When we first met, I warned you someone would take over if Bradenton didn't care for you properly. Since you are here with me alone, clearly you need someone better able to take you in hand."

The room scorched like an inferno. This man didn't adhere to the dictates of the world. Instead, he seized power, took what he wanted. "Who are you to claim yourself my protector?" she stormed. "You have no authority over me."

"As you have so often pointed out, I am not a man who waits

for power to be bestowed."

She shifted, yet his hold did not waver for an instant. It should have been uncomfortable in his arms, hard, rough and inhospitable. Yet instead it was strangely comfortable, comforting even, his chest broad and warm, his hands carefully placed to support without harm. If he wasn't her sworn enemy, it would have almost been... nice.

No. She couldn't forget his misdeeds, allow him to weaken her resolve. Stories abound of ladies falling for their captors, caught in a pretend world in which abductor and savior exchanged meaning. She was too strong to allow it to happen to her.

"I am perfectly able to care for myself."

"Are you now?" A faint Scottish burr underscored the words. "Then you have a choice. Either you enjoy this delicious breakfast, or I continue to hold you for as long as it takes to change your mind. I believe eventually you will realize the futility of your actions, or your stomach will remind you." His expression softened. "Do you truly wish to fight this battle? We return to London in just a few days."

She paused. Her strategy seemed reasonable at first, favorable even, yet clearly she would not accomplish her goals. Being in his arms made her achy and unsatisfied. "When we return, you will release me immediately? Your revenge will be satisfied?"

He did not delay. "You have my word the retribution will be over."

He hadn't explicitly agreed to release her, yet surely it was implied. He couldn't just keep her. "All right."

Foxworth showed no lordliness as he gently lowered her to the seat and took the chair across from her. The plush cushion sank underneath her, yet somehow it lacked the comfort of his arms. The next few minutes were filled with silence save for the clinking of dishes and enjoyment of food. The fare was delicious – the eggs light and fluffy, the cakes sweet as they melted in her mouth. The preserves burst with the taste of strawberries and apple, and the tea was honeyed and flavorful, providing the perfect complement to the hearty meal.

Sophia ate her fill, and then some. When she finished, she patted her face with a delicate lace napkin, as Foxworth completed his own meal.

His satisfaction was obvious as he viewed her empty plate. "Did you enjoy it?"

Her numerous sighs precluded any lie. "It was delicious. Where did you learn to create such delicacies?"

"Unlike the pampered gentleman of the ton, many in Scotland learn such skills. It is practical when one doesn't have a dozen servants seeing to every need." He frowned, held out a hand. "I meant no offense. I was not discussing a particular lord, but society in general. The class differences are striking and harsh."

She parted her lips. Most "civilized" men barely looked at those they considered inferior, believing themselves superior simply because of a title, or a fat purse. Of course, they did not choose their birth any more than the poorer classes, and fortune granted them their bounty, not any sort of inherent difference. She'd seen servants show kindness, humility and grace, and lords destroy for diversion.

Who truly was superior?

By his words, Foxworth seemed to realize this. Was he truly on the correct side of social action?

"The dress fits you well."

She smoothed down the skirt, self-consciousness warming her cheeks. "I was surprised to find so many outfits. I assume they belong to...."

"My sister."

Unexpected relief loosened her lungs, and she relaxed. Of course they were Clara's. She must stay here as well, and was of a similar size.

Foxworth inclined his head. "Who did you think they belonged to?"

She would never reveal she believed them to belong to his mistress, or that she cared. "I assumed they belonged to the last lady you kidnapped."

He grinned. "Haven't I made clear you're the only lady I've kidnapped?"

She bit back a scowl. "It is fortunate they are here. I did not have time to pack for my kidnapping."

"How thoughtless of me." He rubbed his chin. "Next time I kidnap you, I shall give you ample time to prepare. A week at least, two if you need it."

She resisted the urge to flick a tart at him. Mainly because they were so delicious. "There will be no next time. In fact, I'd appreciate it if you took me back right now."

He lowered his cup and took a tart. She eyed it. "You've made many such requests. How did that work out for you?"

He hadn't taken her home. Instead he'd...

Kissed her senseless.

Spirited her away.

Held her captive.

In conclusion, not well.

"Yesterday was merely a setback. Today everything is different."

"Indeed?" He ate the tart in two bites. "Did you forget our little disagreement?"

"The one in which you seized me like a pirate?" She stood, tossing the napkin onto the table. Now that her belly was full, it was time to resume the fight. "You take whatever you want, control others without right or responsibility."

"I do not deny it." He stood, pushing the chair back with a scrape. The mood darkened, as he towered a foot above her. "I fight for justice."

"Justice?" She gripped the sides of her dress, crinkling the delicate fabric. No longer able to stand still, she took several steps, turned and paced. "What is just about kidnapping a lady to seek revenge? Endangering a woman to punish her brother?"

"You were never in danger." His voice was now serious. "I won't touch you unless you wish it."

And with that statement, every memory of him touching her crashed in her mind, every kiss, every gaze. Caught in a clandestine look so full of meaning, she could scarce breathe.

He stepped closer. "Is there something you wish to ask me?"

Would you kiss me?

She cleared her throat. "When will you release me?"

"In several days, when Bradenton has time to reconsider his evil deeds. Of course, I have suitable diversions planned while you are here."

"Diversions?"

Proposed Schedule:
10am Kissing.
11am Kissing.
12pm Kissing
1pm Ki–

"What sort of diversions? What do you plan to do with me while me are here?"

It was the wrong question.

His gaze darkened, as every single thing he could do to her flashed through her mind. Heat flooded her cheeks, as the temperature notched up a thousand degrees. "I mean what are you going to do me?"

Worse.

"I mean what are we going to do with each other?"

Bloody hell.

His fiery gaze proved he recognized every thought in her wicked mind. "What would you like to do with me?"

What she wanted to do with the Untamed Duke, in no particular order.

1. *Kiss him.*
2. *Kiss him.*

3. Kiss him.

4. Kiss...

She fought for strength. "I would very much like to kidnap you back to London so you can enjoy the consequences of your behavior."

"Not to be disagreeable, but your last attempt at kidnapping did not end well, at least not for you."

Ah, yes. He'd reversed their positions and kidnapped her instead.

Disappointing, to say the least.

She jutted up her chin. "I am certain I can get better with practice."

"Would you like me to tie myself up so you may have a go of it?"

"It would be the gentlemanly thing to do."

Amusement glinted in his eyes. "You need not be unhappy here. The estate boasts a well-stocked library, a full music room and extensive gardens, which you may explore."

"Do you have a room with weapons?"

"I'm not certain I should answer that question."

The smothering gloom lifted ever-so-slightly. Perhaps this could be an opportunity, the chance to sample activities her overprotective brother didn't allow. Of course it would only be for today. During their tour she would find the weak spot in his "prison," and formulate the best path forward.

Tomorrow she would escape.

SOPHIA WOULD ESCAPE.

At least she would make the attempt, which he would then stop in no uncertain terms. It was a secret she gave away no less than a dozen times during their tour, as she tried every door, studied every window. She inquired about the building, the roads, the town. By her self-assured expression, there wasn't a chance she wouldn't succeed.

She wouldn't.

Besides her questions, she showed polite interest in the rest of the estate. Her eyes lit up at the gardens, blooming heartily from his caretakers' botanical expertise. She ran her hand along the gleaming instruments of the music room. She looked twice at the library, and said she wished she had time to read the books. When he pointed out she had days, she merely shrugged.

Which meant it was time to show her the only road leaving the estate.

They reached the small path, which led to the narrow bridge over the wide, fast-moving river. She stared.

The large gate that blocked her way was crafted of thick lumber and heavy iron. Secure and sturdy, it towered straight to the sky, with nothing to act as handhold or foothold. Even he would have difficultly scaling it.

She bit her bottom lip. "Was this really necessary?"

"Do you not know the answer to that?"

She stared at him. "Then I may as well be honest. No matter how you imprison me, I will escape."

With a pointed look, he pushed the thick, smooth wood. It didn't give an inch, not even when he added pressure.

Her frown deepened. She looked to the left and right, down a river that stretched for miles. "Where's the next bridge?"

"This is a sparsely populated area, with few towns." That was true, yet the nearest bridge was still only hours by foot, closer by horseback. If she set out at a brisk pace, she could be in the next town by luncheon. It was not something he would mention.

By her clenched fists, he assumed she was trapped, just as he'd intended. "Is there another way back to London?"

He pointed to the forest on the other side of the estate. "How comfortable are you with wild animals?"

She glared. "I'm managing you."

"Tsk, tsk, Lady Sophia. That's not a very... *tamed* thing to say." He pushed off the gate, stalked her. She flinched, but didn't retreat. That was his brave lass. "Some predators bite."

Her eyes narrowed into little slits. "I'm accustomed to dealing with those who falsely seek control."

"Are you?" He cracked his knuckles. "And I enjoy chasing unsuspecting prey. It's almost as much fun as catching them."

Her face pinkened, yet still she stood tall. "I'm not afraid of you."

"You should be."

He had to prevent her escape for her own safety. A woman alone in unfamiliar territory was treacherous, and he hadn't exaggerated the peril of the forest. Dangerous animals lurked there, and she could easily become lost among the dense vegetation. "Even if you don't have a healthy fear of predators, the forest is not a feasible path. You'd have to travel days in the wrong direction, bringing you home far later than I planned. This bridge is the only route back for miles. When a great storm felled it one year, I stayed for weeks, until it was repaired."

Of course, only because he didn't want to leave.

Her expression turned pensive. "You repaired it yourself?"

"No." He grasped its smooth side. "I don't have the necessary materials. Fortunately, the townspeople pass here regularly. I enlisted their help to build a new one."

"You mentioned a town earlier." She gazed over the bridge. "I do not often have the opportunity to visit to new places. I shall like to explore it."

"I'm afraid that's impossible." He did not need to feign his regret. He would have liked to have shown her the charming town and its kind people, but no doubt she'd slip away the moment they arrived. "The townspeople do not know I am a duke. How would I explain you?"

"We shall say I am your cousin. I assume they do not often visit London."

"Most of them haven't travelled further than the next town," he admitted. Of course, there was always the risk someone would recognize her. Moreover, he couldn't take the chance she would escape. "I'm sorry, Lady Sophia."

She sighed. "There must be something I can do to get back to

London."

"There is. Simply wait a few days, and I will take you back myself." He lowered his voice. "Give up, Lady Sophia, You're not going to win."

She took a deep breath, angling her face toward the sun. The light glinted off her creamy features, turning her hair almost translucent. Against the endless green of the land, she was an enchantress of the Earth.

"I think it's time to see the weapons."

And delightfully feisty. He chuckled, gesturing her forward. "As you wish, my lady."

She took one long last baleful look at the bridge.

He smiled.

They walked back in silence, yet a surprisingly comfortable one. She kept a strong profile, a confident tilt to her head, as she stomped forward. When she stepped onto a weak part of the ground, he instinctively grasped her. She started, yet didn't pull back, her expression betraying the same confusion that plagued him whenever they touched. Whatever he felt, affected her as well. "Thank you."

She slowed after that. It felt strangely right, as they strolled under the shining sun, gently brushing against each other. He had to release her to open the door, yet they stayed close as they traversed extensive hallways, until they came to two tall wooden doors carved with an ancient Scottish sword. He unlocked them, and gestured her forward.

She walked in and stopped.

She pivoted slowly, taking in everything. Gleaming swords of all shapes and sizes lined the walls, punctuated by knives, daggers and other impressive weaponry. Some gleamed with modern design, while others were dented and discolored with time's passing. The extensive display included armaments passed down from his ancestors, as well as pieces he'd collected in his travels.

"Teach me how to sword fight."

That the statement did not surprise Kenneth was as surprising as the statement itself. From any other lady, it would have been inconceivable, yet from Sophia, it was all but expected. "Do you wish to challenge me for your freedom? You would lose."

"Don't be so certain about that." She stopped at a broadsword almost as large as she and touched its bejeweled hilt. "I'm a quick learner."

"That is undoubtedly true."

She looked up sharply, yet he kept his expression sincere. Did she not realize how highly he thought of her? Still, the thought of her playing with swords was a bit too much to bear. He would not take the chance of her injuring herself, at least not now when he hadn't enough time to instruct her properly. "Wouldn't you prefer a different pursuit?"

"A more feminine pursuit, don't you mean?" She traced her hand across the blade, snapped her fingers back. He caught her finger, even as she pulled away. Satisfied there was no blood, he released her.

She stared at him. "It is not uncommon for females to encounter danger, yet we are given no tools for defending ourselves. You have often complained about my forays into jeopardy. If I could protect myself, I would be safer."

Her argument held indisputable logic. He had showed Clara the basic techniques for escaping a threat. Elementary moves wouldn't work against someone skilled, of course, and an element of luck existed, yet they gave a chance where none existed. "Has Bradenton taught you nothing about defensive maneuvers?"

She visibly tightened at her brother's name. "Edmund believes he can protect me all on his own. Of course, no one can be there all the time, especially a man with such great responsibilities."

She was making excuses. Bradenton should have known she would put herself in danger. If it had been his sister, he would have made certain someone, or several someones, was watching her at all times.

"I will teach you to defend yourself."

Surprise lit her eyes. "You'll teach me to wield a sword?"

"No." At her waspish expression, he held out a hand. "At least not on this trip."

"This is our *only* trip." She glared. "You mentioned something about defending myself?"

"I can teach you techniques to escape an assailant. They are not foolproof, however, and depending on your opponent, may not work." He lowered his chin. "What I'm saying is they will not work on me."

She smiled sweetly. "Would I try such a thing?"

"Without a doubt."

She shrugged, yet her eyes shined. "You cannot blame me for using every available resource."

"Not at all, yet I am well versed in the ways to overcome these moves." He leaned forward. "If you attempt them, I shall have to take my own defensive maneuvers."

Her expression sobered as he allowed a wolfish smile. "Actually, come to think of it, maybe you should try them."

She stuck her pert little nose into the air. "Are you going to teach me, or is making me fall asleep with endless chatter one of your strategies?"

He chuckled and gave into the urge to move closer. "Are you ready?"

"I am." She stood taller. "Show me."

He walked closer and closer and closer.

"What are you doing?" She gasped as he captured her. "Let go of me!" She struggled in his arms, all lush softness and feminine curves. It affected him in ways he couldn't show, casting emotions he didn't understand. This was to teach the lesson of course, not because of how perfectly she fit.

"Stop struggling," he commanded.

He must have startled her because she obeyed.

"Struggling will only exhaust you," he instructed. "Instead, move like this." With one hand keeping her close, he positioned her with the other. "Try to distract him. Do something unexpected, target vulnerable areas and use his balance against him."

She listened carefully, and tried the technique. Then again, and again, not stopping until she performed it perfectly. Within minutes, she had mastered her first defensive skill.

He covered different techniques, effective against various types of assaults. She was an apt and skilled student, doggedly tenacious and unfailingly precise. She listened attentively, mastering the skills with unrelenting persistence. An hour and then another raced by, and in the end, she possessed at least some tools with which to fight.

Not that he would allow her to face danger again.

On one particularly successful trial she nearly managed to unbalance him. He moved just quickly enough to escape a rather unsavory fall.

"I almost won!" She was breathing heavily, her cheeks tinged pink, her eyes alight with excitement. She never looked so glorious, or so beautiful.

He tapped her arm. "Almost, but not quite. You will not best me, lass."

"We'll see about that." She studied him. "Would you put a wager on it?"

"A wager?" He stood back on his heels. "I am not releasing you, if that is what you wish." The chances of her besting him were infinitesimal, yet he was unwilling to risk it.

For a moment disappointment flashed, but then she brightened. "If I best you, will you teach me to sword fight? I'm sure I can handle that weapon." She pointed to a sword in the corner.

He followed her gaze. With its blunted edge and diminutive dimensions, the sword was unlikely to do major harm, even if used incorrectly. It was actually made for a child, although he would not share that. It was indeed the perfect tool to teach her.

Of course, she would not best him. It was almost too bad. Perhaps he would teach her anyways. "I could be persuaded to give a lesson, if you promise to obey everything I say."

She blinked. "Don't I always?"

He looked upward. "You literally never listen to what I say."

"Then why ask?" she chirped breezily. "It shouldn't matter. The sword is of little danger. Do we have a wager?"

"All right." He grasped her wrist. "If you can escape my hold, I will teach you to spar."

She gave a satisfied smile. Then...

She kissed him.

CHAPTER TEN

Journal of the Duke of Foxworth:

Power is my greatest weapon.

I must never relinquish my will, my senses, my strength. Discipline is vital, for I have seen the consequences of submission, evidence by my mother's surrender to the man who forever owned her. Too much depends on me to fail, and too many need me to allow weakness. I must remain strong, no matter the temptations, no matter my desire.

No one will ever enter the fortress that is my heart.

KENNETH TASTED LIKE brandy and pure power. Somehow even more intoxicating, and just as strong, he usurped her senses, shattered her control. She began as aggressor, yet he immediately took command, holding her secure as he pressed closer.

They parried back and forth, dueling factions mirroring the war within. Somewhere deep, a voice reminded her that she did this for a purpose. She informed the voice that the purpose could wait an hour or two. Yet the voice was insistent, breaking through the fog upending her senses. She pulled back, only slightly, yet Kenneth immediately loosened his hold.

Breaths came one after the other, as she held onto him like a raft in a storm-lashed sea. His gaze held a thousand nameless emotions, his arms still encircling her. She blinked and pulled back. As the gentleman he claimed to be (despite a rather unnecessary kidnapping), he let her go.

Entirely.

She took a deep breath, looked up into his eyes and said…

"I win."

He stared in undisguised shock. After an eternity and a half, said, "I can't believe it."

"Why not?" She grasped her dress, walked lightly around him. "You said to use whatever resources available to distract my assailant. Since there was no sand to throw in your eyes and no rope with which to trip you, I choose this. You released me, thus you forfeit. And I am the victor."

"Indeed you are." In his voice, surprise and wonder tangled with unmistakable admiration. "You are quite extraordinary, Lady Sophia."

She swallowed. He plotted revenge against her brother, kidnapped her, yet when he complimented her, something else lurked…

She swept past him. "Let's get started. You have a lot to teach me."

He stayed still for a moment, before following. "Are you ready?"

Was she ever.

They parried back and forth, and the first lesson she learned was that sword fighting was far more complicated than it looked. How he moved so fast, she didn't know, as he blocked every strike she attempted. When he bested her for the hundredth time, she leaned against the wall. "This is impossible."

He studied her, as if searching for invisible injuries. "Are you well? Do you wish to stop?"

She straightened, lifted her sword. "Of course not."

Yet he remained where he was, at ease with the stick he was using in lieu of a sword slung over his shoulder. "We should stop. You'll be sore in the morning."

She was already sore, as overtaxed muscles threatened to give. Sweat slickened every inch of her body, skin tender from a hundred hits, yet she hadn't made a single successful thrust. She lifted the sword higher...

"We should discuss the kiss."

She froze.

He must have known she would, as he easily grasped the sword. Thoroughly exhausted, she said nothing as he replaced the two weapons back into their holders.

He smiled upon his return. "Distraction can also work for convincing stubborn ladies to listen."

She frowned, studied the floor. "You brought up kissing to distract me?"

"Not entirely," He leaned casually against the wall, perfectly relaxed, as if he'd just awoken from a refreshing night's sleep. "The kisses are now happening with astounding regularity. Shouldn't we discuss them?"

Her heart stopped briefly, then resumed with a thud. How could she explain what she didn't understand? "It's not something one discusses."

"Actually, I'm pretty sure it's something one doesn't *do*."

She looked up sharply.

"Not that I hold any regrets." He held out a hand. "Yet shouldn't we talk about it?"

"There's nothing to discuss." She wiped clammy hands on her skirt. For her next lesson, she would inquire about pants. "I used the kiss to distract you, so I would win our wager. There was nothing beyond practical implications."

"Your only motive was to distract me?"

"Absolutely."

Only it wasn't true.

Other reasons why she kissed him:

His kisses were delicious.

His body was irresistible.

She had the willpower of a tree frog.

She cleared her throat. "I was only creating a distraction, as you instructed."

"And the other times we kissed?"

"That was because…" *His kisses were delicious.* "I had a perfectly rational reason each time, I assure you." *His body was irresistible.* "There was nothing more to them." *She had the willpower of a tree frog.*

He pressed forward. "What if I kissed you now, with no need for distraction, and no rational reason?"

"I would say…I would say there is a perfectly logical reason."

"Really?" He searched her carefully. "And what is that?"

His kisses were delicious, his body was…

She stayed frozen as he stalked closer. Something urged her to flee, yet something far stronger ordered her to stay. Then he was leaning down, stopping but a hairsbreadth away. "Is there a good reason to kiss?" he murmured.

She should deny him, roar an unequivocal and certain no. Yet instead a single word emerged, "Yes."

He swooped down, capturing her lips. It was a passionate onslaught and a slow burning fire all at once, a tangle of sensual ambush and tender assault. He enraptured her, holding her captive, as he drew her closer. Instinctively she raised her hands, yet instead of pushing him away, she splayed them against his chest, kneading, caressing, exploring that irresistible body. Under her palms, muscles tensed, as hard and powerful as the metal swords surrounding them. She breathed in his scent, moaning as he deepened the kiss.

The world melted away. Around them, the gleaming blades turned into a sea of silver, as she breathed in his power, giving hers in return. Large hands threaded through her hair, kneading her neck, massaging her scalp. He held control, yet the power was careful and deliberate, granting not vulnerability, but safety, protection.

It was perfection defined, yet somehow it was not enough. Breathy moans and restless sighs whispered delight, and it took a moment to realize they came from her. Restlessness invaded her soul, the desire – no need – for more. A strange ache weakened her, as already sensitized parts grew even rawer. She writhed at the unfamiliar sensations.

Until he pulled back.

It was sudden and quick, even more so than the beginning. She gasped for air, as the world swayed like a ship on a raging sea, yet she didn't fall. Though his lips had abandoned her, he still held tight, supporting her, sharing his strength.

She opened eyes weighted with uncertainty. He stood tall before her, his expression as severe as the sharpened blades.

"Why did you pull back?"

The scandalous question came on its own, as she touched tender yet traitorous lips. They were swollen and achy, heated like the rest of her. What was he doing to her?

Now she pulled back. For a moment, his hands tightened instead of loosened, as he easily held her captive. "Let me go."

He hesitated, then obeyed, yet a spark of defiance flashed. As if he wouldn't always let go.

Stormy eyes proved his wavering control. "We need to talk."

She swallowed, turned away. "Nothing has changed."

His voice burned. "You truly wish to assert that? After the ki–"

"Do not say it!"

He raised an eyebrow. "Matters have changed. Or perhaps they were always this way, and we are only just realizing it."

She backed up a step, not fleeing of course, yet making a strategic retreat. His presence stole her senses, and the closer she was, the more he affected her. "There are no implications and no consequences."

"If someone knew about this, we'd be instantly betrothed."

So true. "Then it is fortunate no one is here. Soon we will return to London, and no one except my brother will know we were together. He is not the type to force me to marry, and he will not know of the kisses."

"And if someone else discovers the truth?"

She stiffened. "That won't happen unless we tell them. I certainly have no plans to do so, and assume you do not as well."

A muscle ticked in his jaw, and he didn't respond.

He agreed with her, of course. He knew what would happen if the world discovered the truth.

If the secret escaped, she never would.

She stepped back. Only this time, he matched it with a step of his own, until her back came against the solid edge of the table, stopping her retreat. She gripped the wood behind her. It was smooth and hard, unrelenting and unbending. She clutched at it, then stopped.

What was she doing? She was not some wilting wallflower who allowed a man to intimidate her. In a single fluid movement, she ducked under his arm, and turned to face him. She stood tall. "You sir, are untamed."

If she hoped for anger, or annoyance perhaps, she was to be disappointed. Instead he responded lowly, "Perhaps you know me after all."

Yes, she did. This man had *kidnapped* her. She could pretend to be his guest, converse and even jest as if on a society visit, yet in truth she was his prisoner.

The sooner she escaped, the better.

KENNETH STABBED THE air, running his sword through the invisible heart of a nonexistent foe. Sweat dripped down his bare torso as he backed away and lunged again, refining his technique, dancing in precise movement. He practiced regularly, both for exercise and skill. He would need them more than ever when he returned to London and dealt with the men who attacked him.

He still couldn't believe the rogues had bested him. If it hadn't been for Sophia, who knows how it would have ended? When he returned, he would take more drastic action, not stopping until he secured them a place behind bars.

For now, Sophia stole his entire focus. He'd planned to keep her comfortable and secure, yet somehow her enjoyment now mattered just as much. Her passion enlivened him, her strength, intelligence and bravery enraptured him. Watching her sword-fight tested his control like nothing else. The more time he spent with her, the more she drew him in.

And the more letting go became simply unacceptable.

Despite her beliefs, he wanted her happy. If she wanted adventure, he could provide it, albeit safely, of course. Some adventure actually increased her safety, such as teaching her to defend herself. Unfortunately, he had an idea of her next adventure.

Escape.

He parried once more, then returned the sword to its scabbard. Wiping the sweat from his brow, he dried his hands on a course cloth. He turned and strode through the open door.

The hallway was dim, lit only by the occasional candle and the moonlight streaming through the tall, pointed windows. He walked quickly yet deliberately, keeping his steps silent, his bearing focused. It was the middle of the night, yet he hadn't been able to sleep. He had made certain Sophia was sleeping before he left, and kept the door ajar while he practiced. She hadn't tried to escape.

Yet.

But she would, and it was imperative he stop her. His first thought had been to lock her in her room. It would ensure she stayed safely in his care, effectively preventing even an attempt at otherwise. Yet such measures would incur her wrath, undoing the progress he'd made in reducing her animosity. For the first time today, they'd acted as companions, if not friends, and her perpetual scowl had all but disappeared. Which meant he had to find another way to keep her safe.

After careful consideration, a simple solution won. If he couldn't use a lock to confine her, he'd use himself. He stopped briefly at his room, retrieving a thick quilt and thin pillow, before continuing to her chamber. He reached the door and peered inside.

He released a breath at the sight of the petite form on the bed, unaware of the tension until it seeped out of him. Ever since he'd received his title, unchecked apprehension had been his constant companion, like a coiled snake curled in his belly. With the addition of Bradenton, and now the men who'd attacked him, the turmoil had heightened. Yet somehow when he was with her, it was not as sharp.

He backed out of the room, stopping as his reflection glinted off the mirror. Softened features stared back at him, vulnerability he couldn't afford. He tightened.

He couldn't let her distract him from his mission. Logic and reason would determine the path forward, not emotion.

He closed the door. Positioning himself directly next to the entrance, he sprawled on a makeshift bed of hard floor. He would remain strong, powerful, unreachable. One Hawkins had already upended his life.

He would not allow another to do so.

A MASSIVE OBSTACLE blocked her path to freedom. Not the gate, which still loomed in her future, but something far more challenging.

Foxworth lay on the floor, directly outside her door.

Her plan had faltered from the beginning, when she'd lain awake for hours before falling into a fitful slumber. She'd hoped to get a few hours of sleep before embarking, yet her mind churned with memories of the life-changing day. Briefly, she'd considering escaping at night, yet scaling the gate in the dark was just too dangerous. Even if she made it past the bridge, she could not hire a carriage while everyone was still abed. Thus she planned to sleep as swiftly and briefly as possible, rise early enough to break free and arrive at the town just as they started the day's business.

Thankfully, Foxworth was still asleep. Yet his powerful form lay pressed against the doorway, blocking her way. She would have to jump *over* him to escape.

She clutched her dress. She was back in her own clothing, her hair tied back in a simple knot. She bent her knees, but straightened a moment later. To even hope of clearing him, she needed a running start.

She moved back several feet, rubbed her hands together. A breath in, a breath out, hands clenched and flexed. *Three, two, one...*

She lunged. Faster and faster, until inches before him, she leapt. The world stopped as she soared, then she was coming down, down, down...

Just past him.

She landed on four limbs, the breath whooshed from her lungs, her muscles contracted under the weight. Her heart caught in her throat, beating so fast surely it would wake him.

A noise sounded behind her.

Was she already caught? Her breath hitched as her captor shifted to his side, and then back again. His eyelashes fluttered.

No. If he awoke, everything would be lost. He may render the consequences he never-endingly threatened, cast unsurmountable measures to ensure she didn't escape. This had to work.

A second passed, and then another. Yet even as her breathing shallowed, his deepened, and his movements lessened. Even relaxed, his power was evident, yet it was tempered by a serenity consciousness didn't afford. She fought the urge to reach out, to run her hands through his thick locks, to trace the sun-kissed skin and hardened muscles. This man was a danger to her, and more importantly, her brother. She needed to escape.

She pivoted, moving as slowly as necessary and as fast as she dared, her steps whispers against the hard ground. She glanced back at the end of the hallway, yet Foxworth remained on the ground, silent and still. It didn't vanquish the danger.

The predator would chase.

HE AWOKE WITH a jolt. From the numbness of sleep to full consciousness, Kenneth became immediately alert, every sense poised, every muscle ready. The blanket had shifted, the ground cold and hard under his back, his muscles sore from the uncomfortable cradle. He hefted himself up, shielded his eyes against the brightness.

Why was it so bright?

He turned toward the window. Sunlight streamed through the gelatinous pane, its brilliance signaling a far later time than his typical rise. Of course, he did not usually conduct late night training sessions, or lay awake for hours, plagued by memories of the lady sleeping a doorway away. He turned and froze. The door was ajar.

He jumped up in an instant, raced forward and pushed the door. It slammed into the wall with an echoing boom, yet there was no one to awaken, and no one to startle.

The bed was empty.

He pivoted, taking in every corner, every hiding space, any and every location where one may hide. Yet his search proved in vain. Somehow she had escaped.

How had she made it past him? The window? Alarm urged him forward, yet the windows were latched from the inside. He strode back through the door.

Had he truly been so exhausted, he slept through her escape? Anger joined the fear, not at her, but at himself. It was only natural for her to flee. That he didn't prevent it was inexcusable.

Now she was out there alone, possibly in danger. Fear surged, as he pounded down the empty hallway, the boots he'd never removed echoing on the hard tile. He broke into a run, sacrificing moments to glance through the house to ensure her absence. Only silence greeted him, yet something had changed. A dagger was missing from the armory.

With an oath, he raced forward. Not only had she escaped, but she was armed. The latter was more of a concern for her, for although the dagger was small, its blade was wickedly sharp. An unfamiliar wielder could easily get injured.

He burst into the warm day. Blue-tailed birds chirped happy hellos, yet they did nothing to calm the storm brewing inside. He circled the house, yet there was still no sign of her, as he approached the gate.

It was open.

With any other woman, it would have seemed impossible, yet Sophia had proven herself far beyond the ordinary. He growled. Did she truly think she could escape? She may have slunk past him, yet she would find no easy passage from the small town.

Time to recapture his prey.

SOPHIA STARED AT the plump gray horse through the open doorway.

"Are you certain she's awake?"

The shopkeeper rubbed the animal's back. It didn't appear to notice. "Hard to tell. Sometimes she even falls asleep while walking. Just stops in the middle of the road."

Perfect. The only horse available took naps. While walking.

She sighed. The day had started out so well. After literally jumping past Foxworth, she'd run to the armory and retrieved a dagger. Useful for protection, it provided an even more immediate benefit:

It was perfect for picking the gate's lock.

She'd arrived in town at daybreak, taking the well-worn path from Foxworth's estate, as pride and hope cheered her forward. Yet both had faded as she visited one establishment after the next, in an attempt to secure passage to London, with no success. Minutes and then hours passed, and now she was at her last hope, a general store with everything from bonnets and ribbons to medicines and peppers. The store was filled to the brim, yet its offerings were neatly organized and surprisingly broad. One of which was hopefully transportation.

"And she could pull a carriage to London?"

"London?" The gray-haired man gave a raspy bark of laughter, as the corners of his eyes crinkled. George, as he'd introduced himself, was of an age as Lady Drummond, yet far softer, his face etched with permanent laugh lines. "This little lady couldn't make it to London in three lifetimes. When you said you needed to get to the big city, I thought you meant the next town over. They have *two* pubs."

Sophia closed her eyes, opened them. "Is there anyone who can take me to London?"

The man smiled. "Of course. Perry can take you."

Sheer relief eased her stomach, and she grasped the smooth counter. "Oh, thank goodness. Where can I find Perry?"

"He's not here yet." George tipped his hat. "But he should be arriving any month now."

"Any month?" she echoed.

"That's right." He gave a toothy grin. "He comes every six months or so with supplies from London. It's been about five months, or has it been four?"

She didn't have a month. She didn't have a week, probably not even a day. She may not have a minute.

"There's no one else who can help?"

The shopkeeper shook his head apologetically, stopped and brightened. "What am I thinking? Ken can take you."

"Ken?" Even the horse acknowledged the suggestion with a gentle whinny. "Do you think he'd be willing to help? I can pay handsomely as soon as we reach London."

"Ken won't take your money, no matter how much he helps you." The man's smile widened. "A real gem, he is. He's not around often, but he makes a difference all year round. I don't know how we would have made it without him."

Finally, a turn of good fortune. "Where can I find him?"

"You're in luck. According to my bride, he's just arrived."

"Who arrived?" An elderly woman glided from behind a curtain. With a soft smile, she touched the man's shoulder.

He turned, and their eyes locked. And for just a moment, it was half a century in the past, a young suitor gazing at his blushing bride. "This is Rose." His eyes shined. "Isn't she beautiful?"

For the first time since she arrived, Sophia gave a true smile. The woman's face was weathered with age, yet her eyes were a brilliant blue, her expression soft and kind. And she was indeed beautiful. "Most definitely."

The older woman's cheeks turned pink. "Married more than five decades, and he still calls me his bride."

"And you love it."

The deepened blush gave credence to the words. "Oh hush. Your grandson will hear." She pointed to an attractive young man stocking the shelves. He saw them and smiled.

Sophia grinned wider. This love match was no one's secret.

George pointed at her. "I was just telling her about Ken."

"Such a darling young man," his wife gushed. "Always willing to help with anything, no matter if you need advice, money or someone to shovel hay next to you. The Scot may be a giant on the outside, but his heart is even bigger."

The Scot?

A giant?

Oh. No. Oh.
No.

"I don't suppose there are two giant, wealthy Scots nearby."

"Two of them?" Rose laughed. "I assure you, there is only one Ken."

"He has a great deal of resources," George added. "I'm certain he can arrange for passage to London."

He already had. In three days time, with the cost of upending her senses. "Thank you for your assistance. I'm certain I can find my way. Incidentally, how far is that next town you mentioned?"

George looked at her curiously. "It's a bit of a trek, at least half a day on foot. You're far safer putting yourself in Ken's hands. He'll take good care of you."

"Indeed, you'll be quite safe." Rose smoothed down a row of fabrics. "No one can best him."

She had bested him... thus far. She backed away. "Thank you.

If I see him, I'll most definitely inquire."

"He won't be hard to find." The shopkeeper straightened the glass bottles on the counter. "Just look for the man who stands a head taller than everyone. Big fellow."

"Huge really."

"Quite imposing."

Walking to London was looking more attractive by the minute. "Thank you for your assistance. I must go."

"Did you say there was a man who helped people?"

They all turned. A pale young woman stood by the door, with hair so light it was almost white, red-rimmed eyes and severely pinched features. A cloak of concern lay heavy upon her hunched shoulders, as she wrung her hands. She wore a tight cap, hole-stricken slippers and a plain brown dress, its hem frayed with wear and its bottom edged in black.

Deep purple bruises marred the length of her arms.

Sophia tightened. "Are you all right?"

The two elderly shopkeepers looked on with compassion, as their grandson frowned severely. "Can we help you, my dear?"

The woman's eyes darted back and forth. "This was a mistake."

She turned, but Sophia pushed forward. "Wait."

The woman froze, but did not turn.

What to do? The sun was already far on its journey across the sky, and Foxworth could appear any moment. Still, how could she leave the troubled woman? "Rose, is there a place we can speak, in private?"

"Of course, my dear." The kindly shopkeeper gestured them forward, towards a small room in the back.

The younger woman moved slowly, her eyes guarded with fear. Sophia smiled, conveying warmth, solidarity. "Everything will be all right."

The woman bit her lip, clenching and unclenching her hands.

Sophia reached out, yet did not touch her. "No one is going to hurt you, I promise."

The woman paused once more, then gave a nod so slight it was almost imperceptible. She followed Sophia past a thin curtain.

The storeroom was cluttered with countless items, from foods and fabrics to jars holding unknown substances. It tangled in a thousand aromas, yet an open window let in the scent of roses, as well as a breeze of cool air. Sophia moved as far into the room as possible. The woman entered, but stayed far back, like a deer poised to flee.

"I'm Sophia. What's your name?"

"Molly." Her voice little more than a whisper, the woman's lower lip trembled.

Sophia's heart lurched. That lip had been recently split. "It's a pleasure to meet you, Molly. Can you tell me what happened? You're obviously afraid of something." She took a slow step forward. "Did someone hurt you?"

The young woman sucked in a breath of air, confirming what was so painfully obvious.

Somehow Sophia showed none of her fury. The woman needed calmness and composure, not her anger. "It can help to speak about it."

"I... I can't say anything."

"Sure, you can," Sophia implored. "Don't be afraid. No one can steal your power." Yet in a world in which men legally owned women, it was not always true. It's why she worked so hard to change society.

Molly gave a humorless smile. "What power do I have, especially when compared to my stepfather?" Her eyes widened, panic blazing in their liquid depths.

"It's all right." Sophia held up both palms. "Tell me what happened. Please."

For a moment, it seemed as if Molly would flee, yet instead she started speaking in a low, clear voice. She revealed the cruelties of her abusive stepfather, her only relation since her mother disappeared under mysterious circumstances. She talked about how they fled their small town after men threatened him. About how he *hit* her, day after day.

The woman finished her story with a river of tears, and, for just a moment, Sophia wished Kenneth was here. She swiftly pushed the thought aside. "You must get away from your stepfather."

"How?" The woman's gaze darted back and forth to the tavern outside the window. "When he's done guzzling the last of our money, he'll come for me."

"You're going to refuse to leave. At your age, he has no legal right to you." Sophia gestured to the bustling street, boisterous with conversation and laughter. "There are good people in this town. I can make arrangements for you to stay, if you wish."

"If only that were possible." The slightest edge of wistfulness entered the woman's voice. "A local seamstress is looking for an assistant. I thought…" Her voice trailed off. "It doesn't matter. He's never going to let me go."

Yes, he was. "We'll find a way. After this, inquire about the assistant position. I'm sure there's a room for rent somewhere in town."

For an instant, hope lightened her eyes. A moment later, it vanished. "I don't have any money."

Sophia fingered the hidden pocket with her pin money, from a lifetime ago. "I can help with that," she promised.

Molly hugged herself and shook her head.

How could she make the woman see her own strength? Perhaps… "Would you like to learn how to defend yourself?"

"Defend myself?" The woman looked up sharply. "What do you mean?"

"I've learned some techniques to stop an attacker. They won't always work, but they could make you feel a little less vulnerable."

Molly's expression was skeptical. "Can you really teach me that?"

Yes. Did she have time? Most assuredly not.

But she would do it anyways. "Absolutely."

"I... I–"

"Give it a try," Sophia said softly. "What have you got to lose?"

Molly hesitated, but then lifted her chin and showed something every woman deserved: hope. "All right."

They set to work. The next hour was spent practicing all the self-defense techniques, which Foxworth had taught. Molly mastered the basics, and even more importantly, gained a spark of confidence with every successful move. When they finished, Sophia told her about Foxworth and explained how to reach his estate. Despite his overbearing tendencies, he could help the young woman, should she need it.

She was the only woman he wanted to kidnap.

Sophia offered to go with Molly to confront her stepfather, but she refused. Whether she wanted independence or was trying to protect her, she preferred to go alone, and Sophia respected her wishes. She made her promise to speak in a public place, and call for help if she needed it. With hopefully a new future, Molly departed, and Sophia returned to the store.

The elderly woman looked up from her fabrics and smiled. "That was a nice thing you did."

"It sure was." George's eyes twinkled. "Why do I get the feeling you've helped people before?"

"It was nothing." Only as Sophia watched Molly stride outside, poised with newfound confidence, it clearly was something. Perhaps this was the way she could make a difference – provide self-defense instruction for ladies once she returned to London. Of course, she'd need more than a day's worth of lessons herself. If she were actually staying, she'd ask for Foxworth for more lessons.

The tightness in her chest could not possibly be disappointment.

"Is Molly going to ask Ken for assistance?"

The reminder of her kidnapper sobered her immediately.

"She's going to try on her own, but I told her about Foxwo– Ken. She'll find him if she needs him."

Rose nodded, then her gaze drifted. Her smile widened. "She won't have to look far."

Oh. No.

"This is good fortune indeed."

Don't turn around. Don't look.

Sophia edged forward, towards the back exit, yet two heavy footsteps sounded for every one of hers. Tingles traced her spine as her predator delved closer... and closer... and closer.

She never made it to the door.

A form towered behind her, massive, powerful, commanding. Then a hot breath against her neck. "I've found something that belongs to me."

Foxworth.

CHAPTER ELEVEN

The Private Diary of Sophia Hawkins

Remain strong.

Do not forget why you are here, and at whose command. Remember your allegiances, the truths you hold in your heart. You must stay strong, focused and brave, as you navigate these uncharted territories. He is demanding far more than he purports, and if you allow yourself to soften, you will succumb to the danger that lurks.

He demands your surrender.

K ENNETH NEVER EXPECTED the surge of emotion when he captured his prey.

Relief. Satisfaction. The desire to never let her go.

Sophia watched him with wary eyes, edging back until she collided with the counter. She reached behind her, braced herself, but it didn't matter. Her temporary escape was over.

She was his.

"I see you have met Sophia."

The shopkeepers looked back and forth between the two of them. The elderly man knitted his brows together. "You know each other?"

"Of course she knows me," Kenneth rumbled.

"Indeed, I do," she swiftly agreed.

"We are married."

"Married?" The old man grinned.

"Married?" The old woman clapped.

"Married?" Sophia gasped.

The couple looked at her, and she looked at him. "Of– of course. I am his wife."

His wife.

It sounded right.

It was not what he'd meant to say, or even consciously thought. He was going to claim her as his cousin, visiting from London. It was imminently logical, allaying suspicion while allowing them to move freely about town. Of course, claiming they were married brought other problems, such as how he would explain her absence the next time he visited.

Perhaps he'd just bring her with him.

"We didn't know you were married." Rose was as shocked as he'd ever seen.

"We thought you were a bachelor," George added.

"Indeed I was," Kenneth confirmed. "This is new."

"Very new," Sophia echoed. "We just got married. Quite literally. In fact, it feels like mere seconds ago."

"Don't be silly, my dear." He rubbed her back in a slow, circular motion. Muscles tensed, and he splayed his hand wider. "Surely, it's been a full minute now."

"Time does go quickly." Rose's eyes sparkled. "It feels like just yesterday I married my George. But when the connection is there, it's irresistible."

"We don't have a connection." Sophia waved both hands. "We don't even like each other."

At the couple's startled expression, she flushed. "I meant we don't like each other like *that*. You see... he and I... we... it's a marriage of convenience." She gave a shaky smile. "I brought refinement to the marriage, and he... he brought tyranny."

"What?" Rose gasped.

"I'm sorry?" George stuttered.

Foxworth folded his arms across his chest.

"I meant he's tyrannical about my safety." Sophia mumbled.

If he wasn't so frustrated by her escape, he might have

smiled, but instead he stared at her with the full force of his power. Most people would have cowered. She glared right back.

She was glorious.

"A man with such a precious wife must keep her safe." He stepped around her in a slow circle. "It's my duty to keep you healthy and secure. To make certain you *behave.*"

Her expression turned thunderous. "No one dictates how I behave."

"Are you sure?"

She opened her mouth, but Rose spoke first. "We were arranged, too, if you would believe it. I fought my papa, but he knew George was the right man for me. There are some things you simply can't fight."

Love? Kenneth rocked back on his heels. The shopkeeper was mistaken, of course. Love was vulnerability, weakness, pure and utter loss of control.

"It's not the same." Sophia looked as troubled as he felt. "Ours is not a love match."

Somehow her words only increased the agitation burning his stomach.

"I still don't understand." George looked between the two of them. "If you're his wife, why are you seeking passage to London?"

So his little escapee sought to flee the small town. He could make an excuse, find a way to explain, yet instead he gave her a stern look. She would learn not to run from him again.

He would always catch her.

"I should like an explanation."

She opened her mouth, closed it. "I... I thought you had already left."

It didn't make any sense, and by the couple's confused look, they didn't think so either.

"You are mistaken, my dear. We are returning to London in a few days. *Together.*" He grasped her hand. "Don't worry. I will ensure you do not wander off again."

Her eyes blazed. "That is unnecessary, Your Gr... I mean Kenneth."

He halted at the use of his name. First names were rarely spoken among the ton, indicating an intimacy, a far deeper connection. "I like when you say my name," he murmured.

Her eyes widened, yet he was not untouched. Her escape affected him far more than he'd ever admit, not because he'd been bested, and not even because of his revenge. Knowing she'd wandered through unfamiliar territories, alone and without protection, sent fire through him.

"I told you there was a connection." The old lady chuckled softly.

"It's as obvious as the summer rain." The old man sighed.

"Oh no," Sophia protested. "That was–"

"Kenneth, you're here!"

"How splendid!"

"We're so glad to see you."

Sophia took a step back as people poured into the tiny shop, her eyes darting back and forth. He squeezed her hand, instinctively shifting to stand in front of her. Dozens entered the store, with more waiting outside.

He smiled warmly. "It's wonderful to see everyone again."

"And you, as well." A tall man with wavy blond hair and tanned skin stepped forward. With quiet confidence and unconditional kindness, Jonathon served as informal leader of their little town. "We received your surprise shipment last week. How can we thank you?"

Kenneth slid a glance to his would-be wife. Her expression remained neutral, even as curiosity flared in her eyes. "It was nothing. You've always been kind to my family."

"That will never change, no matter what you do." Jonathon replied, as the others nodded. "Please do not feel obligated."

"Of course." They were a proud and hardworking people, yet life was challenging in the small town. His aid made a difference, and he had no plans to discontinue it. "I enjoy helping."

Jonathon gazed at him for a moment more, then relaxed. His wife, a pretty redhead named Mary, stepped forward. "We were hoping you'd come so we could thank you properly." Her smile widened as Sophia peeked out from behind him. "It seems there is much to celebrate."

For a moment, Sophia gripped him tighter. He squeezed her hand softly. "Allow me to introduce my wife, Sophia."

Unease flared as everyone turned to her. Many ladies looked down their noses, quite literally, at anyone without a title, or at least a reasonable connection to one. Everyone awaited her response.

Sophia smiled pure sunshine.

"When did this happen?" Mary demanded with a wide grin. "We didn't even know you were pursuing a bride."

"When it's right, you just know." He traced a finger down Sophia's arm, eliciting a shiver. *Delicious.* "I simply couldn't let this beautiful woman escape."

For a heartbeat, she stared at him. In the next, she was all smiles, as she turned to the townspeople. "It's a pleasure to meet you." She traveled from person to person, with a genuine greeting and a kind word for each. She was sweet and sincere as she ensnared everyone within minutes.

Including him.

When the introductions were finished, Mary rubbed her hands together like a general preparing for battle. "We must have a celebration. With the provisions from last week's shipment, it will be grand indeed."

It did sound grand, certainly more than a stuffy ton affair, with its unkind gossip and guests eager to outdo and outmaneuver. If he were alone, he'd agree instantly. "I'm sorry, but–"

"Thank you so much," Sophia broke in. "We'd love to attend."

Not good. "If you'd allow me a moment to talk to my wife." He tempered his gait, guiding her to the corner instead of stealing her away as instincts desired. "What's your game, Sophia?"

"I have no game," she said quietly. "It would be impolite to say no."

Perhaps, yet if the townspeople discovered the truth, the consequences would be far graver than mild disappointment. "They are good people. I will not allow anything to upset them."

"Neither will I." She gazed at him carefully, as if seeing him for the first time. "They obviously adore you."

Her scrutiny was distinctly uncomfortable. He looked away. "I am simply a man with resources."

"Yet few people make the effort," she murmured. "But you do, I imagine in more ways than one."

He looked back at the townspeople, who made no effort to hide their interest. When he helped others, it brought a joy he could scarce explain. "It's the responsible thing to do. I have a feeling you do the same."

Her flush gave credence to the statement.

He straightened, cleared his throat. "We should return to the estate. If they realize the truth—"

"What does it matter?" she interrupted. "They'll learn soon enough, when you return without me."

When he didn't respond, she paled, yet notched up her chin. "Think of how disappointed they'll be if we turn them down."

The crowd's expressions were expectant and hopeful...

"The least we can do is accept their kindness," she implored. "You said I would enjoy myself during this... vacation. Did you mean it?"

She made a wily opponent, this clever woman. And an even more attractive partner. He exhaled. "All right."

She beamed, and in an instant, it was all worthwhile. "But I'm keeping this." He grasped her hand.

And this time, instead of pulling away, she smiled.

HE HAD NOT allowed her out of his sight.

Not while they conversed with the never-ending parade of townspeople eager to meet the woman who snagged the town hero. Not while they travelled from house to house, gushing over babbling babies and offering congratulations to newlyweds. Not while they visited several housebound residents, at Foxworth's – Kenneth's – insistence.

How could this be the same man who kidnapped her?

He was kind and gracious, generous and considerate, charming grandmothers with humorous stories, inspiring young lads with wise advice and sharing boisterous conversation with everyone. He treated her not like an escaped prisoner, but like the cherished wife they pretended she was. And not just in public, but in the brief moments of solitude, when no audience watched and no consequences loomed. She would never admit it, but their conversations were enjoyable, delightful even. Most of all, *dangerous*.

She couldn't remember the last time she had so much fun.

Now they were visiting Jonathon's farm, a modest collection of neatly tended fields and animal enclosures. Above them, the sky was an endless blue, the sun golden as it warmed the air. Birds sang cheerful greetings, fleeting dashes of blues and reds flitting from tree to tree.

When they arrived, Kenneth immediately offered to help, as he had at every home they visited. Unlike most lords, whose greatest physical strain involved tossing a deck of cards, he was unafraid of hard work, whether hefting lumber, pulling out tree stumps or corralling animals. He toiled in the sun and in the fields, next to men a thousand classes below a duke, as part of nature as the wild animals and ancient trees. And when he smiled... her heart stumbled.

Clearly Kenneth thrived in nature's glory, with people who showed no false pretenses. Yet he was also intelligent, as evidenced by his knowledge on subjects from science to society to farming. The townspeople believed him extraordinary.

Perhaps she did, too.

A gentle breeze caressed her arms, bringing her back to the present. She sipped the cool, crisp lemonade, sighing softly as she leaned against the smooth balustrade. Beyond the handrail, tiny sprouts fluttered, their leaves reflecting diamond dew.

"Isn't it amazing?"

That she didn't flinch was a credit to her control. Somehow she even managed a neutral expression as her *husband* ascended the wooden stairs, his sleeves rolled up, his body glistening in the sun.

He looked even tastier than the lemonade.

She pushed aside the traitorous thought. "What is?"

"The seedlings." Another wind blew, and the plants swayed once more, as if taking a bow to his compliment. "They are so tiny, yet soon they will be three feet tall, producing food to sustain a town." He gripped the railing. "It's astonishing how something so small can bloom into something amazing."

They locked eyes, and suddenly they were no longer discussing plants or sprouts or farming at all. The sunlight reflected golden highlights in his hair, cast his skin a beautiful bronze. "It reminds me of Scotland. The ton is so different than my home... my *former* home." For a moment, sadness shimmered, as surely and strongly as those plants would soon grow, with stems of regret and longing.

He'd lost more than she realized. She was accustomed to the ton, with its stark class differences and confusing concoction of social rules. For someone used to green fields, blue skies and genuine smiles, it was a harsh change.

"Why did you come to London?"

He tightened, betraying surprise at the question she hadn't meant to ask. "The dukedom, of course."

She shielded her eyes from the sun. "A dukedom provides choices; it doesn't take them away. You could have remained in Scotland, or even relinquished the title altogether."

He gazed back at the fields. "It's not as simple as that." His voice was low, the Scottish burr rising. "My heir is a wastrel and womanizer, who spends his money freely at the gambling table and even freer on dangerous frivolities. No doubt the estate would be bankrupt within the year, and those under its care in dire straits. As for taking the title and simply ignoring it, that is not in my nature."

No, it wasn't. This man gave freely, with both his assets and his time, to an entire town. He would never neglect a responsibility, no matter the sacrifice.

"It's also why I must secure a wife and my own heir. I cannot risk the dukedom falling into my cousin's hands."

A tangle of emotions splashed in her stomach at the image of Foxworth with a little boy, swinging him in his arms. She twisted a curl that had escaped its pins. "Do you have someone in mind?"

His eyes sparkled in the sun, as for just a second, a mysterious gleam appeared. "Actually, I do."

The obvious question danced on her tongue, yet the words wouldn't come. Who was he considering for his duchess?

When Jonathon returned, the opportunity was lost, yet her curiosity remained. The rest of the day passed swiftly. They spent a touch longer at Jonathon's farm, before visiting other homesteads in the area. Even as she fought to ignore his charms, the untamed duke usurped her attention. He was kind, considerate and witty, almost irresistible. By his own admission, he hunted for a wife. No doubt every eligible lady in the ton wanted the position.

Everyone except, of course, her.

He was her enemy. Even if forged by misunderstandings, Edmund was unlikely to allow her to marry the man who kidnapped her. If scandal broke, he'd almost certainly find someone among his many friends, who would accept the sister of a duke and her handsome dowry.

Yet none of that mattered. She wanted, no deserved, a love match. Surely one couldn't bloom in such contentious circumstances.

Yet for just a moment, something whispered, *What if?*

She forced the thought aside once and then a hundred times as they continued their visits. As the sun began its slow trek to the horizon, they strolled back to town, so close they brushed against each other, accidentally of course. They talked about that day, and many other days, although not about her brother or his father. It was enjoyable and comfortable, and, if she were honest, a bit delightful.

Just like him.

He was chuckling as she shared how she once managed to eat an entire summer's worth of apple tarts by hiding them in plain sight. They were almost at town, when shouting pierced the air. They raced over the dusty ground, entering the wide main street.

"How dare you run away! You belong to me." A man's voice cracked, the words slurred by the inimitable influence of spirits.

"I belong to no one." A waver betrayed the woman's fear. "You have no rights over me."

A crowd had formed in the center of town, hiding the speakers. Yet their voices were clear. "You're coming with me."

"No, I'm not!"

Sophia's heart skidded. "Molly."

"Do you know her?" Kenneth grasped her hand, holding her back from dashing into the street. Even as she struggled to escape his grip, she relayed the morning's events, leaving out her impromptu instruction on self-defense. His jaw set, his expression increasingly grim, as she finished the story.

"I have to help her!"

"We will."

Sophia pushed forward, but the crowd was too thick. "We must pass," Kenneth boomed, and suddenly the audience was parting, moving in two opposite directions. They ran forward.

Sophia's heart shuddered as the combatants appeared. It was indeed Molly, slender and slight, staring up at a beefy man with scraggly hair, leathery skin and a coyote scowl. His clothes were torn and stained, and he teetered as he glowered at the small woman. "We're leaving." He pulled with a heavy jerk, and Molly stumbled.

The crowd gasped, and Kenneth lunged forward. Yet before

anyone could step in, Molly hooked her foot behind the brute's leg. He flailed for a moment, releasing his captive as he stumbled. Backwards, backwards, backwards...

Straight into the horse trough.

The man sputtered and splashed and cursed enough to make a vicar faint. Molly gave the faintest smile as the crowd laughed, and for just a moment, a spark of power danced in her eyes. Yet her expression turned wary as the man pulled himself up, stood to his formidable size. He turned to the small woman.

And instead faced a very furious, very powerful duke.

Kenneth did not say a word. Did not attack. Instead he grasped the man by the scruff of his collar and *helped* him forward, towards the edge of town. Everyone watched, and although words were lost in the distance, the man turned as pale as a debutante's gown. Then the ruffian turned and *ran*.

There were indeed matters an untamed duke was perfect for.

"Honey, are you all right?" The elderly shopkeepers stepped forward, their grandson close behind.

Molly stood tall. "I am perfect."

"Yes, you are," the grandson breathed.

Molly turned to him, and he turned bright pink. "I mean, I'm glad you are well."

A thousand knowing looks were exchanged.

Immediately, dozens of offers emerged from dozens of kind citizens. Soon Molly had a room for lodging, enough food for a week and an appointment with the seamstress to discuss a position. By the time Kenneth returned, she was smiling widely, yet it faltered at the sight of the large man. Then, she straightened.

"You needn't worry about him." Sophia patted his arm. "My husband only likes to kidnap me."

As everyone laughed, Kenneth's gaze sparkled. "Who could resist kidnapping such an enchanting woman?" He turned to Molly, and his expression sobered. "Your stepfather decided to move on without you. He will not be bothering you again."

Molly brought a hand to her lips, her eyes glowing with tears. "I don't know how to thank you." She took Sophia's hand. "Both of you. He never would have given up without your convincing. Sophia, thank you for teaching me how to–"

"We're so glad to help," Sophia jumped in.

Too late.

Kenneth folded his arms across his chest.

Molly's smile widened. And then Sophia was smiling again, and even Kenneth gave a begrudging grin, after informing her they would discuss it later. Yet his eyes matched the delight in her chest. And as he took her hand once more, something became *inescapably* clear:

There was a connection, after all.

SOPHIA HID HER true self.

She concealed sweetness behind strength, vulnerability behind a will of iron. Her spirited nature was nothing less than magnificent, her passion extraordinary. If Sophia hadn't intervened, Molly may never have resisted her stepfather, turning into another unknown tale of tragedy. She truly was a hero.

Yet Sophia was a woman of many facets, and her sweet side was just as beautiful: the blushes she couldn't hide, the sweet melody of her laughter, the way her eyes softened when children were near. She bestowed smile after smile, no matter whom she addressed. She wasn't too pretentious to tidy an old woman's house, too snobbish to tell the latest London news to the young village girls or too haughty to catch a runaway piglet. While most ladies would have been agog in horror, counting the number of swoons on both hands, she laughed merrily, her sun-kissed cheeks as pink as the little piglet.

In one sun's journey, everything had shifted. She treated him as a friend, or perhaps even the husband he pretended to be. She joked and jested, teased and conversed, in this little town where he was not a duke, and she was not the sister of his enemy. They were simply two people, reveling in the beauty of life.

It was all too easy to play the part of couple in love.

Now she was off with the ladies, getting pampered and primed for the evening's event, while he waited outside the tavern. Miss Sally, the town's seamstress, had insisted upon lending Sophia her newest creation, an ornately described gown fit for a queen. Sophia had deferred at first, yet the woman was so hopeful, she agreed. It was yet another kindness.

He shifted on his feet, nodding to a young couple. A few times today, Sophia gazed at the road leaving town, yet her expression was more thoughtful than longing, and she made no attempt at escape. Still, he made the ladies promise to keep close watch on her. They'd laughed, and Sophia gave him a pointed look, which he promptly returned.

Of course, if she escaped he'd catch her before she made it to the next town.

"Are you ready to see your bride?"

He looked up as Jonathon and his wife approached, bearing twin smiles. "I cannot wait."

They separated, revealing the woman behind them.

Magnificent. Glorious. Breathtaking.

No words could truly describe the beauty before him. Her cheeks were pink, her lips full and red, her hair cascading down her back like a shimmering waterfall. The silky purple gown floated around her like an ethereal cloud, with delicate puff sleeves, an overlay of embroidered lace and a décolleté that made him wish they were alone.

She was spectacular.

He stared for approximately a year and then longer. "I would say you are stunning, yet no term truly encompasses your beauty. Extraordinary, unsurpassed, a diamond of the first water, so true and yet insufficient."

She blushed. "Thank you, Your Gr... Kenneth." A stumble betrayed her nervousness, bringing a gentle pinkness to her cheeks. "You need not say such things."

"I say them because they are true." For once, he allowed her to see the emotions he ever-hid. "You are the most beautiful creature on earth."

Sophia flushed deeper, smoothing down the skirt. "The gown is beautiful." She turned to Sally. The seamstress' eyes shined with unabashed delight. "You rival my London modiste any day."

Sally put a hand to her heart. "You do not know what that means to me. I hope to bring it to London to sell one day."

"Perhaps I can help with that," Kenneth murmured, even as his eyes remained ever-riveted on Sophia. "I would be very much interested in purchasing it, if my bride would like it."

Sophia parted her lips. "It is extraordinary. It would be the talk of London."

Sally's eyes grew wide.

Sophia smoothed down the skirt. "Of course I can pay–"

"Do not finish that sentence," he warned.

For once, she listened to him.

He thought back to what he paid for Clara's latest dress. Tripled it. The seamstress blinked, as if he'd offered the moon, sun and several stars as payment. "It's too much."

"Not at all." By the happiness in Sophia's eyes, even the celestial offerings would be fair. "No doubt you will get numerous commissions when my bride wears it in London."

Eyes as wide as the stars, Sally could only nod.

He returned his attention to the woman who was his for tonight, perhaps for far longer. Sophia shivered as he placed her hand on his sleeve and rubbed her chilled fingers until they were as warm as a hearth. They glided over the rough ground like it was the smooth tile of a mansion, strolled past the tavern's main room as if a spacious foyer of a ton event. They passed the threshold to the back room.

Sophia gasped.

The space was lit by moonlight and candles. Brilliant displays of wildflowers bloomed through open windows, scenting the world in nature's perfume, while shimmering fabric dripped down the walls, cascades of silk waterfalls. Homemade quilts and white lilies adorned a dozen tables, flanked by wooden chairs, each with a thick ribbon tied in a bow. A beautiful melody drifted from a young girl at the town's only pianoforte – a gift from Kenneth when he learned of the child prodigy – accompanied by half a dozen townspeople with homemade instruments.

Sophia slowly pivoted. "It's the most breathtaking ball I've ever seen."

Clapped hands and brilliant smiles welcomed the announcement. "I quite agree," he agreed in a booming voice. "It is extraordinary." No doubt, it would also cost more than they had to spare. He would double, no triple, his donations this month.

Jonathon stepped forward. "We are grateful for your assistance. Please enjoy the celebration."

Kenneth led Sophia to the makeshift dance floor, as the musicians played a lilting ballad. What the sound lacked in fullness, it more than made up for in heart, fortified by the child's extraordinary talent. Yet Sophia stole his focus as she smiled and laughed with lively abandon, finally sharing her true self. He grinned back as they finished the dance, and then another. As they touched, something in him shifted.

For the first time since he ascended his title, the world held promise, and the future was his to forge.

Molly and the shopkeeper's grandson twirled by, their eyes locked as they danced to the music. The young man leaned down to whisper something, and his partner laughed.

"I do believe something extraordinary has begun," Sophia murmured.

Yes, it had.

After half a dozen dances, they took respite at a large table, filled with smiling townspeople. Sophia included every single person in the conversation, inquiring into lives with genuine interest. She shared her own life, careful to avoid details that betrayed their identities, but including charming stories of her family. When it was over, she had delighted the entire table.

They dined on a delicious feast of local fare, including freshly baked breads, savory stews and steaming pies, before returning to the floor. The next dances were slower and softer, the perfect excuse to capture her in his arms. He held her as close as propriety allowed, and she pressed just a little closer.

"You are an excellent dancer." She studied him closely, as if trying to make sense of some unsolvable puzzle. "Where did you learn such skills?"

"When my mother left England, she brought a little bit back with her." He twirled her effortlessly, caught her back in his arms. "She hired tutors to teach us everything from dancing to language to society rules. It's why my accent is not as pronounced as many of my countrymen."

Understanding shone in her eyes. "She knew you would become duke one day."

On any other day, with any other woman, the words would have stung, yet for once the pain was absent. "If so, she never shared. I knew nothing of my father save that he was an Englishman. I may have never discovered the truth had Adam not sought me out to bestow my inheritance."

Most were shocked when they learned of his mother's deception, yet Sophia merely looked thoughtful. "She must have loved you very much to keep such a secret. She knew you would be happier in Scotland."

A rare peace descended, a glimpse of something he sought for so long. How could a few perfect words matter so much? "I'd like to believe that's why she didn't tell me. She was a wonderful woman, who didn't deserve such a marriage."

She nodded commiseration. "It's difficult when people are arranged."

"Actually it was a love match."

Her eyebrows curved upwards. "It was?"

"At least she thought it was." It seemed impossible, with so many wretched stories of his father, yet the elder Foxworth was once handsome and charming, as he wooed the shy Scottish lass with a plump dowry. "She learned fairly soon of her mistake. It took years for her to escape, and cost her the chance to find another match."

Sophia held him just a little tighter. "Not all love matches end that way."

True, yet such unions were rare and dangerous. His mother gave her heart away, and his father returned it shattered.

He would never give someone that power over him.

He pulled her a little closer. "I desire a logical marriage. A mate with common interests, a similar view of the world and comparable opinions. Not love, perhaps, but companionship."

Her eyes flashed, dulling for a moment, before she lifted her chin. "With so many ladies vying for your hand, you shall have no trouble finding one that meets your requirements. Perhaps they shall even write a book about you. They can call it the Wicked Duke."

"The Wicked Duke?" He gave a *wicked* smile. "I would prefer the Triumphant Duke."

"The Overbearing Duke," she countered.

"The Victorious Duke." He winked.

"The Authoritative Duke." She glared.

"The Conquering Duke," he rumbled.

"How about The Untamed Duke?" she declared.

"Agreed."

He spun her again, in perfect harmony to the music. What would she say if she knew he had already found the perfect lady? "Once I learned of my heritage, I had no choice but to relocate myself and my sister to England. I became responsible for two families and a never-ending list of duties. I may not hold a title in Scotland, but I lead an influential family. They need me almost as much as the dukedom."

"That's why you return to Scotland so often," she breathed. "That must be difficult to balance."

She truly understood. They moved without words for a few moments, in perfect coordination. Like a new day, she was full of promise and hope, beckoning a new journey.

She reminded him so much of home it hurt.

"When you are not being an overbearing kidnapper, you can be sort of pleasant."

Amusement rose. "Thank you?"

The corners of her lips ticked up. "What I mean is you are not entirely untamed."

His amusement deepened. "Quite kind of you to say, my lady."

She chuckled softly. "I'm trying to compliment you."

"And an excellent job you are doing." He nudged her shoulder. "I'm growing on you, aren't I?"

"Yes, you are." The words were so low, it wasn't clear if he was supposed to hear them. He grasped her hand and turned it over, tracing her palm. His hold was light, and she could have retreated at any time.

She didn't.

He lifted her hand to his lips and brushed it softly, satisfied when it elicited a small shiver. "You are growing on me, as well, Lady Sophia."

The next moments were spent in low conversation. They spoke of the important and the trivial, about everything from vital political matters to silly childhood tales. She even delved into the topic of social action. Shockingly, they concurred on many subjects, although they didn't quite agree on whether women should be protected at all times.

She seemed surprised to learn how well-versed in English politics he was, and especially that he planned to take an active role in Parliament. When he listed social action as one of his issues, she fanned herself.

"If I didn't know better, I'd almost say you were civilized."

"Never say such a thing," he admonished softly. "What if someone hears?"

She giggled. "Don't worry. Your secret is safe with me. In fact, I would say you are quite extraordinary."

He leaned closer. "Extraordinary?"

Her eyes dilated. "Indeed."
"Indeed."
Closer and closer and closer…
He brushed her lips.

CHAPTER TWELVE

Journal of the Duke of Foxworth:

Seize your future.
    Carve your own path, take the life you want and deserve. Others will challenge your authority, resist you at every turn, yet you must not allow them to pierce your formidable armor. If you give them an inch, they will grasp for all, and your strength will be sacrificed. Do not lose yourself to fate's whims or destiny's dictates. Capture what is yours.
    Do not accept anything less than total surrender.

P URE HEAT SURROUNDED her, undeniable need, raw anticipation. Her body felt heavy, her stomach unsettled, as he caressed her lips, massaging, tasting, testing. They parried back and force like yesterday's duel, armed with far greater weapons. Strong arms surrounded her, keeping her close, holding her against a wall of muscle. She pressed nearer...

The music ended.

Reality crashed down like a tidal wave. They were in public, in front of dozens of people. Everything her mother had warned her about, and everything Edmund had forbidden, flashed in her mind. She was kissing her brother's sworn enemy in front of an entire town!

They broke apart, so quickly she would have fallen had he not supported her. Eyes blazed with scorching intensity, his expression elemental with passion, desire, *possessiveness.* Her dismay must have been obvious, as he softened. "All will be well."

It was untrue, as a hundred people watched them like they were a Theater Royal production. Smiling eyes hid nothing, hushed whispers and romantic sighs proof the memories would last far beyond this night.

He leaned down, and sweat formed underneath her corset. Even now, the force to return to his embrace was almost too strong to resist. "Act as if all is normal," he whispered, "or you shall bring more attention upon us."

As always, his words were a command. Yet he was right. They could not undo the damage, but perhaps they could lessen the impact.

She stretched her lips into a smile so wide it ached, as she stepped back. Coldness swirled at their separation, yet the ability to reason returned. She opened her mouth, faltering with words that wouldn't come.

Kenneth, of course, had no difficulty regaining control. "Please excuse my bride and me. Emotions sometimes get the better of us." He swept his smile across the crowd before turning back to her. "She has enraptured me."

The last words were murmured, yet judging by the renewed whispers, everyone heard. And although they were meant for an audience, something within her shifted. She was indeed *enraptured*.

This was very, very bad.

The old shopkeeper winked. "We know how you feel. Us newlywed couples have difficulty hiding our emotions." He lifted the hand of his bride from half a century ago and kissed her palm. She blushed.

The crowd laughed, and Sophia relaxed as the attention lessened, even as the surreptitious glances continued. "Let's sit down," she whispered.

It was far too dangerous to dance with her all-too-tempting partner. Kenneth did not allow her to go far, as he grasped her hand and led her back to the table, where she pretended he had not upended her world. She would have left right then, yet she could not flee after the townspeople's hard work. So she forced her lips into a smile, talked and mingled and visited until the late hours of the night, when the last of the townspeople departed with brilliant smiles and a hundred thank yous.

Kenneth's hand never left hers as they walked from the town, under a velvet sky dotted with twinkling stars. When she made a half-hearted attempt to extricate herself, he raised his eyebrow and held her tighter. It was not until they passed the town limits, that she broke the silence. "This is a nightmare." Again she pulled her hand back, or at least tried.

He still didn't release her.

"Let go of me."

"There are dangers in the darkness." He clasped her hand more securely. "Sadly, I can no longer trust you to stay close."

"Do you think I'll flee into the night? Dash away to London on foot, with no horse and no supplies?"

He frowned. "Would you?"

If he kept on kissing her, she just might.

Who was she kidding?

If he kept kissing her, she'd kiss him right back.

"Of course not," she huffed. "I'd never make it."

"Undoubtedly, that's the only thing stopping you." His eyes gleamed in the moonlight. "What happened, Sophia? I thought you enjoyed tonight."

He was wrong. She'd *adored* tonight. Yet she could not forget their true identities, and the consequences should anyone discover the truth. "You kissed me in front of a hundred people. It'll be a miracle if it doesn't make its way back to London."

"You overestimate the danger." His neutral expression held no regret. "This is an entirely different world. Even if they visit London, they are unlikely to see us." His side brushed hers. "They do not frequent the exclusive areas."

"Much of London draws the different classes," she countered. "You cannot claim to constrain yourself to the ton's drawing rooms." As pursed lips confirmed the words, she gestured at his massive frame. "People notice you everywhere you go, and not just because of your position or wealth. You stand out like a sword among daggers."

He lifted an eyebrow.

She blushed. "Even if you were not a duke, you are..." She waved her hand, stopped. "Handso– I mean attracti... I mean..." She sighed. "You draw attention."

Amusement danced in his eyes. "The townspeople know me as the son of the Scottish family that has owned the estate for generations. There's no reason to presume I'm anything more."

"If you think they don't suspect you are *more*, then you are underestimating them," She bit her bottom lip. "What are we going to do if they realize the truth?"

He looked at her from under hooded eyes. "I think you know the answer to that."

Scandal. Betrothal. *Ownership.*

"Despite your objections, you enjoyed yourself tonight."

She turned away. "We were just pretending." It was untrue, yet feelings were scraped raw. She would not – could not – admit anything to the powerful duke.

She said nothing more as they continued their journey, walking silently until they reached the bridge. Kenneth opened the gate, firmly guiding her through, before securing the latch behind them. The scent of water swirled from the rushing rapids, hissing and gurgling with danger. During the day, the landscape was calm and peaceful, yet in the darkened night, it played a haunting backdrop.

The manor rose like a beacon in the night. They navigated the distance without interruption, keeping a steady gait as they ascended the steps leading to the entrance. With a heavy key, Kenneth opened the door and ushered her into the warmth and light of the welcoming foyer. He shut the door behind them.

Through it all, he never released her.

She held up their joined hands. "There are no more townspeople to see, no creatures to fear, no dangerous ground on which to fall. Are you going to release me?"

Instead of freeing her hand, he grasped the other. Light from the fireplace danced on his skin, illuminating high cheekbones, chiseled features and determined resolve. "I like holding you." He stood to his full, towering height. "I challenge your claim we were merely pretending."

Her heart skipped a beat. "What else could it be?" Her breathy tone belied the casual words. "We are not truly married."

His gaze was unwavering. "Not yet."

Her heart lurched. Did he mean–

"Even if we aren't married, something undeniable connects us." His voice deepened. "The kisses were not pretend."

Not even a little. Yet she could never share the truth. With every emotion she revealed, he seized more control. "We were playing a role to appease the townspeople." She turned away. "It was nothing more."

He released her hand, yet any taste of freedom vanished as he caressed her cheek. "Are you so certain of that?"

"Yes," she whispered.

"Would you care to test it?"

"Yes," she whispered again.

She moved forward, a mere fraction of an inch, yet he recognized it for the invitation it was. He nipped her lips, then brushed them softer, gentler, as she pressed against raw iron. Solid arms snaked around her back, guiding her into position, as he deepened the kiss, moving his lips against hers in the sensual dance. Places he'd once awoken burst into life, tendrils of fire tracing through her veins. She pressed closer...

Until he retreated.

He pulled back so quickly, at first she didn't even realize. She followed him, yet met only empty air, as he pulled back fully, leaving her without contact for the first time in forever. She touched swollen lips, still tingling with his possession. "Why?" she gasped.

Why had he kissed her? Why did she accept? Why did he affect her so much? The question portrayed a thousand queries, for him, for her, for the world itself.

Why did he stop?

"I'm sorry." Regret burned in his eyes, as he stood taller, wielding his power like a sword. It threatened to overwhelm, yet he would not take all control.

She struggled to focus. "It is best if we avoid each other for the duration of this trip."

"That's impossible now."

Apprehension crept up her neck, like she had fallen into the midnight river, with only a shadowy descent her future. "What do you mean?"

He stepped closer once more, casting havoc upon her senses. It encircled her, ensnaring her in its invisible web. "I can no longer trust you."

He could never trust her, just as she couldn't trust him. Unknown plans blazed in his eyes. "I won't allow you to flee into danger again. To protect you, I must stay far closer."

Images arrived, one after the next, of them *far closer*. Every sense sizzled. "Do you plan to tie yourself to me?"

He gave her a wicked look.

Her heart stumbled. "Don't you dare."

"I'll do whatever is necessary to keep you safe." He rubbed his hands together, leaned down. "No matter what that entails."

He may be powerful, but she had the strength of every woman who believed they were *more*. She would not accept his dictates, would not surrender.

There was only one option, one action to protect herself, her reputation, her very heart. She must escape again.

This time she would be victorious.

HE WAS NOT going to tie her to him.

But it was tempting.

She trudged heavily as they departed the foyer, as they traversed the large hallway, as he escorted her up the stairs. When he took the corridor in the opposite direction of her room, she glanced back in confusion, but he kept her moving with a firm hand on her back.

She said nothing.

When they came upon the largest door in the hallway, he released her briefly to unlock it, then ushered her into the master room. She pivoted slowly, taking in the grand furnishings, the oversized oak armoires, the mahogany desk and plush jacquard settees. Her eyes lingered on the massive four-poster bed. "This is your room?"

"Yes."

She visibly swallowed. "Why did you bring me here?"

The answer was immediate. "This is the only place I can keep you safe."

She fisted her hands. "The only person threatening my safety is you."

"That's not true." He walked closer. "I may have inconvenienced you, yet I have made clear I would never harm you. You endanger yourself."

Her color deepened, even as she glared. "You will not have to worry about me for much longer. I am going to bed. If you dare touch me, I will not be responsible for my actions."

"The same goes for me."

She gaped at him. "I wouldn't dream of touching you."

He lifted an eyebrow, and the color spread to her neck. She watched warily as he locked the door, then placed the key in a hidden pocket deep within his jacket. He turned back to her.

Her anger was a veritable force.

"I'm reconsidering touching you."

He smiled.

"Not in a way you'll enjoy."

He smiled wider.

He strode to the dresser and retrieved a long muslin shirt. "This should be sufficient for nightwear, if you wish to change."

He held out the clothing. "Do not think to escape again. Your escape was an aberration, and I am typically a light sleeper. You will not be so lucky tonight."

She snatched the clothing, then stomped to the dressing curtain. Rustling made every part of him harden, before she returned a minute later. The shapeless garment covered her from ankle to neck, yet she was as beautiful as a princess. She took a step towards the settee.

"Take the bed."

She froze.

He softened his voice. "I will use the sofa. I am accustomed to sleeping in inhospitable conditions."

For a moment, she paused, but then she pivoted and marched to the bed. It was almost as tall as her, yet she hefted herself up in one fluid movement. Placing the gown neatly by her side, she shifted towards the window, providing a tantalizing view of full curves and an alluring backside.

He had lied. The settee was going to be the most inhospitable bed of his life. Not because it was too narrow for his frame, or so short his legs would hang off the end. No, because he had to sleep the entire night without touching the siren twenty feet and an impossible gulf away.

Resisting her would be the greatest challenge of his life.

HER CAPTOR DIDN'T believe she could escape. Didn't think she could elude his intricate web, slink past him once more. He had taken precaution after precaution, seemingly preventing any and all opportunity to leave the gilded prison. He was probably right.

That didn't mean she wasn't going to try.

This time Sophia allowed no sleep. It was easier, and safer, after the day that upended her senses and changed reality. Her jailer stayed up, too, quietly prowling the room, before settling at his desk to tend to some papers. Finally he folded his large body into the settee and squeezed his eyes shut. She waited until his breathing evened and then many minutes more, before daring to rise.

She slid from the high bed, wincing at the gentle thump her slippers made upon the hard floor. Her gaze caught on the lavender dress still folded upon on the bed, the ethereal creation that represented a night of enchantment. She had no choice but to leave it behind.

Leave him behind.

Shadows drenched the room, lit only by the low candlelight and the moonlight streaming through the windows. By the moon's journey across the sky, it was later than she'd hoped, yet nothing could be done. This time she would not be traveling to the closest town.

After yesterday, she certainly couldn't ask the townspeople for help. Undoubtedly they would question her motives and summon Kenneth immediately. She would need to travel to the further town, a substantial yet not unattainable trek. Hopefully, she would be able to gain passage once she arrived. Then she would forget all about the untamed duke.

As if it would ever be possible.

She pushed aside unsolicited feelings. Right now the plan was all that mattered. The first step: steal the key.

Kenneth rumbled softly, shifting in the ridiculously small space. Another rumble sounded, louder, deeper, and not in direction of the slumbering duke. She turned to the window.

A storm was brewing. Dark gray clouds thickened the sky, dense puffs of wool against pure blackness. Lightning flashed, illuminating the billowy atmosphere, before another rumble. Kenneth shifted again, and a pillow dropped to the floor. He sighed softly.

She had to escape *now*. Traipsing through a storm was not preferable, yet she had endured many a tempest during her days in the country, when Edmund hadn't been looking, of course. Once she left Kenneth's land, she could find shelter if necessary. He shifted again as she approached, and she hesitated. The key was deep within his coat, nestled in some sort of hidden pocket.

To retrieve it, she would have to get close.

Not close enough, a traitorous voice whispered.

She took another step, as lightning struck once more, chased by thunder. One foot forward, and then another. What would she do if he awoke? Was there any excuse he would believe?

She could pretend she was trying to steal a *kiss*.

It worked during the sword fight. Of course, it could work all too well, leading to other things. Anticipation whispered through her, as she imagined *other things*.

Finally, she stood above him. Even prone, he was massive, his muscles straining against the thin clothing. His chest rose and fell evenly, and he wore a peaceful expression he never quite managed during waking hours. She fought the urge to touch the planes and angles of his handsome visage, run her hands through his thick locks.

Thunder boomed once more, tearing her from her ponderings. What was she doing? She hadn't time to watch him sleep. She reached down, as lightning flashed again, illuminating her trembling hand. She grasped his coat.

He didn't move, and she released a breath. With deliberate movements, she lifted his coat and traced along the lining, yet the key was nowhere to be found.

She needed to get closer.

She kneeled on the hard floor, edging nearer to the man who was somehow even more massive at eye level. Her hand brushed against his chest.

Desire streaked through her.

Not now.

When this was all over she would seriously consider finding a husband, so she could partake in the pleasures she'd only tasted with this man. Yet even as the thought rose, something rebelled, as the image of only one man – slightly wicked, definitely untamed, all powerful – vanquished all others.

The key had to be here somewhere. She'd seen him tuck it into his coat. A thud sounded from up above, and then another, as a thousand raindrops poured from the skies. In seconds it was a deluge, pounding against the roof like an out-of-control drummer, streaming down the windows like a waterfall. She moved to the cadence of its beat, underscored by thunder's drum. She pushed a little further, and something solid moved under her hand. Triumph glistened as she grasped the key. *Victory!*

His eyes opened.

CHAPTER THIRTEEN

The Private Diary of Sophia Hawkins

The impossible.

I do not believe in the word, do not accept that which puts limitations on my dreams. Just because something seems impossible, does not mean it is not worth trying.

Of course one must be careful. Most in my position would surrender, wait for others to grant them freedom. They would do as their captor says, be an obedient lady. I have never been an obedient lady.

Who knows what he will do if he captures me?

NOT A SLIVER of guilt arose.

Just because he'd been conscious from the moment Sophia padded out of bed, pulled to awareness by the distinctive combination of storm and the scent of violets, didn't mean he was obligated to reveal himself. Instead, he'd stayed silent as she moved in the shadows, her lithe body outlined in the moon's dim light. Did she realize the thin fabric molded to her silhouette, defined generous curves that beckoned for his touch? It had taken every bit of strength to stop himself from joining her in the midnight dance.

Her presence required no guesswork. Clearly another escape attempt, despite the results of her last and the futility of the next. Yet this woman did not let the mere impossible stop her.

Watching her had been pure torture, yet when she approached, desire surged to new heights. That he managed to stay still, mimicking the quiet of slumber, attested to his self-control. Yet she had rapidly stolen the last when those slender fingers traced his chest.

He opened eyes to a liquid blue gaze. Her lips parted, and she gave a tiny gasp. He clamped a hand on her wrist.

Mine.

A thousand emotions swirled, in his chest and in her gaze, confusion, frustration and challenge, yet most of all, pure, unadulterated desire. Uncertainty changed to determination, vulnerability to strength. She leaned forward...

And kissed him.

He surged forward, taking her with him, as he switched their positions. Her boldness enflamed him, her touch burning through his clothing, as he pulled her flush against him. She was softness and strength, sensitivity and passion, as she tested his control like never before.

And once again, a maddening voice reminded him he was a gentleman. Not by the title he abhorred, but by the honor his mother instilled. He did not deflower maidens.

At least not without wedding them first.

He tried to pull back, yet *she* didn't allow it. She clutched at his shirt, and he kissed her deeper, stealing a moment to explore hidden treasures. He traced over curves, soothed planes, caressed crevices. He cupped the underside of her breast.

She sucked in a breath of air.

He closed his eyes, opened them as his conscience finally wrangled control from the rake within. Under him, she watched with wary eyes, her cheeks flushed with passion she couldn't disguise.

Disgust flared as she scurried off the settee and backed away from him. What had he been thinking? She'd accepted the other kisses breathlessly yet stoically, yet she was still an innocent. There was a correct order with ladies, and he had missed the most important step.

"I'm sorry," he rasped. "I know you are a lady."

"Indeed I am." Her voice was high, her breathing still labored, as she edged further away. "This wasn't supposed to happen."

That was a matter of contention, yet the timing was indubitably wrong. Just like him, she didn't often show her vulnerabilities.

"I would never do anything you didn't want," he said softly. He stayed motionless, his voice low, even as she moved further away. "I hope you realize that."

She stopped as her back came flush against the door. "I do understand." She notched up her chin.

That was the moment he realized her game.

The key. He patted his coat, but its absence was there for him to *not* feel. She flung open the door, lunging the moment a sliver of hallway appeared. He leapt, but the air fought him as he sprinted across the room, and she slipped through the door just as thunder boomed. The lock clicked shut.

The blasted woman had trapped him in his own chambers!

"Sophia!" he bellowed as he rammed against the door. The reinforced wood gave no quarter, yet a slight creaking betrayed wavering resolve. "Don't you dare leave." He lunged again, and the creaking loudened. The barrier would not last long.

Long enough for her to escape?

Perhaps.

"Open the door," he commanded. "You have no chance of escape."

"That's not true." Her voice was muffled through the wood. "This time I know what to do."

Did she realize he was breaking out as they spoke? He lunged again. "Do you think to leave me here forever?" It was an immense exaggeration. In minutes, he would be free.

And she no longer would be.

"You needn't worry. I'll inform the townspeople to come to you. In fact, I will send several to ensure your safety."

He shouldn't be satisfied, yet somehow it mattered that she

cared enough to protect him. He rammed the door again, denting the wood, and a long crack appeared. It would be costly to replace, yet far less valuable than the treasure who was trying to flee.

Thunder roared as rain pelted, the water pounding like thousands of tiny bullets against the thick pane. Lightning flashed, and a bolt of fear overshadowed his anger. "It's far too dangerous to venture into this storm."

"I've weathered storms before." The low voice came through the doorway, the tone certain and strong. "I'm not afraid."

He was. For a man who feared little, the thought of something happening to this woman was *devastating*. "You could get struck by lightning, or fall into the water. At the very least, you will face the consequences for risking yourself once more."

"My fear of your consequences is no stronger than my fear of this storm." The words were bold, yet a slight edge belied their poise. "A locked door separates us, and I have the only key."

"Do not do this." He pushed slower now, silencing the warning of his efforts. "Open the door, and we shall forget this ever happened. It's only a few days more. Despite your claims, you were happy yesterday."

"Therein lies the problem." Her voice was so low, he was not certain he was meant to hear. "I cannot afford to be happy. Goodbye, Kenneth. Your revenge has been satisfied, and our business is concluded. Forever."

No.

"Don't leave," he barked, yet there was no reply.

She was gone.

But not for long. This was not over, by any means. He would recapture her, even if she made it all the way to London.

He was never letting her go.

HAD HER PLAN worked? It seemed impossible from the beginning, unfathomable once he awoke. Yet she recalled his lesson: Use whatever resources available to distract your opponent. There was no better distraction than a kiss.

Unfortunately, the sensual web had also ensnared her. She could have grabbed the key in seconds, yet she could not resist his sensual attentions, the tantalizing touches that made her yearn for things that could never be hers. The man she could never keep.

He thought he shocked her by touching her breast. It was true – in the most delicious way possible. It had taken all her power to resist, poised on the edge of something remarkable. His touch sparked unquenchable sensations, unfilled needs desperate for more. Thankfully, it also shocked her back to reality, allowing her to escape.

Somehow she had made it.

A shadow of regret lurked, ludicrously, for her kidnapper. His concern about being trapped gave her pause, yet she would ensure his safety. Like she promised, she would send people to check on him, paid of course. It may not be necessary. She hadn't missed how the door shook with his efforts, cracking and creaking with undeniable force. It was sturdy, yet he was a powerful man.

Thunder cracked above, and she quickened her pace. At the next strike, she hitched up her skirts and ran, racing to the tattoo of the pouring rain. She reached the door, grabbed the handle and pulled.

The world was alight with nature's fury. Wind came from all directions, twirling and swirling in gusty waves. Lightning flashed, illuminating a waterlogged land of streams and valleys. The rain slanted down in racing sheets, stinging as it angled through the doorway, soaking the ground instantly.

She took a deep breath. She may have dashed through sun showers, but she had never faced such wrath. How could she escape in this?

She must fight. That she would escape him seemed impossible, yet no more than her earlier attempts. After she passed the bridge, she would find a place to hide, seek shelter from the rain as the deluge eliminated her tracks. When the storm passed, she would travel to the next town.

Suddenly, a crash sounded from the manor. Then, heavy footsteps. She flexed her muscles and leapt.

She had underestimated the storm.

This was immediately clear as thunder crashed again, as the world flashed in a nonstop electric display. A spider web of light leapt from the velvet sky to a nearby tree, engulfing it in flames before the rain extinguished it to a smoldering mass. It was nightmarish scene of shadows and danger, placing her center stage in a fireworks show, as she played both performer and audience in a world of peril.

The heavy scent of rain mixed with the noxious odor of charred wood, scratching her throat and scraping her lungs. Her wet hair lay plastered against her neck, as icy water dripped into her eyes, distorting her vision. She blinked it away a hundred and one times as she ran over the uneven terrain, leaping over rocks and dodging hail. Then... her foot caught under a fallen branch.

The ground came rushing at her. Jagged rocks sliced her palms, piercing the thin shirt and skinning her knees. She pushed herself up, yet stayed in place, straddling the darkened path to danger and the manor whose lighted windows beckoned like a safe harbor. The choice that seemed so certain now wavered. The price of her life was too high for a few days of freedom.

Sophia!" The storm swallowed Kenneth's roar, yet its fury reached her. He had emerged from the estate, and was now soaring towards her with almost superhuman speed.

Suddenly she was in motion again.

Reason and logic vanished on the quest to freedom, her only goal the independence denied not just by this man, but every man who would dare control her. Her hunter commanded her to stop, ordered her to obey, so she pushed harder, further...

A bolt of lightning struck mere feet away. She screamed as the air *sizzled*, fighting to stop, even as the momentum pushed her forward. Shadows hid the danger before it was too late.

She plunged into the river.

CHAPTER FOURTEEN

Journal of the Duke of Foxworth:

*Do not forget why you are here. Do not lose sight of your goal.
Do not allow another to steal your focus, or unravel your resolve.*

*Sophia challenges me at every turn, threatening my control
as none before. There is something about her, something I want
so very much. The thought of letting her go becomes more impossible by the day.*

I know what I have to do.

HIS HEART STOPPED.
    His breath caught.
His world shattered.
As Sophia plummeted into liquid darkness.
"No!"
He didn't remember running. Hardly heard the roar that
drowned out the thunder. Barely felt the burst of speed, as the
ground transformed from soaked grass to blue waves in an
instant.

He jumped in after her, diving into the depths of the noxious,
slimy water. It smothered like a thousand sweltering blankets,
swirling him like a child's top. Muscles screamed as he maneuvered the churning depths, fighting the river's brutal attempt to
take control. He fought his way up, bursting thorough the
surface. As he gasped a breath of rain-filled air, he frantically
searched the violent waves.

Sophia was nowhere to be seen.

He dove again, blinded by darkness, motivated by hope. That she had already been swept away was not something he would consider. She was still there, waiting for him to rescue her.

She would be all right.

He fought the dense, frigid liquid. Sharp vegetation sliced his palms, sending the metallic taste of blood into the water, as the powerful current urged him forward like a horizontal waterfall. He searched spindly plants, threaded around silvery fish and over jagged rocks, until suddenly something smooth floated by. Triumph surged as he grasped what could only be fabric, as he pulled a supple form into his arms...

She wasn't moving.

He had to get her to the surface! He pushed up, yet something captured her down below, clutching her in a deadly tug of war. Lungs screamed as he kicked with feet that felt weighted with lead, pulling against the never-ending current. Sounds dimmed, white fog clouded his mind. The world grew quiet...

Fight! With a last burst of strength, he pulled once more. The shirt tore free!

He soared up, up up...

They burst into the raging storm. He gasped a breath of sweet air, coughing as he spit out the wretched water. Sophia did the same, breathing in huge gulps as she emptied her lungs. Never had a pained sound been so sweet.

"It's all right. I've got you." Holding her with one hand, he used the other to paddle them to shore. He grasped the craggy bank, lifted her onto land. She was cold and shivering but breathing and alert, and most importantly *alive*. But still not safe.

He scooped her up, holding her against his chest, as he hurtled back to the house. Behind him, lightning brightened the world in nonstop flashes, never-ending thunder adding its beat. Another crash roared, different than thunder, then a booming splash. He didn't look back as his precious cargo burrowed into him.

A minute and an eternity later, they reached the manor, its

door whipping wildly in the wind. He caught it with one hand, holding tight as its sharp edges tore into his palm. He pushed forward, leaping into the safety of his family estate.

For a moment he stilled, exhaling pure relief. Yet the danger was not over, as iciness surrounded them, the frigid water chilling from within. Sophia started to tremble, slightly at first, then more violently. He had seen strong men succumb to such injuries.

He had to get her warm.

Slamming the door, he raced forward, moving from memory as he navigated the darkened hallways like a childhood maze. He burst into his room and placed her on the heavy cover, sacrificing but a moment to stoke the fire. He returned and grasped her, yet her limbs seemed crafted of ice. She had been unnaturally silent through their journey, a condition far more dangerous that any hysterics.

She was so very cold.

"Speak to me, Sophia." He removed the ruined slippers, pulled off the soaked stockings. It was only when he began to peel off the shirt that she protested. "What are you doing?"

That raspy whisper brought untold relief. "I won't touch you more than necessary, but I have to get you warm."

Her teeth clattered so loud, it was audible over the never-ending pounding of the rain. "Do you have a hundred blankets?"

Only she could make him smile at a time like this. "A thousand if you'd like." He carefully pulled the fabric from her damp body. "I'll take good care of you, lass."

He moved quickly and methodically, removing all clothing before drying her with a thick cloth. It was not how he imagined seeing her naked for the first time, and although she was the most beautiful creature on earth, his only urge was to care for her, to get her warm. He wrung her hair twice, absorbing the moisture, before sliding a dry shift over her head.

He brushed a hand against her cheek. "How are you feeling, lass?"

"A little better," she whispered.

Relief as he'd never known it liquefied his muscles, as his heart finally dipped from its crescendo. He grazed his knuckles against her arm. She winced as a droplet of water dripped off his shirt and onto her.

"You're still wet." Her eyes widened, as if she only just realized he carried half the river. Yet in truth, he barely noticed the dampness. The heavy physical activity had kept him warm, and he was accustomed to the cold temperatures of Scotland.

He gave a soft grin. "I am well."

"You most certainly are not. Why haven't you changed?" She tried to wave her hand, but he'd tucked it securely in the blanket. "You need a hundred blankets, as well."

He smiled. "Yes, my lady."

He traveled to his chest and retrieved a pair of clean black pants and a crisp white shirt. Ducking behind the screen, he dried himself, not realizing how cold he was until the warmth of the dry fabric covered the chill. He strode with renewed vigor, emerging to find Sophia vastly improved. A healthy pinkness had overtaken her ashen pallor, and the trembling had lessened to a modest shiver.

She even produced a weak smile. "You're supposed to be wearing a hundred blankets."

It would take far more than a dip in the river to convince him to wear a blanket. "I'm fine." He sat on the edge of the bed and touched her arm. "Men do not need such things."

"So you're impervious to the cold?" Despite her state, she managed a wry smile. "You should take better care of yourself."

"Men also do not need to be cared for." A lock of hair fell across her cheek, and he gently swept it away. Yet instead of retreating, he stayed.

Her eyes shined. "I believe couples should care for each other."

Something shifted within him, amidst emotions he couldn't name, as he sat next to this beautiful woman. She was covered in a shirt and two blankets, and he was fully dressed, yet a moment had never felt so intimate.

It almost felt like a love match.

He cleared his throat, removed his hand. A love match was impossible. His mother had sacrificed everything for his father and had paid for it the rest of her life. He could never risk his heart.

It didn't mean he wasn't planning on keeping this woman.

No other option was possible. A match with Sophia was most logical. She was practically raised to be a duchess, with all the necessary abilities and skills. They communicated well, got along famously. They were compatible in every way.

What could be better revenge?

He frowned deeply at the final thought. If revenge was the journey's reason, why did it now seem so wrong?

"What are you thinking?"

The softly spoken words brought him back to the captive who had captivated him. "How very sorry I am."

She sat up, or at least she made the attempt. He placed a firm hand on her shoulder, keeping her secure. "You will not exert yourself tonight."

For a moment she looked ready to argue, but then she relaxed back with a sigh. "Why are you sorry?"

"I never should've allowed you to get hurt." He flexed his fingers. "I should have protected you better."

"As much as it pains me to say this, and believe me, it pains me..." She exhaled deeply. "This was my fault. I never should have ventured into the storm."

"No, you shouldn't have." A vision flashed, of her plunging into the river, disappearing underneath the inky waves. The fear he would never forget. "You will never put yourself in danger again."

For a moment, defiance sparked in her eyes, but then she grimaced. "I have no desire to tempt another storm. If you hadn't been there..." She swallowed, blinked.

The urge to comfort her was all-consuming. "It's all right," he murmured. "You're safe."

"Only because of you." Her voice cracked. "I didn't mean to go into the water. I didn't even see it..."

"All is well." He lowered his voice. "I will always be there."

"You cannot say that."

He could indeed, for she was his. She just didn't know it yet.

She took another quivering breath. "I can't believe you jumped into a raging river to rescue me. You could have been killed."

He laid a gentle kiss upon her forehead. "I told you I would keep you safe."

She burrowed into his touch, casting the all-consuming urge to pull her close and never let go. Yet she didn't belong to him – yet. And when she did, he would not allow emotions to take control. "What type of kidnapper would I be if I let you get hurt? It's specifically forbidden in the kidnapping handbook."

The words elicited the desired smile. "Wouldn't a book on kidnapping etiquette say it's impolite to kidnap?"

"I'd rather not say."

"Are there any other rules of kidnapping etiquette you've broken?"

"Only a hundred or so."

At her soft chuckle, he drew back with mock sternness. "Of course, you've broken etiquette as well."

"Have I?" Her eyes glittered. "Was I supposed to play lady in distress?"

"Exactly," he shared. "Perhaps I shall write my own book on etiquette for kidnappers."

"And I shall write a book on etiquette for the kidnapped." She laughed again. "I am certain they shall be instant sensations."

After another chuckle, they settled into a soft silence. Her breathing evened as he sat next to her, holding her as her eyelashes fluttered, as she slowly surrendered to sleep. Then he did what any gentleman would do: tore himself away.

As he lay on the miniscule settee, emotions scattered like the storm still raging outside. It was a miracle she was uninjured, with no visible harm from her treacherous journey. If he had arrived a minute later...

Stop. He had made it in time, and she was well. Now he would ensure she never did anything like that ever again.

Protecting her would be his greatest responsibility.

THE BRIDGE WAS gone.

Well, not exactly gone. The supports still stood on either side of the river, the wood was still present, the nails and rope visible. Yet instead of a coherent whole, the wood was splintered into a thousand pieces, the rope was a tangled ball and the supports were jagged pieces of metal.

No one was crossing the river any time soon.

Sophia stepped towards the bank. Next to her, Kenneth watched with wary eyes, clearly poised to grab her if she delved too close to the water. He needn't worry. She had no intention of navigating the perilous rapids ever again. "The bridge is gone."

He regarded her as if she'd remarked the sky was blue, or the grass green. "It would appear so." He prowled beside her, his steps easy and assured, even on the rocky ground.

She blinked and closed her eyes, opened them to unhidden amusement.

"Were you hoping it would suddenly appear?"

He was entirely too jovial for a man who just lost the only feasible path to civilization. "It would be nice."

She clutched her skirt, carefully stepping around the stumps of fallen trees. Despite the earth's chaos, the sky was as serene as a sleeping babe, the sun shining brightly, with only a few wispy clouds sailing the blue expanse. A gentle breeze had replaced the night's fierce wind, and the air smelled clean and fresh. It was a moment of rebirth, a reawakening, as nature celebrated night's end. "You said the bridge has failed before. How long did it take to rebuild?"

"Not long." He picked up a piece of debris and tossed it onto the shore. Then another, and another. "It should only take one."

She relaxed. "One week isn't that bad—"

"Month."

A month?

A month!

She stomped after him. "There has to be another way."

He stopped and gestured to the surroundings. His muscles bulged with every movement, which make her stare, which made her angry for staring, which made her look away, which made her indignant for looking away, which made her turn back, which made her notice how his muscles bulged with every movement, which made her stare—

"Does there appear to be another way, Lady Sophia?"

She frowned as he interrupted her staring. She glanced back at the land extending for miles, the dense forests in the back of the estate, the wide river still flowing in rapid gurgles. There would be no magically appearing bridges.

She was trapped.

"Your mother will not be back for some time, correct?"

She paused at the unexpected comment. "Yes, thank goodness. It's bad enough making poor Bradenton suffer, but my mother—" She halted. "How did you know she was away?"

He turned away from her. "I heard it somewhere."

Could he actually care about her mother's sensibilities? It was not the sort of thing a typical kidnapper considered.

Yet he was not a typical kidnapper.

Do not soften, she chided herself as she hurried to catch up with him. Kidnapping was not his only transgression. Priscilla's words flashed in her mind, alongside an image of the journal he had likely stolen. He may still be planning to expose them.

Even if she couldn't escape him, perhaps she could at least prevent that calamity. "What about the journal?"

His amusement faded. "You accused me of taking a journal before. I've only ever stolen one thing. You."

She narrowed her eyes. "Don't you mean borrowed?"

"Borrowing indicates you are going to give something back."

She swallowed. *Ignore him. He is just trying to unbalance you.* "Priscilla has a journal, which she brought to the masquerade. Someone stole it."

"You're fighting for something that doesn't even belong to you?" Suspicion seeped into his gaze. "Why do you assume I have it? Is it because I'm the villain of your story?"

"You're no villain." The protest came on its own, immediate and instinctual. Despite his transgressions, he wasn't a bad man, just a thoroughly misguided one. He believed her brother to be the villain, but in truth, both were heroes.

A cool wind blew, and he edged closer to her, rubbing her arms, warming her instantly. She inhaled dewy air.

"Tell me why you believe I have the journal."

She pursed her lips. She could evade him, and probably should. If Kenneth didn't know about the guild, it was vital he remain ignorant, for it posed yet another method of revenge.

Only if he could help retrieve it, perhaps it was worth the risk. "Priscilla saw someone take the journal, a man with your general shape and build. As you know, few men are as..." *Muscular. Powerful. All-too-tempting.* "Unfashionably well-formed as you."

He lifted an eyebrow, and she blushed. "A mask hid his exact features, and his costume was indistinct. She chased him to the carriages, but he escaped before she caught him." She took a deep breath. "The crest on the carriage was yours."

He stiffened. "Is she certain?"

"It was dark, and several of the crests were similar. Still with the man's size, the coach and your motives–" She grimaced. "It seemed like a forgone conclusion."

Something flashed in his eyes, before they shuttered a moment later. Did he know who took it? "Why is the journal so important?"

"It's private." She broke eye contact. "No one should read another person's journal."

He folded his arms across his chest. Ah yes. She had read his journal. And his father's journal. And if she hadn't been interrupted, she would have read every single one.

"I quite agree," he drawled. "Could you imagine looking through someone's private musings without their permission?"

The heat started at her neck and spread through her entire body. "There are exceptions."

"Indeed." He edged closer to her. "Perhaps he has a good reason."

Undoubtedly he had a reason, but good? Doubtful. "Do you know who took it?"

"I'm not certain." He looked down at her with unrevealing eyes. "If I am to help you, you need to tell me more about the book."

She exhaled slowly. Sharing the secret of the guild was a step too far. "It contains nothing of consequence, yet they are personal matters. I cannot break my friend's confidence."

"Why would Priscilla bring something so sensitive to the masquerade? It seems like an unnecessary risk." His voice deepened. "Unless others are involved."

Sophia hesitated just long enough to confirm his suspicion. "It does not matter who is involved, only that it is returned. The journal is not bad itself, yet in the wrong hands, dozens of people could be impacted."

"Dozens?" He stopped, turned to her. His voice was lower, deliberate. "Who?"

Priscilla. His sister. *Her.* "I can only tell you it is imperative it's returned."

His gaze hardened, yet he didn't press further. That he would investigate was now all but certain, yet whether he would ultimately aid or sabotage remained to be seen. If he learned the ladies were part of a secret society of social action crusaders, there would be no way to predict his reaction.

She stepped over a fallen log. Despite the calmness of the day, restlessness infused her. She had a month's forced vacation, with no way to contribute to the guild's cause.

Unless...

Perhaps the trip could be useful. She had already learned the basics of self-defense, instruction that gave Molly the courage to escape her attacker. So many women could benefit from such knowledge, yet a day's lesson could only go so far. With a month of training, she could learn enough to teach others, perhaps create some sort of school...

"Since I am stuck here with you, I should get a benefit."

He lifted an eyebrow.

And she imagined every benefit he could bestow in clear, detailed imagery. It involved lips, hands...

Not really a lot of clothes...

She cleared her throat. "That's not what I meant."

His gaze darkened.

Maybe it was what she meant. Because really, what could be better than lips, hands...

Not really a lot of clothes...

She pushed herself forward, too quickly, as her foot slid into a branch. Her dress caught, and she fell forward...

Straight. Into. Him.

Strong hands caught her, spanning her waist. Bulging muscles shifted, tightening and flexing. "Are you all right?" he murmured.

She nodded a lie.

"Were you imagining something between us? Some benefit?"

Yes. Lips, hands, not really a lot of–

A thousand shoulds swirled in the air. She should chastise him. Should flee. Should tell him they would never kiss again.

Instead she pressed closer.

"Would you like to show me what you were thinking about?" he murmured.

She couldn't.

She shouldn't.

She wanted to.

She did.

His lips were as warm as the sun burning above, as tender as the breeze dancing with the leaves. He smelled like oak and fresh dew, with just a hint of spice. He cupped her cheek, stroking the soft skin under her neck, bringing warmth, security, delight.

He explored with abandon, freeing her hair from its pins, grazing her neck with his teeth. He was everywhere at once, and yet not enough, as he surrounded her, brought her deeper into an embrace of pure power. A soft moan escaped, as sensitive spots molded against unyielding hardness.

"Is this what you want?"

"Oh, yes."

Oh no.

She opened her eyes, blinked at a world so bright, it hurt her eyes. Pulled back from the forbidden. "I didn't mean to kiss you."

"Yet it is what you want." It was a statement, not a question, irrefutable truth belying any denial. How easy it would be to surrender, to allow him to do as he wished. She would love every second, yet the aftermath would destroy her ability to make her own path. Would he demand more?

Demand her?

She could not deny the obvious, not to him, and not to herself. She had to focus on those who needed her. "I want to fight."

That stopped him. "I'm sorry?"

"I want you to teach me to fight."

Confusion overtook the raw hunger in his eyes. He retreated ever-so-slightly, allowing a dose of sanity to return. "I did teach you how to fight."

She stepped away, resuming her journey to the manor as if they hadn't just paused for her ravishment. One step after another, eyes straight ahead, away from the man who would usurp her control. "You gave me one lesson. I want more."

In the corner of her eye, his expression softened. "You need not be afraid, Sophia. No one will harm you."

His gaze pulled at her like an invisible rope. "I'm not afraid."

"You're not?" Now he moved closer, casting dueling urges to

approach and flee. Another step and then another. "Molly's situation was difficult to witness, yet she is well, and her stepfather will never bother her again. Do not worry about your own safety. You are well protected."

She licked dry lips. "Of course. Few would challenge my brother."

"I wasn't talking about Edmund."

She almost missed a step, managed not to fall into him. Ignored her disappointment.

This was why she needed her own power: to snatch it back from men who would dare claim it. "I wasn't referring to me. I was talking about all the women of society. Do you know how many women are abused?"

He visibly tightened. "Far more than either of us imagine, no doubt."

"Exactly." She clasped her hands. "Some are abused by the men sworn to care for them, others by strangers in broad daylight. They have no way to escape, and no one to help. I've seen it many times, even experienced the threat myself."

His eyes narrowed into little slits, as suddenly, his entire demeanor changed. Gone was the gentleman of the ton, in his place, a warrior. "Explain."

She swallowed a suddenly parched throat. "Someone on the street accosted me." Or rather someones, a fact she would not mention. "It is of no matter. I got away before anything happened."

"It is a grave matter." He stared at her, a pure Scottish laird. "Tell me, Lady Sophia, where were you when this incident occurred?"

Perhaps now would not be the best time to mention she traversed the slums regularly.

When she didn't respond, he folded his arms across his chest. "Matters of your personal safety will change once we return to London."

Not if she had any say in it. "My point is it happens everywhere, and women should learn to defend themselves."

He stared at her a moment more. Just when she was sure he'd deny her, he nodded. "Very well. I shall help you hone your defensive techniques."

"You will?" She didn't quite manage to hide her shock. *While she was at it...* "I also want you to teach me how to sword fight."

His gaze immediately turned suspicious. "Please don't tell me you plan to arm ladies with swords."

"Of course. I thought we could roam London, rounding up criminals. We'll call ourselves the Distinguishes Ladies of Sword Fighting."

"I don't know whether you are serious or jesting."

Neither did she. "I do not plan on teaching every lady in London how to sword fight."

Just the ones who were interested.

He grimaced. "I suppose there wouldn't be any harm in teaching you sword fighting, so long as you refrain from displaying your skills at Almack's. Please tell me that is your final request."

"Not even close."

"Any chance it doesn't involve danger?"

"Probably not."

He rubbed the bridge of his nose.

She smiled. "I want to learn how to ride astride."

He grimaced. Likely he would provide the same response Edmund had given when she posed the question. How riding astride was wholly inappropriate, most improper and simply not done by ladies of the ton.

"All right."

She started. "Did you say all right?"

"Why not?" He shrugged. "Riding sidesaddle is nonsensical and dangerous." He took a step around her. "You've crafted me as a man who lacks empathy, doesn't listen and ignores conflicting viewpoints. I am different than you believe."

Yes, he was.

And the more she learned about him, the less she could dislike him.

"Maybe you can teach me something in return for all my instruction." His gaze turned mysterious. "Something you learned at your guild perhaps?"

She moved her hands behind her so he wouldn't see her clench them. Did he suspect the guild was not as she portrayed? "If you wish to learn about *sewing*, I shall be happy to teach you. Yet I would like to start with riding, if that is acceptable." She was still restless from last night's storm, and even more so from their kiss. Physical activity was the perfect foil.

"I'm afraid I can't teach you right now." He gestured to the fallen trees marring the landscape. "I must clear the debris and address a few important matters."

Could "important matters" relate to the journal? "Would you like me to assist with the trees?"

This time his smile was genuine. "Do I not look strong enough to move a few branches, lass?"

"You're certainly strong." She closed her eyes, opened them to wry amusement. "I mean you are reasonably strong." Then because her sense had apparently been stolen by the lightning, she licked her lips. Then she looked at his lips. Then she wished his lips were on her lips.

She needed to get away from him. Well, first she needed another kiss, but then she needed to get away from him. It took all her strength not to demand that kiss. "I shall ride by myself until you are ready."

"Absolutely not."

Just when he wasn't being an overbearing aristocrat. "I will do as I wish." The wind blew a lock of hair over her eyes, and she swiped it aside. The wind blew it right back in her eyes.

Before she could react, he tucked it behind her ear. "We will ride later. Rest now. You are still recovering from your ordeal."

Why did men always think ladies needed rest? "I am quite well, and more than capable of riding a horse."

"Yet not astride. I shall be there to ensure your safety the first time."

Dominating men and their authoritative tendencies. She opened her mouth to tell him exactly what she thought of it when she halted. Why was she arguing? She'd lived long enough with Edmund to know the best strategy for dealing with overprotective men.

She smiled.

He frowned.

She didn't say a word. Instead, she pivoted and headed towards the manor, ignoring the weight of his stare on her back. That he was suspicious was without a doubt, but it didn't matter. Time for him to learn she would do as she pleased.

Even if she was trapped.

SHE WAS TRAPPED.

He was not.

Kenneth had not exactly lied. The bridge was obviously impassable in its current form, and it would indeed take a month to craft a new one. No other bridge was close. Yet "close" was a relative term, and Sophia did not ask precisely how long it would take to reach the next crossing.

They could be back in London within two days.

In a thousand opportunities to share the truth, he kept silent a thousand times. He needed time to learn more about his reluctant guest, to discover why she affected him. He could claim retribution as his motive, yet it would be untrue. Even with precautions, every minute together carried risks. He abated the risks as best he could with a letter to Adam, wrapped around a rock that he threw to the townspeople this morning. He wrote of his plans and asked that he contact him if matters deteriorated enough to force his return.

He just couldn't bring himself to return her. Not yet.

Not ever.

Kenneth hefted one broken branch after the next, tossing

them in a haphazard pile. Besides the bridge, there was no substantial damage, yet plenty needed clearing. He could have waited until later to do the work, yet he needed a few moments to regain his focus, especially after Sophia's revelations. He hadn't taken the journal.

He knew who did.

Or at least it appeared that way, if memories from the masquerade proved correct. A man with a tall and formidable build similar to his own. A man who shared his carriage that night. A man with a mysterious book.

Adam.

His cousin's demeanor had been mysterious, odd even. If suspicions were correct, why had he taken the journal, and more importantly, what did he plan to do with it? His cousin was an honorable man, who would never steal anything without good reason. Sophia had mentioned dozens of people. His sister Clara was included in her groups of friends, and in the guild. Was she somehow involved?

It warranted immediate investigation.

A horse's neigh broke the silence, as if bestowing its agreement. Dropping the last piece of wood, he brushed off his hands, already circling the edge of the house. He emerged onto the field and stopped.

Sophia stood out like a shining star, riding atop a large horse, wearing a shirt, pants and pure feminine power. Astride for the first time.

Horse and rider soared over the ground with wild abandon, like a favorite speeding down the home stretch of a horse race. Her excitement was palpable from afar, yet small wobbles revealed her lack of expertise. Clutching the reins, she urged the horse even faster.

He tightened as a corner appeared, as she took it far too sharp. The horse skidded one way and then the other, scrambling to compensate for the narrow turn. It regained its footing, yet dashed wildly, as it jerked its head and its rider violently. It careened straight towards a fallen tree.

Kenneth yelled to her, yet the wind swallowed his words. The horse reared...

And tossed its rider.

CHAPTER FIFTEEN

The Private Diary of Sophia Hawkins

Adapted from Rules of Etiquette for the Kidnapped, First Edition

In order to successfully resist a kidnapping, it is vital to adhere to the following steps:

1. *Never cry, swoon, sob, beg or cajole.*
2. *Instead protest, argue, and demand compensation in the form of useful lessons.*
3. *Resist your captor at every turn.*
4. *Above all, do not fall for your kidnapper.*

T UMBLING ONTO THE hard ground can really change one's perspective.

Quite literally, unfortunately, as the world turned topsy-turvy, as she tumbled and bumped, rolled and rollicked until she was on her back, gazing up at the clear, blue sky. Metaphorically as well, as jumping into riding astride (also quite literally) provided results that were disappointing at best. The only bright spot? The horse was unharmed, looking mighty pleased with himself, after divesting himself of his rider. He tossed his head and turned away.

Seems even the horse disapproved of her methods.

She flattened her palms on the rocky ground, wincing as sharp pebbles scratched her ungloved hands. She pushed herself up, dusted off the pants she had found in Kenneth's room and stood. Then the *storm* arrived.

Entirely different from last night's tempest, this force of nature was no less powerful and far more furious. Dust and debris filled the air, as he approached her personal space and beyond. *Then he captured her.*

He was checking for injuries. It was obvious by the methodical way in which he worked, the focused gaze as he felt for bumps, bruises and scratches. Yet as firm fingers traced sensitive skin, powerful hands molding tender curves, her body did not care about his motivations.

It wanted more.

"Are you all right?" he demanded.

The short answer was "no," and the long answer was "not even a little." His touch burned every inch, travelling through the thin shirt and over her entire body, overtaking all soreness. Her body became heated, swollen and sore. It was all she could do not to push into those hands, invite him to sooth the spots that most yearned for his touch.

The concern in his expression deepened. "I shall take you to bed at once."

It was the wrong thing to say.

A thousand images flashed: Him. Her. The Bed. So many combinations thereof. If he carried her inside, she wouldn't have the power to stop herself from demanding something a lady shouldn't even know about. And that was a very bad idea.

Even if her traitorous body thought it was a very *good* idea.

"I am well." She pushed herself back, but he didn't allow it. "You may release me."

"Why didn't you answer?" he demanded. "Why do you look so out of sorts?"

Because of his...

Wandering hands.

Powerful body.

Sensual promise.

"I fell off a horse." His gaze darkened. "As you can see, I'm fine," she quickly added.

His gaze turned as intense as lightning. She looked down at herself and froze.

Well, that explained it.

In her haste to ride, she had glanced in the mirror for scarcely a moment. Everything appeared reasonably covered, even if the fabric was a little thin. Yet she hadn't considered how the outfit would appear when silhouetted by the sun.

Shadows became outlines, crevices shone in exquisite detail. Fabric rounded curves, hugging in all the right, or wrong, places. When pulled taut, the effect was even greater.

She was all but indecent.

"You promise you're not hurt?"

She swallowed, nodded. "Not at all. I was just thinking."

"About what?"

Him. Her. The Bed. So many combinations thereof.

Understanding transformed his expression, as unease vanished, replaced with clear desire. His eyes smoldered, bringing pure heat. He edged closer.

She couldn't decide whether to push him away or pull him near. "What are you doing?"

He slid his hands around the nape of her neck. He traced her spine, and she arched into him, flattening against the wall of muscle. Pinprick sensations blazed through the fabric, as her breasts brushed his chest. Blood flooded vulnerable spots, swelling, sensitizing, ripening.

Heat engulfed her as the warrior leaned down, his eyes blazing emerald fire. "Do you know you belong to me?"

Her response was lost in the kiss.

It was like returning home, to the place you're destined to be. He held her as if she were a rare and precious gem, a delicate treasure. It was delicious temptation, slow torture, as she urged him closer, faster, *more.* Yet even as she quickened her movements, he continued as before, no doubt a consideration to her soreness.

What sort of kidnapper was so conscientious?

They parried back and forth in the sensual duel, as he became bolder, more daring, exploring ever-closer to the feminine spots that ached for his touch. She gasped as he caressed her lips and body, as she capitulated to his administrations. She closed her eyes, surrendering as he nuzzled needy spots.

An eternity passed before he slowly leaned back. Yet it was an eternity too little, as unquenched thirst lingered, tender cravings only he could fulfill. She fought to remain coherent, as he surrounded, enveloped, *dominated*. The question he posed before the kiss, and the answer she didn't have, danced on her tongue.

Passion burning in his eyes, he murmured, "We should stop."

"Most assuredly not." She pressed forward.

This kiss was even more delicious than the last, as she urged him forward, showing him without words what she wanted, needed. He touched everywhere – her swollen lips, her vulnerable neck, on top of her clothing, *under* it. He stopped another three times, perhaps five, before she finally stayed back. Because if she didn't, this wouldn't end here, may never end at all. He was still her captor.

Somehow he read her resolution, even as his eyes blazed. She should feel satiated, yet it was not enough. His earlier question burned:

Do you know you belong to me?

It was untrue, at least at present. Little was required for it to become reality, for their worlds to become irreversibly intertwined. Yet she couldn't think of it now, when her body still burned from his sensual administrations. Pushing all thoughts of untamed dukes and kisses from her mind, she announced, "I'd like to ride again."

Widened eyes betrayed surprise, even as admiration shone. "You want to get back on the horse?"

"Of course. That is what one does when one falls off something." With a deep breath of courage, she reached towards the reins.

A hand clamped around her arm. She gripped the thick leather harness so tightly it scorched her raw hands. "I have to get back on." She blinked, unbidden emotion welling inside of her. And suddenly the moment was about far more than a horse. "Please," she whispered. "I don't know how else to live."

She swallowed emotion, as he stayed still, regarding her carefully. He released her arm, yet not her, moving down to grasp her waist. In one smooth motion, he lifted her onto the horse.

"You are an extraordinary woman, Lady Sophia," He caressed her waist, his gaze gentle. Then he cleared his throat, and his expression turned stern. "Yet it doesn't mean you shouldn't take care. Until you are accustomed to your seat, you will only ride on straight, easy paths."

She grinned. "Those are perfect for racing."

Exasperated amusement lit his gaze, and the mood lightened. "Must everything you do involve danger?"

She thumped her chin. "Why, yes, it must."

His lips twitched. "Most women enjoy calm activities, yet you prefer danger, with one exception. Tell me, is the sewing guild your only safe activity?"

Do. Not. Laugh. "Indeed, my lord. I find it most… calming."

"Do you? Perhaps later you can tell me about it." His eyes betrayed nothing, yet something told her this was no random question. Did he suspect the sewing group was more than it seemed?

She would reveal nothing, yet better to agree than raise suspicions. "Yes, Your Grace."

"Your Grace?" He frowned. "Are you humoring me?"

"It is a distinct possibility, Your Grace."

"Will you stop calling me Your Grace?"

"Certainly, Lord Kidnapper."

He growled, yet his expression betrayed sparkling bemusement. "I like Your Grace better."

"You should have thought about that before," she said cheekily. "Henceforth you are permanently known as Lord Kidnapper."

"Even if I go riding with you?"

She stopped. Pretended she didn't really, really want him to join her. "I suppose I can think of another name. How does The Untamed Duke sound to you?"

"Like the name of one of my sister's romantic novels."

Indeed.

"How about The Duke Who Steals Ladies?"

He rubbed his chin. "The Duke Who Stole Lady Sophia may be more appropriate."

She looked upward, yet could not summon any true anger. "I suppose I can call you Kenneth, although it is highly inappropriate."

He looked at her pointedly, or rather he looked at the lips he'd just kissed/caressed/fondled. "That's what you are worried about being inappropriate?"

She had the grace to blush.

"I shall go riding with you if you promise to stay out of danger." He patted the horse lightly. "I do not want to find you in the river's clutches again."

She shivered. She had no intention of going anywhere near that river again, at least not until a sturdy bridge spanned it. Yet danger was an inherent part of her life. Perhaps a compromise could be made. "How about I promise to be careful for the duration of our stay? Would that be sufficient?" Since escape was impossible, there was little to tempt her towards danger. Once she returned to London and the *Distinguished Ladies of Purpose*, however…

His eyed held unhidden doubt. "You promise to be safe while we are here?"

She nodded.

"And you won't risk your life in the few minutes it takes me to saddle my horse?"

"I would hurry if I were you."

He chuckled, yet all amusement fled as he leaned in. As the

air turned serious, his voice was low, somber and *dangerous*. "If I ever see you risking your life again, I shall do everything in my power to ensure it's the last time, even if it means curtailing your freedom. Do you understand?"

Indignation tightened muscles, yet she showed none of it. "Perfectly."

He nodded and turned, walking to the stables.

She exhaled. Once she returned to London, she would live her life exactly as she pleased.

Danger and all.

HIS HEART STOPPED today.

At least temporarily, when the horse sent Sophia soaring across the field, slamming into the uneven ground. By fortune or fate, she landed in a grassy spot, in between two jagged rocks pointing upward like daggers. He didn't remember running to her, or his thoughts as he touched her far more intimately than appropriate. He'd attributed her aroused state to injury, yet clearly it was the affliction that affected them both.

Now even hours later, alone in his room, the memories returned in a never-ending loop. How did she captivate him so? Pure fear, not tempered concern, jolted him when she slammed to the ground, and his heart galloped even as she protested she was hearty and whole, proven by her uninjured state. The moment replayed in his mind again and again, alternating with the other times she'd put herself in danger. She thrived in peril, and his efforts to stop her had proven woefully inadequate. Henceforth, he would do more to protect her from herself.

Whether she liked it or not.

At least she was safe for the night, securely tucked into bed. He had allowed her to move from his room, reluctantly, relocating her to the chamber next door. He managed to only check on her three times.

He gazed out the window of the large master bedroom. Outside the air was cool, but not cold, with a gentle breeze flavored with the scent of night roses. A nocturnal bird sang a pining melody, its harmony joined by dozens of night creatures. Despite the late hour, energy burst within him, unresolved longing for what he could not have.

He needed to expend energy. Physical exercise not only strengthened his body, but also tempered his emotions, and he normally partook every day. Perhaps a late night dip in the water would help, not in the river, of course, which raged endlessly, but in the calm, clear spring that bordered his property. Laps in the naturally warm water made for a pleasant yet challenging exercise.

He took a moment to scribble a note and place it on the table, should Sophia seek him in an emergency. He strode from the room, just managing to pass his guest's room without checking on her again, then made his way through the manor and stepped into the cool, comfortable night.

He strolled through the cleared paths, taking his time as he travelled the short journey. The night's weather was as flawless as the previous night's was turbulent, with a bright moon presiding over a cloudless sky. A breeze ruffled his hair, soothing raw senses, as the lake appeared behind a copse of trees.

He stopped and closed his eyes, basking in the purity of the natural world. The ton ignored such treasures, instead focusing on false splendors of little substance. The superficial riches they worshiped were like paste to the raw beauty of nature, their pursuits of wealth, titles and land unending, while they devalued the true worth of goodness, kindness and charity.

Not Sophia.

She showed what others didn't. Sincerity and compassion, kindness and respect, to everyone, no matter a person's position in society. She didn't care how much money was in a man's pocket or what title was attached to his name. In a kingdom of goodness, she was royalty.

Desire for his enchanting captive flared once more, as he reached the bank of the glittering water. Grasping the hem of his shirt, he divested himself of the garment, followed by his pants and even his underthings. He usually swam in the nude, and yesterday's outfit was still damp from his little *dip* yesterday. Of course Sophia was asleep, and the lake was not visible from her window.

He leapt into the crystal clear springs, opening his arms wide to the welcoming warmth. He cut through the water, sliding in its silky embrace, propelling himself forward with smooth, even strokes. As Sophia's image reentered his mind, he swam faster, through the winding springs, under a miniature waterfall. A cascade of violet blooms massaged his back as he glided under a hanging tree down a meandering path.

He swam one lap and then another, and then another and another. Yet no matter how fast he raced, he couldn't outrace the image of his captivating guest. She thought he had stolen her.

She had stolen him as well.

SOPHIA STARED AT the wall above her, counting the number of times the owl hooted in the distance (26), the number of roses painted on the cream colored walls (142) and the number of times the fire crackled in the deep marble fireplace (309). She examined the cherry wood furniture, tossed on the four poster bed and snuggled into the silky sheets. She watched the tall trees swaying in the night breeze.

Yet she was no closer to sleep than before.

This was Kenneth's fault. When he had stolen her, he had also stolen her attention, good sense and even her ability to sleep. She tried all the methods to cure insomnia.

Counting owl hoots turned into counting kisses.

Counting roses turned into counting the number of times she wished they kissed.

Counting fire crackles turned into counting the number of kisses they might share before this trip was over.

She leapt onto the hard floor, wincing at soreness from the previous day's misadventures. She had no destination in mind as she donned a soft lavender dress, slid her feet into slippers and bound her hair into a soft knot. She padded to the door, and stopped.

Whatever she went, she would avoid anything *too* dangerous. It would not do to go back on a promise, even to her kidnapper. After all, he hadn't deceived her. He'd made perfectly clear he was going to kidnap her.

Then, he did.

She'd promised to avoid danger, not remain in her room like a prisoner. Surely a walk on the grounds posed no peril.

She grasped the door handle. Half expecting to see an uninvited duke slumbering outside her door, the empty hallway came almost as a surprise. Still, she moved quietly past his room, then quickened her stride as she padded through the hallway and descended the long staircase. She reached the front door and stepped into the night.

Like a soothing blanket, the wind wrapped itself around her, as if apologizing for yesterday's tantrum. It was scented by roses, their dark red blooms visible against the emerald bushes, even in the moonlight. The river was far enough to provide a comforting cadence, a gentle backdrop to the lilting nocturnal birdsong.

A rare peace descended, as she strolled through enchanting gardens, under a brilliant star-studded sky. She wandered without destination or direction, always keeping the estate in view. Getting lost would definitely meet Kenneth's definition of danger, and no doubt she'd find herself sleeping next to the formidable duke again.

She ignored the sudden urge to become hopelessly lost.

Like her steps, her thoughts wandered down meandering paths. She liked her life in London, yet it was a cacophony of nonstop movement, a never-ending performance with every exchange watched, every mistake seized. Kenneth scrutinized her, yet with good intentions, her safety and security his primary goal. At times, it almost seemed he cared.

Just as she cared for him.

He was not the man she had imagined, not even close. He was honorable and good, kind and compassionate. He showed his true self in his interactions with the townspeople, as he gifted his time, efforts and funds. If not for his revenge...

Impossible. The revenge was as much part of him as the good. Whatever feelings she had for Kenneth, she loved Edmund. She must remain loyal to the man who helped raise her.

She stepped over a fallen log and sat down upon its crusty side. With a deep breath, she closed her eyes.

Water splashed, and she jumped. She immediately pivoted to the river, yet it was too far to be the source. She rose as the splash sounded again, then slowly advanced. The moon was large and bright, illuminating her path as she slunk through velvety leaves. The wind whistled, tickling the trees, as the sound grew ever-louder.

The swaying trees drew apart, revealing a glimmer of water, like the surface of a looking glass. A natural spring glistened amidst a canopy of flowering vines, shining under the full moon and countless twinkling stars. It extended in meandering swirls, with waterways delving beyond the trees.

The floral scent grew stronger, so lovely it was almost intoxicating. Dozens of majestic trees arched above, moss and flowers dripping down their branches like fluttering butterflies. Lilies bordered the edges, in whites and yellows, their fragrant scent beautifying the air.

Sophia hopped over a small dip in the ground. The spring was shallow along the edges, with a wide shelf of fine sand before it deepened to a fathomless bottom. She stopped only long enough to pull off her slippers and stockings, then stepped forward. Yet just before she reached the inviting pool, she hesitated. It would not do to get the dress wet. With his uncanny instincts, Kenneth would take one look at the damp bottom and immediately deduce what she had done.

Before she could think better of it, she grasped the hem of her dress and pulled it over her head. The night wind blew, yet its coolness only invigorated her. She folded the dress neatly on a rock next to her stockings and slippers, smoothed down her shift and stepped forward.

Unlike the river's jagged shore, the rocks here were softer and rounder, interspersed with soft moss that tickled her feet. She moved slowly in the relative darkness, careful to avoid tripping on the slippery floor. She braced herself for a shock of cold that never came, as the water remained deliciously warm, like a fresh bath poured from steaming buckets.

She sighed as she glided forward, until her ankles, and then her calves were submerged. She fought the urge to travel further, to immerse herself entirely in the natural bath, yet then she would have to fully unclothe, and unseen dangers could prowl the unfamiliar waters. She settled for sitting on a flat-top rock, her legs dangling in the water, her palms flat against the smooth surface behind her. *Pure bliss.*

Water splashed again, and she smiled as tiny silver fish danced a waltz to the melody of the night birds' orchestra. More splashing came, further yet louder, cast by something far larger than the little fish. She studied the darkness. Then, she froze.

Someone was there.

Moonlight glinted off a powerful form in the distance, cutting through the water like Poseidon, lord of the sea. He moved with the grace and power of a shark, his muscles rippling as he pulled forward with one arm and then the next in bold strokes. He was massive and he was dominant, a predator of the waves.

Kenneth.

She'd recognize his formidable form anywhere, yet she never imagined this. How did he move with such effortlessness, defying the water's pull? He conquered it with ease, just like he vanquished every other challenge in his path.

Move. Stay. Go. Remain. A thousand conflicting urges paralyzed her, as she stayed still on the smooth rock, even as he stalked closer. He emerged from the shadows, and she sucked in a breath.

He. Was. Nude.

A shark couldn't have moved her now, as she stared at the man who ruled not just the land, but the water as well. He was power defined, master of his world. He always seemed immense, always massive, yet the true measure of his power shone like never before. His shoulders were broad, his back muscled. She looked lower…

In the wet world, her throat dried.

My goodness. One didn't really consider such things, and she certainly had nothing with which to judge. But really…

Wow.

As a lady, she should turn away, should not stare, should not avoid blinking for even that momentary interruption to her one person show.

She never really listened to shoulds.

He turned, ever-so-slightly, yet it set him on a different path, one that brought him closer to her. Suddenly, he was on a journey with her as the destination, yet still she couldn't move. And then it was too late.

He stood before her, a warrior king rising from the mist. Water dripped down his body, outlining bare skin, corded curves and exposed angles. Her skin prickled as droplets moistened it, even as she pushed herself up to stand so far beneath him. He towered above her, his gaze piercing, as their eyes locked.

Then he leaned down and whispered, "Time for consequences."

CHAPTER SIXTEEN

Journal of the Duke of Foxworth:

Adapted from Rules of Etiquette for Kidnappers, First Edition
In order to conduct a successful kidnapping, it is vital to adhere to the following steps:

1. *Hide all emotions.*
2. *Do not allow distractions.*
3. *Maintain control in all situations.*
4. *Above all, do not fall for the lady.*

WAS SHE AN apparition?
A conjuring of his imagination?
An ethereal creature sent to bewitch him?

Perhaps all three, yet as he drew himself up, senses proved she was all too real: quickened breaths, cheeks flushed with emotion, the intoxicating scent of violets.

She was a sparkling star in the moonlight, her skin flawless, her ruby lips plump and inviting, her eyes brilliant. The shift clung to her like a second skin, outlining a trim waist, slender legs and oh-so-tempting curves. She was pure beauty, an enchantress of the night, and she was *his*.

He could forgive himself for thinking her otherworldly. She had taken residence in his mind, trickery of an artful imagination. She could have been fate's way of reminding him of its power, that his path lay in destiny's clutches. She could have been a waking dream, a fulfillment of never-ending wishes. Yet close enough to touch, she was all too real.

For a moment, he stood motionless, staring at her, before he managed to reach the nearby rock where he placed his towel. Her eyes tracked every movement, as he tied it around his waist and returned.

Most ladies would have fled the instant they spied him, or, having been caught, reacted with mortification and endless apologies. She did neither, as she stood like a queen, resplendent in a cotton shift. He swallowed, tightened. It would be so easy to reach out, pull her near...

Control yourself. By her response, she was not here for that, and even if she was, it wouldn't matter. He could wait. He would wait. He didn't want to wait. "You shouldn't be here."

"I couldn't sleep." Her voice was a breathless whisper, as she tilted her head in the starlight. Her gaze dropped, her pupils dilating as she stared at his chest, before she snapped it up.

"Would you like me to get dressed?"

"Absolutely not." She blushed the color of a blood rose. "I mean yes! Of course, yes. Absolutely, positively yes."

The blush deepened.

Her gaze burned into him as he retrieved the rest of his clothing and donned his pants. Did he imagine it, or was there a flash of disappointment in her eyes? Then her gaze tracked to his bare chest, and she brightened.

She tested his control like no other.

"Explain yourself."

She drifted her fingertips across the water's surface, casting tiny circles into every-expanding rings. Such was her influence on him, the slightest touch rippled to chaos. "I have nothing to explain."

"Why did you defy me again?"

She lifted her hands, inadvertently splashing them both. Bubble-eyed fish scattered in silvery disarray. "I wasn't trying to escape."

"Perhaps not," he acknowledged, "yet you were in the water."

She lifted a delicate shoulder. "You cannot compare a placid spring with a raging river. I simply wanted a walk." Her lips quirked into an impish smile. "Do you think me so clumsy as to drown in a foot of water?"

"It's the middle of the night." His mood darkened, as a thousand scenarios played in his mind, all culminating with her injured and alone. "You shouldn't be exploring by yourself, and certainly not in unfamiliar waters. What if you slipped and hurt yourself?"

"By your definition, any solitary activity is dangerous. Should I stay attached to your side for the next month?"

"It would be my preference."

It was true, for so many reasons. She inspired unease with every daring misadventure, fear from a man who feared little. Who knew what peril she courted in London? She needed someone to watch over her.

Permanently.

"What if you became lost?"

She lifted her hands. "I kept the estate in sight. You can even see the roof through the trees. I must live my life, Kenneth, just as you live yours."

As a duke, it may seem like he had every choice in the world, yet his life was not truly his own. He'd been the head of the family for as long as he could remember, responsible for so much and so many. Protecting others was his greatest responsibility, yet at times it yielded difficult choices. Of course, she wasn't officially his – yet.

He could force the issue. Could confine her to the estate when he wasn't by her side. It was tempting, yet perhaps it was not the best method. As she said, she needed to live her life, and a nocturnal walk was not truly unsafe. "I understand your need for freedom."

She parted her lips. "You do?"

"If I say yes, will you hold it over me?"

"Forever."

He hid his smile. "Next time you crave a late night sojourn, wake me and we can go together." He raised his hand to stop the oncoming protest. "Unless you do not enjoy the company?"

Her eyes drifted to his chest again, and she licked her lips.

Clearly, she was trying to end him.

She cleared her throat. "All right, but only while we are here."

He neither agreed, nor argued. Of course, just because they returned to London, didn't mean he wouldn't still guard her.

"I know the next thing I want you to teach me."

He grimaced. "War strategy?"

The impish smile returned. "Perhaps another time. For now, I wish to learn how to move through the water."

"You want to swim? I'm surprised, after…" His voice trailed off, yet the words did not need to be said. After she almost drowned.

Flashes of her sinking struck again, the cold murky water, the moments she disappeared. The horror, the fear. Yet even as he grew rigid, she stood straighter. Fear did not defeat this woman.

"It must feel glorious to move like that, like flying on earth. I've spent time in Bath, yet they allow little more than relaxation. No one ever offered this." She breathed deeply. "Should I get into trouble again, I wish to be able to rescue myself."

He would always be there to rescue her. The thought was immediate, yet it wasn't quite true. With so many lakes, ponds and watering holes, a simple fall risked tragedy. "I will teach you on one condition. You must never attempt to navigate the river. The current is far too strong." He lowered his voice. "I am serious, Sophia. I would have your word on this."

She didn't hesitate. "I promise."

He believed her. Like him, her honor was paramount. "All right," he agreed. "Tomorrow, we can start."

"What about now?"

"Now?" She wore only a thin shift, her courage and moonlight.

"We are both wet, and the moon is bright enough to light the way."

He resisted the immediate denial. If they stayed in the shallow area where the water was clear, he could easily see her. A traitorous voice whispered, *He could teach her better if she wore nothing at all.* "Do you promise to stay close?"

"I will stay as close as physically possible." She paled. "I mean I'll stay close, but not that close. Certainly not as close as possible, because that would be..." She stopped, shut her eyes. "I mean close enough to be safe."

"Of course."

She placed her small hand into his large one. He grasped it for a moment, steadying her as he moved them forward. The bottom of her shift swirled in the water, revealing small feet, shapely ankles, slender calves. Something shifted in his breast, as she entrusted herself into his care.

She wasn't trying to end him. She was *going* to end him.

HER WILLPOWER HAD dissolved an hour ago. Focus on the water, she told herself. Focus on technique, position, breathing, anything and everything that wasn't the towering man sculpted from pure muscle.

Instead she focused on the towering man sculpted from pure muscle.

By the time an hour had passed, she'd made excellent progress in focusing on the towering man sculpted from pure muscle and far slower progress in swimming. That was to say, she still sank like a rock. Only she sank slower now, which was progress if one wanted to enjoy a leisurely sinking instead of just getting straight to the point.

Yet no matter how many times she sank, her instructor remained positive and optimistic, certain she was moments away from navigating the water like the fish that danced around them. He was skilled and kind, patient and understanding, as he assured her a hundred and one times. And when she started to sink, he was always there to catch her.

"Let's get you into position."

That was how it always started.

And like before, instead of saying "No, thank you, because if you touch me one more time, I may not be able to resist kissing you," she smiled and nodded.

Then his hands were *everywhere*.

He positioned her on the liquid bed, supporting her stomach with hands so huge, they nearly encircled her. When she shifted, his knuckles inadvertently brushed the underside of her breast.

And so she shifted. *A lot.*

He ran a hand down her legs, demonstrating the technique again. She heard half of what he said and felt twice of what he touched, as the thin cloth provided little barrier. He touched her bare leg.

Senses flooded with desire.

"Do you mind if I move your clothes for a moment, so I can demonstrate how to kick?" He slid his hand down her leg.

"I don't mind!" She lowered her voice. "If it can help me learn."

"Don't stay so rigid," he instructed, grasping her leg. "Move with the water."

She dutifully obeyed, paddling one arm in front of the other just like he'd showed. He splayed his fingers on her belly.

She gulped a mouthful of water.

She choked as he patted her back, holding her up as she coughed. He rubbed her shoulders, making soothing noises, as she heaved in a breath of air to dislodge the watery film coating her throat.

"Are you all right?"

No, she was not. Physically, perhaps, yet senses were scrambled, undone by his endless touches. Like a storm-lashed ship held by an anchor, she clutched at the warmth, the beacon of strength. His grip never loosened as he turned her in his arms.

"Are you well?" he murmured.

A moment or a thousand passed. "I don't know," she answered honestly.

"Neither do I." He breathed in deeply, and she brushed against him. Her breasts felt heavy as the wet fabric clung to them, as she pressed against his chest with only the translucent cloth separating them.

"What do you do to me?" He leaned lower.

"The same thing you do to me." She closed her eyes.

The first taste was extraordinary.

He brushed her lips, as he firmly took control with an intoxicating blend of whisper soft touches and firm strokes. He massaged her body, her mind, *her*. Yet she was a willing participant, surrendering as he softened her with intimate caresses she couldn't resist.

Only a sliver of clothing and a sheen of water separated them, yet she ached for more. His gentle hold tightened, and he wrapped his hands around her to bring her closer. Her body pressed flush against his, tantalizing friction with every movement.

The watery world brought them closer than ever before. They were no longer separated by a dozen layers of clothing and the heavy burden of society. Here, in their enchanted pool, only the two of them existed.

He licked the seam of her lips, and she opened for him. Yet she demanded as well, exploring, manipulating the heavy muscles under her hands. He stole her control, her senses, her every resolution, as he deepened the kiss. He rubbed her skin, ran his hands through her wet hair, cupped her vulnerable neck. The thin shift gave no protection against his sensual onslaught.

Why was her shift still on?

The thought came on its own volition, like a lightning bolt in an amorphous world. Her wicked mind flashed with images, naked skin to naked skin, bareness to bareness, hardness to softness. The fictional images mingled with true sensations, movements that became bolder by the second. It was unbearable delight, yet something more lurked out of reach.

So why was her shift still on?

The question's second arrival was less fanciful wonder, more potential reality. As they writhed against each other in the sensual dance, each iteration bringing them closer, his presence was everywhere. It was perfection, yet it was not enough. She wanted more, needed more, *deserved* more.

Why shouldn't she embrace passion's ultimate ritual? Society's dictates were arbitrary and unfair, misogynistic by their very nature. She could show the ton, albeit without their knowledge, that she would not be constrained by their skewed opinions on right and wrong, would not deny herself for their unfair decrees. Indeed, making love was a most rational, and even logical, decision.

His hands strayed to her backside and squeezed.

Forget logic and reason.

She wanted him.

Even knowing the break was only temporary, pulling back was an endeavor to require a warrior. "Kenneth…" She closed her eyes, fighting the dual urges to protect sensitive spots and open herself up to his administrations. She settled for a combination, yet when he nipped at her, she gasped.

He sighed, and his movement stopped. Ever so slowly, he retreated. "I'm sorry. I just wanted one more taste."

She swallowed. "How about a feast?"

He looked up sharply.

"I didn't pull back because I wanted to stop. On the contrary…" She breathed in a taste of intoxicating male. "I want to continue."

Confusion joined the need in his eyes… then enlightenment. "Sophia–"

"Do not."

"Do not what?"

"Do not sacrifice our lives to society's whims." She lifted her head. "The ton forbids ladies from what they tolerate, and even expect, from men. A woman can not so much as enjoy a chaste kiss, while a man can enjoy an endless parade of mistresses."

"Our kisses are hardly chaste." He gently stroked her cheek. "Yet you are a maiden."

She placed her hand on top of his. "What does it matter? Everything changes the day I marry, so does it truly make a difference if it is a little sooner?"

His nostrils flared. "What are you saying?"

"I refuse to live with regrets." She took a deep breath. "Claim me."

CHAPTER SEVENTEEN

The Private Diary of Sophia Hawkins

How to get an untamed duke out of one's mind:
Stop fantasizing about seeing him naked.
Stop dreaming about seeing him naked.
Stop wishing you were naked with him.

If all else fails, simply ask to see him naked.

"C LAIM ME," SHE said it again, stronger, louder, infusing all the power of feminine might into her voice.

"Sophia–"

"Do not deny me because of the opinions of others. If this is what you want–"

"Of course it's what I want." Kenneth ran his hand through his slicked back hair, sending droplets flying through the air. "You are all I want, but we can't do this. It isn't right."

"By whose definition?" she demanded. "The womanizing lords who condemn ladies for the tiniest infraction of their rules? The elites who don't notice when men abuse the women they're sworn to protect? The class who would support a debutante's marriage to an old man, so long as the match is financially beneficial?" She raised her hands. "Are those truly the people who should guide our lives?"

He hesitated.

She blinked up at him. "I have followed the rules, been all that is prim and proper." At least she appeared that way. "I know what I want. Do you?"

His eyes were a piercing green, burning with raw emotion. He growled lowly, but it was not against her. As certain as she knew anything, he was fighting himself. "If you wish to stop, it takes but a single word. Anytime."

She nodded, even though it was wholly unnecessary. This was the right path. He was–

He seized her lips.

Whether it was knowing it would reach the ultimate conclusion or another reason altogether, this time was different. No longer could she think, no longer could she analyze. All she could do was feel.

He moved slowly at first, with all the time in the world, and no ending point to elude. Yet unhurried caresses provoked even more excitment, as he traced up and down bare arms, stroked a quivering stomach, peppered kisses down her throat. She explored his body as well, tracing hard curves, molding thick muscles. She gasped as her feet left the ground.

"What are you doing?" She clutched at him.

"Taking you to bed." He nipped at her neck. "Do not worry, lass. I will always care for you."

She opened her mouth to respond, yet he stole her words with another kiss. He stepped to the plush emerald grass, before lowering her onto a *flower bed*. The natural cushion cradled her with its heady scent, yet not nearly as intoxicating as the man who hovered above her, his hands masterfully plying untold sensation from her body. The sensual onslaught came from all directions at once, unbearable and unstoppable. He grasped her shift.

"Yes." She bit back a gasp of delight, as he lifted and swept off the thin covering. The rest of her clothing was gone in seconds, and his as well, until they were skin to skin, without any barriers. He touched her bare stomach, and she gasped.

"Open your eyes," he commanded.

She squeezed them tighter.

"Don't you want to see me?"

Oh. Yes.

She opened them, slowly, deliberately. Her breath hitched.

Breathtaking. He was a masterpiece of human and fantasy, an artist's rendering in reality. His handsome visage was splendor in the moonlight, as he gazed at her with brilliant eyes. "Do you have any idea of how beautiful you are?"

Her answer was lost as he descended once more. Sensations once muted by cloth now came without obstacle, casting fiery heat, leaving her body aching, wanting, needing. He was a master pianist, and she his instrument. She writhed as he traced a breast, weighing, molding. Then he reached lower, past her abdomen and lower still...

He caressed her *there.*

Her breaths were a series of gasps, her speech mere moans. When she thought she could take no more, he wrung more delight, more sensation, more perfection. When they truly joined, she was ready. A tiny pinch was the only pain, soon overtaken by unfathomable pleasure.

There was more. *So. Much. More.* He moved above her, with her and in her, as she endlessly gasped, as the sensations came quicker, higher, stronger and greater.

Until finally, the world burst with the power of a thousand stars.

It was unbelievable and immeasurable, physical sensations of which she never dreamed. Yet something else emerged on that bed of flowers, something far deeper than the physical realm. A connection formed, a bond, borne of emotions she could not name.

And it whispered, *unescapable.*

HE EXPECTED A battle.

An argument at least, a protest of why she could not accept his claim. A denial of what was between them.

He never expected her to surrender.

His intentions were clear, her acceptance obvious. She would be his duchess, even if scandal did not force a match.

How else could he interpret her request to claim her?

Sophia stretched on the covers, sighing softly, charcoal lashes fluttering against rosy cheeks. Her hair slipped down her naked back, spreading over tantalizing curves, outlining her feminine gifts. He resisted the urge to explore, instead allowing her to settle back into slumber. There would be time enough later. This enchanting creature was his.

He'd carried her inside after she fell asleep under the blanket of stars, lulled to the realm of dreams by the birds' soft melodies. She hadn't stirred as he journeyed back home, nestling into the silky sheets of *their* bed. He never considered bringing her anywhere but his chambers, where she belonged.

When she first propositioned him, he'd told himself he was a gentleman, then again and again, yet she was as strong as he, and her reasoning broke down barriers as powerfully as any sword. She was right about society and its unfair dictates. Still, he never would have agreed had he not known what it meant. She was agreeing to a match.

How could he say no?

They had not spoken of the future, yet that was to be expected. Sophia was a strong woman, proud and unyielding, and no doubt admitting her surrender would be unpleasant. Her actions revealed what words didn't.

He considered returning to London immediately, formalizing the union before the entire ton, as instincts urged. Yet Bradenton would be furious, and may even attempt to refuse the match. Kenneth needed time to solidify their bond.

Their bond. Tension rose within him, before he forced it away. She was his perfect companion, smart and strong and benevolent. They would have a productive and amicable marriage. If something lurked deeper – feelings, emotions, wants – they would be ignored. He'd seen the pain such sentiments wrought.

Time to commence a campaign, an onslaught even, the most

important of his life. He would share his true self, and learn about the magnificent woman he claimed. He would overcome her resistance, show her the life he could provide, while keeping her safe, of course. And when it was all over, he would have his bride, and his revenge.

What could be better?

HOME.

It was her first thought as awareness came, as sunshine bathed her in brilliance and warmth. Peace surrounded her, the all-encompassing feeling that all was right with the world. She fluttered heavy eyelids, allowing a sliver of illumination, then opened her eyes wide. She was not in her bedroom in the family townhome, or even in the room Kenneth provided. She was in *his* room, in *his* bed.

Somehow it felt like home.

She was still naked, the cover her only consolation to modesty. Her body was sated and sore in the most delicious way possible, yet longing still simmered, hidden underneath the surface. She closed her eyes and relaxed back into the covers. "I wonder how often one does that," she sighed.

A hand splayed possessively over her stomach. "I think thrice a day an appropriate number."

She gasped and opened her eyes.

"It's only me, lass." Kenneth's voice warmed her like hot chocolate on a cold winter day, smooth, sweet and delicious. Their physical connection sparked, accompanied by other sensations: comfort, kinship, something deeper.

She frowned. It was unacceptable. Their joining was about attraction and physical need. It was not – could not – be more.

For the tiniest sliver of time, something whispered, *Why not?*

It was impossible. Kenneth had kidnapped her, cast her as a pawn of revenge. Even if she desired the match, Edmund was unlikely to allow it. And while she prided herself on living as she wished, her brother wielded his own power, which he flexed quite often. If he was truly against a match, triumphing against his wishes would be a daunting task.

Yet she would fight, if that were the only obstacle. Yet something far greater stood in their way....

Kenneth didn't love her.

It may be the realm of romantic novels, yet she desired a love match. Someone who loved her beyond compare, someone who cared beyond position and wealth. Someone who felt as she did.

She tightened sore muscles. She couldn't, wouldn't, think of the tangle of emotions her captor left in his wake. The untamed duke did not believe in love matches. She would accept no less.

Of course, that didn't mean she couldn't enjoy herself while she was here. So long as she kept her heart safe behind a stone wall, she could explore new delights. The sunlight brightened, and she shielded her eyes, regarding the man who introduced those delights. "Have you been here all night?"

"Of course, lass." His smile was soft, genuine. "I enjoy watching you sleep."

Heat crept up her neck, even as the unease deepened. Why was she acting the blushing debutante? She lifted her chin. "I shall like a turn to watch you sleep."

"Would you now?" He moved forward, and the cover slipped down, revealing his broad chest, a well-defined stomach and, well, *my goodness.* "Sophia?"

"Yes?" Swiftly, she looked up. "Did you say something?"

His eyes lit in amusement. "Is something distracting you?"

"Nothing at all."

"Are you certain?"

"Indeed."

"Are you lying?"

"Indeed."

He chuckled, pulling her back into him, nestling her in the cocoon of his strength. She shivered as muscular arms wrapped tight around her. "You can watch me sleep later."

"Actually, I'd much rather do something later." She cringed, closing her eyes. One fantastic joining, and she craved it already.

"Can I assume you are pleased with last night?" He hesitated. "Have you any regrets?"

Her emotions were a knot of contradictions, yet regret was not among them. "No," she said honestly. "Do you?"

"Need you ask, lass?" His eyes crinkled at the corners, amusement clear and present, amidst rarer emotions: satisfaction, contentment, happiness. "I just want to make sure you accept the consequences of our actions."

"Of course." She no longer had the burden of her maidenhood, or the heavy anticipation of the relations between man and woman. "You are exceptionally skilled." Heat burned the nape of her neck. "Can we pretend I didn't say that?"

He placed a hand over his heart. "Are you saying I'm not skilled?"

A thousand memories of a thousand touches blazed. And the temperature increased a thousand degrees. "Of course you are skilled, yet dukes have enough to fill their heads."

She winced. Why had she mentioned the title he abhorred, the source of inevitable pain? Yet the peace in his eyes never wavered. "I am glad you agree with the path we shall now take."

Did she agree they should make love so many times it would make a rake blush?

Yes.

Certainly.

Surely.

Positively.

Definitely.

Undoubtedly.

Unquestionably.

She waved her hand mildly. "I suppose I could be persuaded."

Of course, any and all relations would remain solely about physical satisfaction. Clearly he agreed, since he brought up nothing of the future. A wisp of a not entirely pleasant emotion rose.

"I'm glad you think so." His expression betrayed a flash of surprise. "I wasn't sure you would. Now we can be honest with each other."

She paused. "I thought you've been honest with me."

"I have, lass." No subterfuge lurked in his eyes. He released her, and she shifted to face him. "If you recall, I even revealed my plans to kidnap you."

Yes, he had. Which made his success all the more frustrating. "Yet you are not forthcoming."

"I do not always grant information that compromises my control," he admitted. He rubbed his forearms. "Yet we both now know our path."

Their path? Was that what he called last night? "I am most... pleased with our path."

Something akin to relief lit his eyes. "When I mentioned honesty—" His eyes had regained their sparkle. "I was speaking of you."

"Me?" She placed a hand on her chest. "I am honest." *Sort of. Mostly. Certainly as much as most brigands.* Yet her dishonesty was for a good cause, to aid those in need. If the ton knew of her actions, she'd never be permitted to continue.

He lowered his gaze. "Do you remember kidnapping me? Or at least attempting so?"

She parted her lips. "You kidnapped me first!"

"But I was honest about it." He shrugged. "It is always polite to provide advance notice of a kidnapping."

This was the oddest conversation she'd ever had. "You cannot be serious," she gritted out. "Next time I shall put a notice in the papers. Would that satisfy you?"

"It would help."

"One of us has clearly lost our minds. Perhaps both."

He didn't deny it. "And what of your numerous escape attempts?"

"How was that not honest?" She held up her hands. "I made no secret of my desire to escape."

"I suppose that's true." He studied her carefully, and his smile faded. "Yet you are hiding something. Some hidden activity or agenda perhaps?"

Her heart thumped. Was the goal of this outlandish conversation to get her to relax so she would share her secrets? Was he merely posturing, or had he discovered the truth of the *Distinguished Ladies of Purpose*? "You've been reading too many stories of intrigue." She tapped him on the shoulder. He reached out like lightning, capturing her hand.

"That was a non-denial if I ever heard one," he murmured. "Tell me, do you hide secrets?"

This. Was. Not. Good.

If he discovered the truth of the guild, everything could be destroyed. It didn't matter that they fought for a good cause, or that no harm came from their activities. He may expose them for revenge, misguided chivalry or both. "There isn't a person in London without secrets. I am no different."

Yet most ladies did not lead a double life, dancing in gilded ballrooms during the day, traversing the shadows at night. The ladies of the guild chose their own roles, from innocuous tasks like convincing lords to support the right measures, to riskier jobs such as scouring the poor areas for people to help. Sometimes they *investigated*. It was dangerous, and it was vital. And it was indeed a secret.

The suspicion burning in his eyes intensified. "It must be quite clandestine to inspire such concern."

He was too clever by half. "You just admitted to not being forthcoming yourself. You cannot expect me to share all my secrets with you."

"Yet you read my journal."

How could she convince him she hid nothing of worth? Her eye caught on the papers that served as her temporary diary. Perhaps she could share some secrets to protect the one that mattered. "How about I show you my journal?"

"Your journal?" He rolled his shoulders. "You keep a journal?"

"Indeed I do. Since my regular one is in London–" She gave him a pointed look. "I've been making do. If I show you my personal wanderings, you will see there is no deep, dark secret."

It was both true and a misdirection. While she wrote her thoughts, she was careful not to mention anything about the guild, especially after the theft of Priscilla's journal. Some of the entries may be embarrassing, but they contained nothing life-shattering for either of them. "Would you like to read it?"

He raised an eyebrow. "Does it outline your revenge for the kidnapping?"

She smiled as she slipped off the bed and walked to the paper loosely bound in a book. Some of it was embarrassing enough she'd have to flee to America, or possibly the moon, yet surely she could find something innocuous. She flipped through the pages and held out an entry. "As you can see, no secrets."

He grasped the book and read aloud, *"The impossible. I do not believe in the word, do not accept that which puts limitations on my dreams..."*

He read until the end, with a raised eyebrow at the last sentence. *"Who knows what he will do if he captures me?"*

He glanced at the bed. "Did the outcome meet your expectations?"

The heat started as a spark, transformed into fiery tendrils flaming up her neck. "That may have worked out better than I hoped."

"I see. What else have we got here?"

She reached for the book, but it was too late.

He read, *"How to get an untamed duke out of one's mind:*
Stop fantasizing about him naked.
Stop dreaming about seeing him naked.
Stop wishing you were..."

"That's enough." She grasped the journal, yet he held it higher. "It seems you do have some secrets."

Flames turned into an inferno. She yanked the journal away

and tossed it towards the table. *Missed.*

Papers scattered across the floor. "Blazes!"

She rose at the same time he did, and they both reached for the paper.

He got there first.

"Ways to escape an untamed duke:

1. *Hide all his clothes while he is sleeping and run. Problem: Likely he'll chase you anyways. Unexpected Benefit: The view will be interesting.*

2. *Sneak out while he is in the bath. Problem: Likely he'll chase you anyways, only wet and naked. Unexpected Benefit: The view will be even more interesting.*

3. *Tie him to..."*

She grabbed the paper.

She needed to turn invisible. Or him to turn invisible. Ideally, they would both turn invisible. Not permanently, but until her mortification died down, in about two (or three) decades.

They stared at each other for two (or three) decades. She gripped the paper tightly, crumpling the thin sheet of disaster. Then, as if he hadn't just learned how interesting his naked body was, she notched up her chin. "As you can see, I've been very honest with you."

His lips twitched, and he stared for another two (or three) decades. Finally he cleared his throat. "Have you? I had no idea you wanted to see me–"

"If you finish that sentence, I may do something I'll regret." Unwittingly, her gaze drifted over his naked form. She tried to look away.

Failed.

"You're not very good at hiding your thoughts," he mused.

"I am quite good at hiding my thoughts." She sniffed.

"Do you think so?" He leaned closer, bringing the intoxicating scent of amber and bergamot. "You're thinking how very much you like seeing me naked."

"That's not true." She was thinking how much she liked seeing him wet *and* naked. And whether he would notice if she poured the pitcher of water over his muscles and enjoyed the view. For two (or three) decades.

Perhaps she could improve at hiding her thoughts.

Yet she admitted nothing as she returned to the bed and pulled up the covers. He sat down next to her, not bothering to hide his nakedness.

If she was really, really, really, really pleased, that was another truth she'd never admit.

He placed a possessive hand on her side. Even through the thick fabric, her skin jumped. "I knew you would try to escape, although I didn't realize the methods you would be willing to try." His lips twitched. "I shall take more precautions in the future."

Did that mean he would be naked less? Because he'd just started the practice, and it was even better than she hoped. At least he was no longer thinking about her secrets.

"Of course, it doesn't mean you're not hiding something."

Perhaps not.

She forced out air, bunched her hands on the soft mattress. What could she do to convince him? "I let you read my diary. Surely that proves I have no secrets."

"Of course it doesn't." His eyes sparkled. "You only showed me a portion of your diary. Your secrets could be written on a different page, or not at all."

She should have known he was far too intelligent to deceive. "You read more than I intended."

He chuckled. "I'll give you that. I especially liked the part where you said–"

"Don't. You. Dare."

Not only did showing him the journal prove nothing, but now he knew she imagined him naked. And wet. And naked *and* wet.

She needed another plan.

"How about I tell you a secret?"

He leaned back, flexing his muscles. "A secret?"

Even though they were quite alone, she lowered her voice. Time for a distraction he wouldn't be able to resist. "Seeing you naked was even better than my fantasies."

His lips stretched into a slow, wide smile. He grasped the cover she held up to her chest. "May I?"

Oh. Yes.

He fisted the cover, tugging the silky sheet away from her. Her skin prickled as it came into contact with the cool air, even as his smoldering gaze warmed her. Ever-so-slowly he drew the fabric down, revealing her swollen breasts, her stomach and the secret she no longer wanted to hide. Rose-hued color bloomed on every spot he uncovered, and soon she was bathed in it. Hot and cold, she was both and then neither, as he forced a thousand sensations.

Then the cover was gone, and they were flush against each other. So close, yet not touching. He reached out with a single finger...

And traced.

He trailed curves and angles, limbs and *crevices*. His lips followed, as he kissed every inch of burning skin, exploring, testing and tasting. Yet she was no passive party to his plundering, taking her fill and more. And when they finally joined, it was even better than the first time, for he remembered every little thing that made her gasp. It was...

Glorious.

CHAPTER EIGHTEEN

Journal of the Duke of Foxworth:

Unexpected.

To call this journey such would be an understatement. I kidnapped Sophia as a path to revenge, yet somewhere along the way, everything changed.

Including me.

I found something on this journey. Something important, something extraordinary. Something I believed inescapably lost the moment they first called me, "Your Grace."

Hope.

S OPHIA DID NOT merely enjoy her time with Kenneth. Did not merely like, tolerate or endure it.

She loved it.

Free of the constraints of strict London society, she'd never been so free. Although an unrepentant kidnapper, Kenneth was also charismatic, fascinating and charming, and he did things with his hands that made *every* part of her blush. He taught everything she asked and more, including a dozen ways to unarm a man. She never quite managed to overcome her captor, but she had numerous methods to teach other women. She also became adept at riding astride, and could cut through the water without sinking to the bottom first.

She learned much from her unexpected teacher. He remained helpful and patient, supportive and generous in both time and effort, although his overprotective side made itself well known.

When she asked if she could jump into the spring from the low cliff, he gave a resounding no. Of course, she immediately jumped from the low cliff. He then lectured her for jumping from the low cliff, at which point she jumped from the high cliff.

The lecture was after that was excruciating, but he followed it with a glorious bout of love-making.

So she jumped from the high cliff again the next day.

This time he told her he would *not* make love to her.

She never jumped from the high cliff again.

As far as lovemaking, they enjoyed relations twice more...

Each and every day.

It was scandalous, illogical and definitely inappropriate. A dozen times she pledged it would be the last, and a dozen and one times she ignored her own directive. He explored parts of her she didn't know existed, brought her to levels of pleasure of which poets could only dream. The physical joinings were extraordinary, yet there was more. So much more.

Long conversations grew from enchanting days, as they discussed any and every subject, light and serious, important and frivolous. Even when he wasn't teaching, they stayed together, learning of each other's worlds in a lifetime of stories. They talked, dined and played games, from charades to cards to everything in between, betting kisses and more. Of course, no matter who won or loss, a kiss and *more* was always the result. Sometimes they simply stayed near each other in comfortable silence, riding over sun-splashed paths or reading in the library. No matter their activities, peace and satisfaction followed, and with it, the inevitable question:

Could they be a match?

The question drifted into her mind, as if on a passing breeze, yet once it found fertile ground, it barely left her conscious. Life here was a fantasy, yet could that somehow transcend to the real world, enchant a life defined by propriety and protocol? If not for his predilection for kidnapping, she could almost imagine a life with the powerful man. Yet even as her emotions churned, he kept his feelings hidden behind an army of one. Her resolve never wavered – she could never accept a match without love.

The days passed as swiftly as the horse she rode ever-swifter. She thought of home often the first few days, and then occasionally the next. By the time a week had passed, so had thoughts of London, and the entire ton, if she admitted it. Edmund did enter her mind, accompanied by regret and sadness. He must be overwrought by her absence, and tearing apart England to find her.

Yet as they delved closer and closer to the day they would step across the ever-growing bridge, dissatisfaction bloomed, unease tempering what should have been relief. For one brief instant, the thought of another tempest destroying the bridge was not entirely horrific. Yet although storms flared, none bore enough anger to fell the passageway, and the progress continued.

She waited with bated breath every time Kenneth returned from checking the bridge. When he shared that more time remained, she would release that breath, and they would make love to begin another beautiful day.

Until…

The day was sunny and blue-skied, the picture of perfection outside the large window. The birds sang their usual melody, as they flitted from wildflower to wildflower, hopping and skipping and playing early morning games. Flowers scented the inside of the chamber, from the roses that mysteriously appeared on the bedside table every morning.

Sophia lay on the bed, atop sheets crinkled from glorious lovemaking, comfortable, content and sated. A soft smile played upon her lips, as she awaited Kenneth's return.

Then everything changed.

Something was different, as the man she awaited strode into the room, fully dressed in a cream shirt and dark pants. It was clear from his hardened stride, the severe slash of his lips. His hair was tousled, his sleeves carelessly rolled up. Storms brewed in his eyes, at severe contrast to the brilliant sunlight.

"The bridge is complete."

She had known the moment he stepped into the room, yet confirmation stole her breath. "When are we leaving?"

"Today."

This time she gasped, fisting the silky sheets. "Why so soon?" The blurted words came on their own, borne of a dismay she could not deny.

Widened eyes betrayed his surprise, and a moment of satisfaction, before his expression returned to neutral. "I didn't think you would wish to wait."

"Of course not." She clenched the sheets harder, and the delicate fabric strained under her fingers. She released it. "My brother must be overwrought."

Kenneth stiffened. A moment passed, and he nodded. "Take the morning to prepare. An afternoon departure will bring us to London late at night, reducing the risk of being caught."

There was no acceptable way to return home after a month away, yet it was the best option. Edmund would not care about her method of arrival, and the servants were loyal and discreet in the well-paying Bradenton household.

"I shall visit your brother in the morning."

Her breath hitched. Did he plan to make amends with Edmund, to apologize? Would he offer for her, not because of scandal, not because he kidnapped her, but because he truly wished to be with her?

At Kenneth's stern visage, all hope vanished.

What was she thinking? Likely he would gloat over his successful campaign, taunt her brother at the well-played revenge. This had always been a fantasy.

Now it was over.

With a deep breath, she slid off the bed. Kenneth's stare burned into her, as she padded to the dresser, picked up the only dress that was truly hers. "I should get ready," she said quietly.

Suddenly, he was behind her. He grasped her arms, taking control with a firm yet gentle touch. Fighting was impossible as he turned her, holding her against the body she knew so well.

"All will be well," he whispered.

No. Nothing would be well, not now, perhaps not ever. She'd pledged to protect her heart, yet something pierced it, to an extent she couldn't explore. She could never reveal the truth. "Of course," she said breezily. "This is wonderful, of course. I cannot wait to get home."

It was untrue. She missed her family and friends, yet somehow London held little appeal. That was, unless she imagined a certain untamed duke by her side.

It could never be.

"Do not hide from me."

What good would come of him learning his plan worked even better than he thought? That he had not only stolen her, but her emotions as well? It would only provide further means of revenge. "I am not hiding."

He softly caressed her cheek. "If you need me, I am here for you. Always."

Always was an unlikely term for hours. He pressed closer, brushing a soft kiss on the sensitive skin of her neck. She should turn away, should resist. Instead, she melted.

As he dipped his head, common sense fled. She could not relinquish their last chance to be together, no matter how dangerous. She may not be able to tell him how she felt, or even understand herself, yet she could show him. So she accepted the kiss, for what was certainly the last time.

It was time to return home.

"WHO IS KIDNAPPING whom?"

He locked eyes with the beautiful woman who was his captive for not much longer. The thought of being apart from her brought sharp discomfort, tempered only by the knowledge that any separation would be short.

She belonged to him now.

Obstacles must be defeated before he could officially claim

her, particularly a furious duke who was more likely to demand a duel than marriage. Had Bradenton been a typical lord who cared more about society's rules than flesh and blood, the concern wouldn't have been as great. A betrothal was the logical solution in cases like these, with the dual benefits of vanquishing any hint of scandal and creating a fortuitous match. Yet Bradenton was anything but ordinary, and clearly he loved his sister. As long as there was no scandal, Bradenton was unlikely to relinquish her.

Only he wasn't letting her go.

The horses neighed, swiping the ground with their hooves and rocking the carriage. Even the equines were ready to depart, as if they sensed the change in the dusty air. Blue skies provided the perfect setting for their voyage, not too hot, not too cold, with a tempering breeze of pleasant undertones.

Sophia was dressed in her own clothing, her hair in a gentle twist, as she once more transformed into a lady of the ton. Yet although she'd been born into the role, it seemed the facade, a mask for the carefree woman who dove into springs from ridiculously high cliffs, then allowed him to kiss her senseless. He longed to kiss the pinched and prim lady until the spark returned. Instead, he ignored the truth no one would admit:

Neither wanted the journey to end.

Only they hadn't a choice. Of course while one journey was ending, another was just beginning. It would officially commence when he visited Bradenton the next day.

"I could lock you in the carriage." She gave a soft smile. "Just for fun."

He smoothed down Sophia's silky hair, satisfaction rising as she leaned into him. She tested his discipline like none before. "I shouldn't have let you read that book on abductions."

"I'm glad you did. It was very educational." She stuck her pert little nose in the air.

And he had to stop himself from kissing it. "You plan to abduct someone, do you lass?"

"Without a doubt."

They both smiled, yet the mood sobered as a bird squawked across the sky, blotting out the sun. "We should depart if we are to arrive tonight."

She breathed deeply, then ascended the carriage, stopping for one last long look at the estate.

He rubbed the back of his neck. He should be pleased with matters, satisfied even. She accepted their path. She may not have said the exact words in the exact order, yet she made her thoughts clear. As soon as the banns could be read, they would enter a logical, sensible and beneficial union.

Exactly as he wanted.

The gentle clop clop of horses thrummed as the carriage jerked into motion. He directed the carriage by instinct, as the world melted away. The ride was smooth, especially over the sturdy new bridge, and it seemed a mere instant passed before they reached town, and a warm welcome from dozens of residents.

Despite her obvious uncertainty, Sophia was all smiles as she greeted the townspeople, and they embraced her with love. They didn't notice her forced smile, or the way her eyes dulled with unexplained longing. The only genuine smile came when Molly appeared, hand-in-hand with the shopkeeper's grandson.

"It's wonderful to see you." Sophia hugged the young woman. "How are you?"

Molly squeezed her suitor's hand. "Perfect."

Sophia's smile widened. Her eyes shone with kindness, her voice warmth, as she spoke to the delighted couple. It was an amazing show of cordiality, for a woman raised in the glacial ton. She truly was a diamond of the first water.

And he was the most fortunate man in all of England.

A voice broke the silence. "You barely know the young couple, yet you are captivated."

Kenneth started. He'd been so distracted he hadn't even noticed George's arrival.

The elderly shopkeeper gazed at him knowingly. "Yet perhaps your wistful expression is for another lady."

Kenneth ran his hand through his hair. Was he that obvious?

Sophia laughed, her cadence as sweet as the candies the townspeople gifted them for the journey. Her gaze softened, reflecting dappled sunlight and pure goodness.

"A true love match," the elderly man murmured.

Kenneth nodded, paused. George was not looking at his grandson.

Impossible. He would never allow such a thing. Yet perhaps...

He straightened, cleared his throat. Whimsical notions of love were for debutantes and children. It was time to leave. He moved behind Sophia and placed his hand on the small of her back, ignoring the jolt of satisfaction when she melted into him. "We must depart."

Muscles tightened. "Of course."

The others nodded graciously. "We hope you can return soon." Molly looked shyly at the young man next to her. "We are to be married."

Her suitor beamed. It was difficult to believe this was the same woman who had barely escaped her abusive past. *Because of Sophia.* "The celebration won't be grand, of course, but I'd love for you to stand beside me."

Sophia visibly swallowed. "I'm certain it will be beautiful," she whispered, her voice wavering. Did she not think he would bring her back for the wedding? Of course he would, and he would pay for a celebration that would indeed be grand.

She looked up at him, her eyes fathomless. "I'm ready to leave now."

Something was wrong, as they said their final goodbyes. She stood tightly, her shoulders stooped, her eyes unabashedly melancholy, as she wished happiness and fortune to them all.

It was almost as if she thought she'd never return.

They didn't talk as they traveled back to the coach, trailed by half the town while the other half watched. They remained silent as he helped her into the carriage, climbed onto his perch. He waved to the people. "We will be back soon," he promised.

Both of them.

Time melted away as they rode through the countryside. The air was warm and temperate, the breeze fragrant with the scent of wildflowers sprinkled on gently rolling hills. They passed few carriages and even fewer towns as he kept the horses at a steady, yet not punishing pace, giving them brief but frequent stops for water and rest. Sophia was a least demanding passenger, emerging only once from the carriage when he insisted she take refreshment at a small inn.

He began to ask her intentions, or her interpretation of his, a hundred times, yet the words wouldn't come. So instead he stayed silent as he led her through the inn, staying close the entire time. After their stop, they picked up the pace, as the daylight waned, turning the sky into a fiery rainbow of golden oranges and reds. He donned the same coat he had worn on his escape as the night fell, as the lights of London appeared in the distance. No one would see the Duke of Foxworth arriving by carriage, or the precious cargo who would slip into Bradenton's townhome.

The beat of the horses' hooves remained steady, as they changed from the soft padding of grass to the heavier cadence of London's roads. He tightened his grip as he came to the intersection, which would lead to her brother's home or his, forcing himself to turn towards her family home, away from where she belonged. It would not be for long.

And then they arrived.

Every muscle was a tightly wound coil, every instinct clamoring to stop what must be done. He pushed forward, ignoring the protests of stiff limbs as he stepped down after the hours-long journey. He reached for the door handle, yet it moved before he could touch it.

Time stilled.

She stole his breath, his focus, his attention. Beautiful features glowed in the moonlight, a hundred emotions hidden in her clandestine gaze, a thousand messages he could not decipher.

She should have already slipped away, so swift and silent an observer would think her nothing more than a spirit. It was dangerous standing outside her brother's townhome, cloaked only in dark coats and even darker shadows. Yet she didn't move.

"Are you ready?"

She stayed still for a moment, staring at him with uncertain eyes. Then, because he couldn't stop himself, he reached out, grazed the petal soft skin of her cheek. He leaned down...

And stopped.

He couldn't do this. Couldn't risk her reputation, her happiness, no matter how much he wanted to keep her in his arms forever. He must bide his time, wait until the moment he could claim his duchess before the world. So he stayed still, his head bent down as he stole a single moment more. When she edged away, something in his heart cracked just a little.

He grasped the carriage. "Best make haste. We should not risk scandal now."

Her chest rose and fell, as she gave yet another nod. Then she pivoted... and fled.

He didn't know how long he remained in that deserted street, standing as still as the fence she slipped behind. A dog barked in the distance, then the wind blew past him, bringing just a hint of the scent of violets.

He straightened. The separation was only temporarily. Tomorrow he would visit Bradenton and offer for Sophia. He would explain all the reasons why the marriage was rational, logical and, most importantly, required. His heart would not get involved.

As he ascended the empty coach, he ignored the voice that whispered...

It already was.

CHAPTER NINETEEN

The Private Diary of Sophia Hawkins

Rules.

They are the lifeblood of the ton, the written and unwritten guidelines by which we must abide. Any deviance has severe consequences, not merely upon the perpetrator but upon any family so unfortunate to share blood. Follow every single rule, and you will be safe, they claim.

Not true.

How many rule-followers has scandal caught, by misfortune or fate? How many have been targeted by those who thrive on others' pain? How many are damaged simply by relation? So many, despite painstaking diligence.

It is why I do not follow rules.

THE TOWNHOME WAS exactly as she remembered.

The settees were still high and velvety, the mahogany furnishings richly stained, the adornments priceless and unique. Jewel encrusted antiques lined intricately carved shelves, including a rather extensive selection of vases, amidst oversized furniture that whispered untold luxury. The air still smelled fresh and clean, scented with gardenias and citrus. Indeed everything was the same.

Everything, that was, except her.

Somehow she was a stranger. It was a peculiar feeling, in the abode where her mother lived, where her father once ruled. Her brother's wife had become a sister, and both she and Edmund not only welcomed her, but expected she stay until the moment she wed. Yet somehow, it no longer felt like home.

Not like Kenneth's home.

It was ridiculous, preposterous even. Kenneth's manor had never been home – indeed, it had been her prison. There was nothing special about the stones that forged Kenneth's estate, nothing extraordinary about the land, trees or lakes. The bedrooms, hallways and rooms were unremarkable. It had never been *something*.

It was someone.

Yet what existed was now over. She must refocus her life, carve her own path. One unarguable benefit of the trip had been Kenneth's tutelage on self-defense, which she would now share with other women. She would propose the idea to Priscilla the very next day, if Edmund did not lock her in her room for the next five years. She took a step towards the stairway–

A hot breath on her neck was her only warning.

She gasped as someone grabbed her, as two heavy hands shackled her wrists. She opened her mouth to scream, just as the scent of her captor surrounded her. "Edmund," she cried.

"Sophia?" For a moment he was still, and in the next he enveloped her against his formidable form, as tightly as the time she'd fallen out of the big oak tree in the country. Love surrounded her, as he soothed her just as he had back then, conveying without words the bond between sister and brother. And although it could not make everything better, the world was a little brighter in her big brother's arms.

They stayed like that for a minute and more, before he slowly pulled back. He studied her carefully. "Are you all right?"

Not even a little.

Yet somehow she managed a whisper of a smile. "I am well."

"Are you certain?" For once her brother appeared starkly dismayed, the normally unflappable man fighting for control.

She placed a hand on his arm. "I am."

His eyes lit in stark relief, yet a moment later they flashed with fury. She drew back. He rarely allowed her to see such emotion. "I'm angry at him, not at you. I'm ever so relieved to have you back."

A sliver of guilt sliced through her. It was ridiculous of, course, to feel shame when she had been kidnapped. Yet had she taken more care, Kenneth never would have had the opportunity to take her.

Or perhaps, he still would have found a way.

Still, the remorse grew, although strangely, not for the physical relations she enjoyed. Any privilege a man was afforded should extend to women. Yet she'd been with her brother's self-proclaimed enemy. Had she betrayed Edmund with every kind word they shared?

The urge to confess tightened her chest, even as the consequences paralyzed her. Her brother was a good man, unwaveringly honorable, yet his views on society were unpredictable. She could not reveal the truth if she wanted to keep her options, her very future, hers.

If the chance existed anyways.

Despite her resolution, the guilt grew. Perhaps she could admit something, without revealing everything. "I'm partly to blame."

Edmund stiffened. "I'm sorry?"

She took a step away from him, gazing with unseeing eyes at her mother's collection of fans. "The night I was taken, I followed Foxworth into the garden." She breathed deeply. "If I'd stayed in the ballroom, none of this would have happened."

Edmund's gaze softened, as he placed a hand on her shoulder. "Foxworth is a very determined man. He would have found a way." He stepped away, and his features hardened once more. "The fault is mine. I knew Foxworth was a threat, and I should have watched you closer. I shall not make the same mistake again. Henceforth you will be guarded at all times."

Her breath hitched.

In the distance, a clock struck, with only a few lonely notes to mark the late, or rather early, hour. Edmund exhaled, relaxing again. "There is much to discuss, yet now is not the time. You have returned, and this is a joyous day." He rubbed her back. "You must be exhausted. Off to bed with you."

She nodded, even as her stomach churned. It felt wrong, having her brother care for her as if she were still in the nursery. She was no longer a naive girl, but a woman, strong, independent and powerful in her own right. Not because of the physical relations she shared, but something far more substantial.

"Ken– Foxworth will visit tomorrow."

His eyes flashed fury, proving he hadn't missed her slip. "That will save me from having to confront him."

"We should meet him together."

"No."

She opened her mouth to protest, but he cut her off with a slice of his hand. His voice was curt, clipped and brooked no argument. "I will take care of him."

Dread and fear tangled within her. "What do you have planned?"

"That is a matter for men."

Absolutely not. "Before you speak, there are matters we must discuss. He believes you murdered his father. A journal and his father's man of business confirmed it, but I'm convinced..."

"Enough!" His voice whipped the air. "The former duke was responsible for his own ills, and his own demise. If Foxworth had come to me, I would have explained that. He doesn't want the truth." Edmund's voice was low. "His crime was never about me."

Heat flamed throughout her body. "You're wrong. The kidnapping was only supposed to be a few days."

"A few days?" he snapped. "You've been gone a month."

"That wasn't his fault." She waved her hand. "A storm destroyed the only bridge to London. I saw it with my own eyes."

"I can assure you, the only person trapped was you." His eyes blazed. "I will discuss the matter with Foxworth tomorrow. If your concern is a forced marriage, rest assured, I have no intention of giving you to him. That man will never lay a hand on you again."

No.

Exhaustion took hold, usurping all of her energy in a moment's span. Too overwhelmed to protest, she nodded, yet it was not a surrender. Tomorrow she would confront Edmund again, convince him to make peace with her former captor. She would find a way to make matters right.

Yet for now she allowed him to lead her up to a bedroom that no longer seemed hers, a luxurious bed that was no longer warm or secure. As sleep carried her away, there was no relief, no happiness.

Only a thousand dreams of a man who could never be hers.

EVERYTHING WAS PERFECT.

Perfectly wrong.

On the outside, all seemed well. She had woken as she always did, to a cheerful maid, hot chocolate and a blissful bath. Yet the maid was not as witty as Kenneth, the chocolate was not as delicious as the country fare and the bath somehow felt cold despite the steam curling from it.

She had *shared* her last bath.

During breakfast, her brother was back to normal, his emotions perfectly controlled. He acted as if she'd just arrived back from the vacation they concocted, not a kidnapping by his sworn enemy. Priscilla also acted as typical, yet by the flash in her eyes, she was privy to her scandalous adventure. Her brother's marriage may have been built on secrets, yet now it was forged by honesty. Exactly the sort of match she hoped for one day.

She was not ready to speak with Priscilla, who would deduce far more than her brother ever would, mainly because he still considered her an innocent babe. Which was why she excused herself directly after breakfast, and returned to her room, where she was currently making every effort to pace a hole into the rug.

Emotions churned within her, inescapable, turbulent, raw. Every time she tried to decipher them, her stomach burned, as if she'd eaten a dozen grapefruits at once, and she drew back. What if Kenneth's visit to Bradenton was not about the feud, but something else entirely?

What if he planned to declare his love?

Flames snapped in the fireplace as something sparked in her chest, even as she stifled it. She couldn't allow her emotions to escape until he shared his. She ignored the voice that said it didn't quite work that way.

How would she discover the truth? Edmund refused to allow her at the meeting that would determine her future. She had demanded, cajoled, pleaded and bribed, yet he remained firm.

She stopped pacing.

Edmund would meet with Kenneth in the front drawing room. If she just happened to be in the chamber next door, near the adjoining wall, with her ear pressed against the wall, she wouldn't really be able to avoid hearing them.

She took a deep breath. Soon she would learn Kenneth's plans, then just perhaps she could explore the emotions she glimpsed within herself.

She couldn't wait.

KENNETH DID NOT sleep until the fashionable hour. Did not stay abed until the typical ton stumbled awake, rushing to apply potions and creams to hide the shadows from their late night debaucheries. Just a whisper after dawn's first light, he left the bed he'd barely slept in, eschewing sustenance completely.

He dressed sharply, donned the usual weapons he kept for protection, plus several extra. Not for Bradenton, but for his father's business associates, who would undoubtedly attempt another assault. He would pay them a visit soon, but for now his focus was on one goal.

Claiming Sophia.

He'd storm Bradenton this very moment, yet angering the

man with a ludicrously early call served no purpose. So he visited the expansive library, where memories of Sophia greeted him, and attacked the mountain of letters that arrived in his absence. Several were from Clara, who was greatly enjoying her vacation, although she complained of having to convince their grandmother to not spend all day locked inside. Several were from their grandmother, who was also greatly enjoying her vacation, although she complained of having to pretend she didn't want to go anywhere to prevent Clara from spending all day locked inside. They would be returning next week, one of the few events to which he was looking forward.

Unfortunately, a significant portion of the letters came from his so-called business associates, who had increased their correspondence to thrice a day, with quadruple as many threats. No doubt they would pay him a visit soon, and this time he would be ready.

But first it was time to make the most important offer of his life.

He left at the earliest reasonable hour, or a bit before, if he were honest. The ride seemed but seconds, before he was rapping on the formidable door of the Bradenton household. If the servants were surprised to see him, they didn't show it, as they granted him immediate entrance.

He was shown to a drawing room of elegant luxury, filled with deep oak furniture, plush settees and oversized vases. Antique fans edged in gold covered the walls, and a crackling fireplace brought warmth, light and grandeur. A selection of fine liquor had been left for him to indulge, yet he took none. He would be of complete mind for the next task.

Bradenton did not keep him waiting long. The powerful duke's eyes blazed, his lips tight, as he strode in, dressed in all black. Most people would have retreated from the pure fury emanating from one of the most powerful men in London, yet Kenneth stood tall, straight. He would need his own power to claim Sophia.

"Your sister is mine."

They were not the words he planned. He'd crafted the perfect speech, practiced it even in the privacy of his bedroom. He'd made it as gracious as possible, perhaps not an actual apology for his father's murderer, but at least an explanation of their extended stay. Yet when he saw the man standing between him and Sophia, instincts had taken control.

Eyes so similar to those of his lass flashed with fury. It didn't matter. By whatever means necessary, he would convince Bradenton to accept his offer.

Kenneth stepped forward. "I am prepared to do the right thing."

"You haven't done the right thing since you first attacked my family," Bradenton snapped. "What makes you think I'd allow you to see Sophia again, much less keep her?"

Do not call out this man. Do not race past him, grab Sophia and steal her away. "I just spent a month with your sister, unchaperoned. A union is the only honorable outcome."

Bradenton's gaze turned as dark as a midnight storm. "I will not sacrifice my sister for propriety's sake. You took your revenge for a crime I did not commit. You are fortunate my wife convinced me that killing a man in a duel, or being killed myself, was not the ideal resolution to your crimes." He glared a thousand daggers. "Do not underestimate my power."

Indeed, power defined the massive man before him. Yet it forged him as well. "You would risk ensnaring your sister in scandal?"

Bradenton's glare became thunderous. "What scandal? My sister has been on holiday this past month, visiting her cousin. You were on a trip to Scotland. By fate or fortune, no one saw you together, and there's not a hint of gossip to suggest otherwise. As you predicted in your letter, no scandal emerged."

This was not the path he hoped to take, or the strategy he thought to employ, yet nothing would stop him from claiming Sophia. "There could be."

An icy glare turned into an avalanche. "You hate me so much, Foxworth, you would destroy Sophia?"

The very notion he could harm Sophia scathed fire through him. He could never hurt the woman he lo...

He stopped, blinked. *Liked.* He liked her, of course. She was an exceptional woman.

"You would destroy her life for revenge?" his host snarled. "Ruin her to get back at me? You claim honor, yet you are no gentlemen!"

Pure red filled his vision. "You talk of honor? You led an old man to ruin before murdering him! You are the one without honor." He strode up to the duke, eye to eye, fury to fury. They were the same size, as they circled each other. "This will be your revenge, Bradenton. You lost your sister to your sworn enemy, and I am never giving Sophia back." He stood with all the power he possessed. "She is mine."

The door opened.

Both men turned, as a tiny tornado stormed into the room. Cheeks blazed pink, eyes flashing fire. Then the woman who would be his duchess stood in pure, feminine fury. "I will never belong to you."

Challenge accepted.

CHAPTER TWENTY

Journal of the Duke of Foxworth:

From birth, I was destined to lead, groomed to one day rule a great family. When my father died, a new role – and life – was thrust upon me, and a position of great power. Though all these and more, I endured and persevered, never forgetting my ultimate goal.

Yet those endeavors pale before the obstacle I now face. Making Sophia mine is my greatest challenge, yet the most important of my life.

I will be victorious.

S HE WAS A fool.

A heartbroken, lovesick fool.

She'd fought for strength her entire life, clawed as much independence as society allowed a mere woman. She'd championed social action, supported those without a voice and strove to better a world that saw her as *less*.

Yet in the end, she was a prize caught between two men's hatred for each other.

"Sophia, are you all right?" Kenneth reached for her.

"You should not be here." Edmund grasped for her.

She backed away from them both.

No, she was not all right. As she suspected he would, Kenneth had offered, yet not from a declaration of love but an avowal of hate. She was no more than revenge's pawn, the ultimate payback for a life lost. Her brother may love her, but he would never see the woman she truly was.

Kenneth took a step towards her.

"Get away from her," Edmund snarled. The two men glared at each other, fists clenched, stances poised in battle. Would they fight a duel in Priscilla's drawing room?

Not if she showed her own power. "Enough!"

"Sophia–"

"Sister–"

"Let me speak." She regarded one, and then the other. "I have something to say to both of you."

Wary eyes flashed, as both predators stalked her. "Speak your mind, but quickly," Edmund growled. "I do not want you in this man's presence any longer. After today, you will never see him again."

"I think not," Kenneth snarled. "You lost the privilege of caring for Sophia. She is mine now."

How dare he?

After countless days of delight, endless nights in each other's arms, how could he turn her into nothing more than revenge? She gathered her strength. "I am not marrying you."

His eyes glinted like daggers. "You haven't a choice."

Edmund opened his mouth, but she stopped him with a raised hand. "I will decide whom I marry. And when. And it will not–" Her voice broke. "It will not be you."

"I compromised you."

She gasped.

And Edmund lunged.

Kenneth leapt out of the way, so fast he was almost a blur. Edmund circled his prey, but Sophia jumped between them. "You will not fight in Priscilla's drawing room." Her voice stumbled, as she drew a shuddering breath. "Please."

The single word halted them, the lust for blood, but not the anger, departing their eyes. As both men stepped forward, she cried, "He didn't do anything I didn't want."

Everyone froze.

She stared at her brother, returning the same power he wielded. "Before you say anything, consider your own life. My actions are no different than you or any other man in the ton. I will not be condemned for living my life."

Edmund hesitated. When he spoke, his voice was low. "I would never condemn you, Sophia. I love you."

She released a breath. He accepted it, accepted her.

Deep down, she always knew he would.

Kenneth watched with an unfathomable expression. Now *she* stalked him. "Despite what we've shared, you still only think of revenge. I will no longer be an instrument in your scheme. I thought...I hoped..." She swallowed. "It doesn't matter now. I want a love match, and this was always about hate." She wrapped herself in the power of every woman who fought for love. "What we had is over."

"My offer has nothing to do with hate." His voice was stiff, as he followed her step for step. "I want you."

"This is not about me," she hissed. "This was always about Edmund."

"That's not true." He shook his head, tousling the locks she'd smoothed so many times. He hesitated, as if weighing his words. "Why do you think we stayed for a month?"

She gripped her dress. "We had no choice. The bridge was destroyed, and the river was too dangerous to cross."

He held her gaze, then glanced to the side. "That's not exactly true."

"What's not true?" she demanded. "The bridge fell into the river. I saw it."

"It did fall." He kept close beside her. "But the river was not impossible to cross. Although you cannot see the other bridges from the estate, they aren't nearly as far as I indicated. Several hours in either direction would have provided a viable path home."

Oh. My. Goodness. She brought trembling fingers to her lips. "How could I have been so senseless?" she whispered. "Of course a single bridge wouldn't be the only method of travel to London." She fisted her skirt. "You said you'd never lie to me."

"I didn't lie. I merely implied it was longer than it was." Yet his wooden voice belied the misdirection. He purposely deceived her.

"Do you not understand it's the same thing?" She took a breath, then another, so quickly, the world started to tilt. She forced her breathing slower. "Did you wish to punish Edmund even more? If a few days hurt, imagine what a month of agony would accomplish?"

"No." He stepped forward. "Bradenton had nothing to do with it."

"Then why?" she demanded. "Why would you make me believe we were trapped?"

"For the same reason I offered for you," he thundered. "I want to be with you."

"Do not lie! All I am is a weapon to wield against my brother." Her voice broke, her eyes blurring with unshed tears. "You don't care for me at all."

"That's not true." He reached for her, but she backed up. He grasped her hand, and the connection immediately sparked. "My words were borne of anger, and I will forever regret them. Sophia, I—"

She snatched her hand away. "Do not pretend you care for me." Her heart cracked and shattered, yet she pushed forward. "My answer is the same as my brother's. I do not accept your offer."

Her heart beat so loud it drummed in her ears, fast, irregular and *broken*.

For a moment, Kenneth looked as if he would throw her over his shoulder and kidnap her. Had her brother not been present, she would have all but expected it.

"You have the answer to your question." Edmund stepped forward, perhaps sensing the same. "Time for you to leave."

For a moment, Kenneth stood frozen, considering another

abduction perhaps? In the next, he strode forward, his steps booming on the hard floor. Her heart lurched as he passed, so close, yet a lifetime away. Instincts urged her to run to him, to leap in his arms and ask him to kidnap her. Yet she stayed still, for all the strong women before her and all the ones after, who would choose their own destiny. They deserved a match of the heart.

Even if hers had to shatter.

No one spoke as he crossed the room. Yet with his hand on the knob, the untamed duke turned. "This changes nothing." Pure power defined the words. "You are still mine."

"I'M GOING TO kidnap Sophia."

"Didn't you already do that?"

"I am going to do it again."

Adam strode into the library, stopping before the grand desk in a stance as straight as the swords lining the walls of an armory. The fire crackled in the marble hearth, warming the room and casting amber light on the rows of antique books. It smelled of opulent leather, rich wood and relentless tension.

"You said were only taking her for a few days." Adam's mild tone hid something far stronger. "Then it became a month. Now you plan on keeping her permanently?"

"Do not judge me, cousin. After all, I'm not the only one with secrets." Kenneth rose from the desk, stepped slowly around its amber drawers. "You stole Priscilla's journal."

His cousin's eyes glinted in the firelight. Guarded, unyielding, yet there was no denial. "How did you know?"

That his cousin did not feign ignorance was a show of their kinship, and trust. He would return it with unfiltered honesty. "Priscilla saw the thief flee in my carriage. She and Sophia both assumed I took it, but they were wrong, of course." He stepped forward. "The book you had that night was Priscilla's journal. I shall like an explanation."

For a moment, Adam remained silent, unwavering and unmoving. When he spoke, his voice was low, somber. "From the moment I learned of your existence, I supported you. I ensured you received your inheritance, sought you when others would steal it from you. I covered for you when you stole a lady of the realm. Now I am asking you to do one thing for me." He leaned forward. "Forget about the journal."

Kenneth stared into furtive eyes, where secrets swirled and hidden motivations lurked. The journal was no small matter; by Sophia's admittance, it affected dozens of lives. Yet his cousin was not one for exaggeration, and no doubt important reasons propelled him. Behind the request, a single question loomed: Did he trust him? "I will agree, on one condition."

Adam gave a curt nod.

"You must promise no harm will come to Lady Priscilla or any of the other ladies. While I have not seen the journal's exact contents, I know it contains secrets with the power to do great harm. I will not allow it to touch the ladies."

Adam's eyes flashed with emotion, gone in the single blink of an eye. "I wish you knew me better than to ask that question."

Kenneth started at the words, spoken so low, he wasn't sure he was meant to hear. Had he inadvertently insulted his cousin?

Yet when he looked up, Adam appeared as strong as ever. "You have my word. No one will be injured, and the journal's secrets will remain intact. On the contrary, my actions serve to further a very important quest. A friend has a vested interest in an individual mentioned in the journal."

A thousand questions churned, amidst stark dissatisfaction. Kenneth didn't know Adam well enough to be certain he wouldn't misuse the journal, and Adam didn't know him well enough to trust him with his secret.

Perhaps that was his fault.

"Of course, I shall keep your secret," he affirmed. "I do trust you, and should have known you had no ill intentions. You are the noblest man I know, and I am honored to be your kin."

Surprise, and satisfaction, flashed in his cousin's eyes. "I would say the same to you."

Kenneth looked up sharply. "Normally, I would cherish such a complement, yet I cannot accept it." He looked past his cousin, at the bookcase where he kissed Sophia. "I kidnapped a lady to seek revenge on her brother. I kept her captive for an entire month. Even now, I plan to abduct her again." He shook his head. "Have I become the villain?"

"No." Adam placed his hands on the desk. "Ignoble as it seems, there was honor in your quest. You sought to punish a man you believed to be a murderer, prevent him from harming others. Your goals were noble."

"That's only partly true." At the beginning, he'd convinced himself it was his only motivation, casting himself as a righteous defender of good. Yet he had taken a careful look at himself these past few days. "You never approved of my actions." He regarded his cousin carefully. "Why did you help me?"

Adam stayed still for a moment. "Because you are my cousin and my friend. A man who I should have grown up next to, a man who, although he eschews London society, is an excellent duke. You take care of your tenets, are kind and generous with those under your care. Your charitable endeavors have helped hundreds."

Kenneth stiffened. "How did you know about that?"

Adam's eyes shined with intelligence. "My specialty is learning about people, and uncovering the truth. I chase those who hide."

A memory of the journal flashed, amidst Sophia's words. Was Adam hunting one of the *women*?

Yet he kept his silence, honoring his promise. Perhaps one day his cousin would trust him with the truth.

Maybe time would change that.

Or perhaps, he would.

"If there's anything I can do for you, Adam, you need only ask. We are family, after all."

Satisfaction shone in his cousin's eyes. "I appreciate that."

He reached out a hand. Adam took it, then surprised him with a brotherly embrace. When he pulled back a minute later, somehow the weight of the dukedom seemed just a little less daunting.

Adam rubbed his hands together. "Now that that's settled, there are a few matters we should discuss. You received numerous messages from your father's business associates."

Kenneth opened his mouth to offer an excuse, yet the words wouldn't form. If he wanted a true connection, he had to be honest. "They attacked me the night I took Sophia."

Adam's features hardened. He traveled to the sideboard, poured two generous splashes of brandy and handed Kenneth a glass. "What happened?"

Kenneth conveyed the story, and Adam's gaze darkened with every sentence. By the time he finished, his normally unflappable cousin was unequivocally furious. Seems he was not the only one discarding his neutral mask.

Kenneth drank the brandy in a single gulp. "I plan to confront them immediately, and this time there will be no doubt our business is concluded. Then I will claim Sophia."

"I'd hoped you were joking about that." Adam seemed only slightly calmer. "What happened during your meeting with Bradenton?"

Disaster. "Matters did not progress as I intended, yet nothing has changed." No obstacle would lessen his resolve to marry his once and future captive. "Sophia will be my duchess."

"So that Bradenton may suffer more?" Adam responded quietly. "You would sacrifice her future for your revenge?"

"Of course not." Kenneth tightened. "Don't you know me better than that?" It was the same question his cousin asked, and the discomfort was just as sharp. Why did no one understand his motivations had nothing to do with Bradenton, or revenge?

"Actually I do know you." The accusation in his cousin's eyes disappeared, replaced with understanding and empathy. "If you cannot be honest with me, at least be honest with yourself. Why is it so important she accepts your offer?" He straightened to his full height. "Why do you care so much about claiming Lady Sophia?"

Because he lo–

Kenneth froze.

The room wavered for just a moment, as life-defining uncertainties swirled. Pushing away forbidden thoughts, he forged ahead. "Because I kidnapped her. Because we were alone without a chaperone. Because I held her captive for a month." The room sharpened. "Any gentleman would make an offer in such circumstances."

If it was true, why did it sound so very wrong?

His cousin's gaze was far too knowing. "Your offer was not accepted."

"It's preposterous." Kenneth braced his hands on a wingback chair, squeezing the leathery fabric until the seams stretched. "Bradenton should be pleased, ecstatic even. Most lords would have demanded an immediate betrothal."

"Bradenton isn't most lords," Adam reminded him "He loves his family, and does not bend to society's rules. I implore you to reassess your revenge. I've known Bradenton my entire life. I cannot believe he murdered a man."

"But the journal–"

"Was written by a drunk."

Kenneth sucked in a breath.

"I apologize for my harshness, yet it's necessary." Adam's voice remained steady. "You didn't know your father, and you certainly don't know Bradenton. Ask anyone in the ton, and they will say the same. Have you investigated the journal's claims?"

Kenneth set his jaw. He'd never been a man to rush into judgment, or action. Yet when he read the journal, uncontrollable fury had sparked, and he'd acted without consideration or deliberation. Sophia claimed her brother couldn't have committed such atrocities. Could there be any truth to her claims? "I suppose a deeper search can do no harm."

"Excellent." Adam leaned forward. "No matter what you discover, consider whether your hatred for Bradenton is greater than your regard for Sophia. Because if not, you could lose her."

Not. In. This. Lifetime. "Losing her is not an option."

"That's what I thought." The sides of Adam's lips quirked up. "When do you plan to confront your attackers?"

"As soon as possible." Kenneth pushed himself away from the chair. "I'm hoping they show up tonight at the Rawlings affair."

"I'd like to help." Adam finished his drink and placed the glass on the table. "I have some friends who do this sort of work. If you are amiable, they can provide assistance."

Instincts demanded an immediate no, yet he hesitated. With Sophia involved, the criminals must be neutralized in whatever way possible. "Do you trust them?"

"With my life."

With another pause, Kenneth nodded his agreement. It was strange and disconcerting, accepting help, yet the expected tension didn't emerge. It felt almost *good*.

Something shifted, as he shook hands with the man who had changed his life, in so many ways. Adam was proving to be far more than a cousin.

Perhaps this was what it felt like to have a brother.

"This life is not as terrible as I imagined." The murmured words came on their own, yet once uttered, it was shocking how very true they were.

His cousin stilled in clear surprise. "I've been trying to tell you that since you arrived."

"I haven't listened." Kenneth ran his hand along the ladder, where he had caught Sophia. She had been so spirited, and so brave. "I resented the title so much, I was blind to the good it represented."

"I know this isn't the life you imagined." Adam put a hand on his shoulder. "That doesn't mean you can't be happy."

No, it didn't.

He gazed at the beautiful adornments of the library. Despite his love of books, he'd allowed even this to be a source of negativity, a reminder of the unjust class differences the ton endlessly exploited. Yet perhaps he could strive to transform society instead. "The dukedom is an opportunity, a chance to do good." He took a step underneath the many volumes. "It's inexcusable for these priceless books to be locked away, seen by so few."

"Your father didn't even read them." Adam selected a book with an ornate leather cover. "He considered them a sign of wealth rather than a treasure to be enjoyed."

"Perhaps we can change that." Kenneth rubbed his hands together, as possibilities shaped. "I could create some sort of library, a place where everyone can share in their riches."

Approval shone in Adam's eyes, bringing a level of satisfaction he'd never admit. "That's a capital idea."

"I can utilize the dukedom in other ways." Kenneth took a step, as his heart quickened. "Use my new resources to better the world." He'd always planned to meet the responsibilities of the dukedom, and he had his charitable endeavors, of course, yet perhaps he could go even further. He could start, rather than join, social campaigns.

Adam returned the book to the shelf, as a smile played at his lips. "My word. You almost seem happy."

Happy. It wasn't something he thought possible after he left Scotland. Yet why not? He contemplated the cousin he almost never met. "Perhaps I've been neglectful in appreciating the benefits of my new life. I am grateful for you and grandmother."

"And we are thankful for you." Adam gestured to the paintings lining the walls. "You haven't met much of our family, but they are good people. When things have settled, we should arrange a gathering so you can meet them. They would like to welcome you properly."

"I'd like that." He'd thought the dukedom would cost him his family, yet with his frequent trips back to Scotland, he hadn't lost anyone. Instead he'd gained a new family.

"I will arrange it." Adam clasped his hands together. "This world is far from perfect, yet there is much to embrace. Of course, just because you accept the dukedom doesn't mean you have to abdicate your life in Scotland."

No, it didn't. His life may now include more traveling and responsibilities, but he didn't truly mind either. If he had a certain lady next to him...

He stood taller. "I've been so absorbed by the past, I've barely noticed the beauty of the present. From now on, I will stop focusing on what I lost and celebrate what I gained. Everything will be different."

This could indeed be an amazing life.

"There's one more thing." Adam reached into his coat pocket and retrieved a small lavender book. "Clara wanted me to give this to you."

Kenneth reached out and took the thin tome. "Clara?"

Adam dusted off his hands. "She gave it to me right before she departed on her trip. She thought it could be of use."

Kenneth turned the book in his hands. Its cover was smooth, with no markings or letters to hint at its secrets. The scent of jasmine and cinnamon drifted by, and his breath caught.

It couldn't be.

"I'll leave you to it."

Kenneth barely noticed Adam slinking from the room, or his quiet smile as he did so. He turned the page, and read:

*Journal of the **Duchess** of Foxworth:*

Love.

It is a powerful emotion, the strongest of all them, some would say. Worth more than any fortune, stronger than any sword, hope is its beacon. It is a power, over which wars have been fought, wealth given and gained, lives redeemed. I thought I was in love with a man who never truly existed, and although it was a façade, it gave me two beautiful gifts, the children I love and treasure more than life itself.

Some said I should give up on love, should eschew the fickle emotion and grasp something sturdier. Tempting indeed, yet I refused to give up hope that I may one day find true love.

It I had given up on love, I never would have found my Alastair.

We are not married, and never will be. Our class is not the same, and that will also never change. Yet our hearts meet as equals, our souls intertwined. My world is more glorious for his presence.

Love gives hope and joy, a home in this often bitter world. It is what I always wished for myself, and for those in my heart. When I left England, I could have succumbed to the bitterness. Instead I started anew, and I am forever glad I did, for I found a man I could be happy with for all my days. Perhaps not in the way the world demands, yet in the way my heart needs.

Love is beautiful and all-encompassing. Of all the things I wish for my children, may they find true love.

The book drifted from his fingers, its pages fluttering like time's passing. He always believed love destroyed his mother, yet had it actually saved her instead?

Memories flitted by, his mother's smiles, the sweet cadence of her laughter. Alastair had been her friend since childhood, the son of a tradesman. As a young woman, she had wanted to marry him, yet he thought she'd be happier in the splendors of London, among the glorified ton. He'd sacrificed his heart to help hers, yet in the end they had both lost.

Yet perhaps their story hadn't ended there, as he always believed. Alastair visited often, and his mother glowed with happiness in his presence. He had been gone so much with his responsibilities, he never realized the truth. His mother never gave up on love. In the end, she found the match of which she always dreamed.

Kenneth traced the elegant script on the pages. "Thank you mother," he whispered. "For this one last lesson you taught me."

CHAPTER TWENTY-ONE

The Private Diary of Sophia Hawkins

Life must continue, even if it will never be the same.

A lady of the ton must consider every move carefully, for scandal is ever-present, hiding in darkened corners, peeking through hedges, listening at doorways. We are endlessly watched, forever scrutinized, always judged. My life has returned, yet I am not certain I want it. In the end, I will not adhere to the destiny they demand.

Time to forge my own path.

"HOW ARE YOU?" Priscilla opened her arms wide. Sophia embraced her sister-in-law, portraying the perfect picture of serenity. The ton must believe they were enjoying each other after a modest absence, not celebrating the end of a kidnapping.

The ton must believe...

The ton must believe...

The ton must believe...

If only she could ignore what the ton must believe.

Yet it was the world into which she was born, and she must never forget how fortunate she truly was. Many were not so lucky to have food in their bellies, a warm bed in which to sleep, a secure home.

They broke apart. "I am well."

A tinkling of laughter, its cadence filled with false mirth, rang through the air. Sophia edged further into the corner, away from the revelers enjoying the magnificence of the Rawlings ball. The night was an absolute crush, with crisp lords and stylish ladies twirling and swirling under the majestic candlelight. A hundred exclusive scents filled the air, mixed with the aroma of the steaming pastries invisible servants peddled. At least the generously sized orchestra was skilled, their music lilting and pure as it covered their conversation.

"Truly, how are you?" Priscilla rubbed her arm, in the same spot Kenneth liked to touch.

Sophia adjusted her pale peach gown. It was tight, itchy and uncomfortable, so unlike the supple fabrics she wore during her trip. She liked *Kenneth's* shirts the best of all. "I'm fine." She waved her hand. "More than fine."

If fine meant she wanted to jump in the Thames and swim until London was far behind.

Her heart was shattered. Destroyed. Broken into a million shards that could never be made whole. Yet she could never share that, not even with Priscilla. "Tell me the news while I was away."

Priscilla frowned at the clear attempt to steer the conversation. Yet she nodded. "This is not the place for this conversation, but we shall talk later. I will supply chocolate and vases." She lowered her voice. "I do indeed have good news. The journal has been returned."

Sophia put a hand to her chest, as the weight of dozens of lives lifted off her shoulders. "That is indeed fortunate. Who took it?"

"I don't know." Priscilla glanced around again, lowered her voice further. "It arrived by courier a week ago, with no return address and no word who sent it. The thief left no clue as to his identity."

"A week ago?" Sophia breathed. "Then, it couldn't possibly have been Ken– I mean Foxworth."

Priscilla's gaze sharpened. "No, because as everyone knows, Foxworth was in Scotland."

Not in Scotland, but sequestered with her, behind one broken bridge and a thousand shattered dreams. Sophia swiftly pressed on, "Has any of the information been made public?"

Priscilla shook her head. "Thankfully, no. There's not a hint of gossip or suspicion regarding the guild. The thief never demanded ransom, made threats or communicated in any way."

"Perhaps it was a mistake." Sophia rocked back on her heels. "Maybe the bandit confused your journal with another book."

"Or perhaps he is simply biding his time." Priscilla edged closer, as her eyes darkened. "Not everything was the same. A page is missing."

Sophia's throat dried. With a secret society of forbidden activities, a single page had the power to destroy lives. "Did it contain information about the ladies?"

Priscilla hesitated.

Not good.

"It revolved around single person," Priscilla whispered. "It described our work with the sanctuary, and its proprietress."

There was only one person that could describe. "Elizabeth?" Priscilla's quick nod provided confirmation. "Was there enough description to identify her?"

This time, Priscilla didn't hesitate. "If the person is smart and tenacious enough, then yes. With our collaboration, it wouldn't take much to discover who and where she is."

It didn't make sense. Elizabeth was not a lady. "Everyone at the sanctuary knows of Elizabeth's work. She has the least to lose if identified."

"Perhaps…" Priscilla's gaze remained even. "Or perhaps there is far more to her than we know."

They all hid secrets.

"Please hide me!"

Sophia started, relaxed as a familiar lady appeared before them. Hannah looked all but disheveled in a pale green dress with emerald adornments. "Crawford is following me again, with most nefarious intent."

Sophia hid her smile. Having been the target of a lord with nefarious intent, she was fairly certain Hannah's conundrum did not meet the lofty standards her kidnapping duke established. "What nefarious purposes is this?"

Hannah's face screwed into utter hopelessness. "He wants a dance."

Priscilla's lips twitched. "Wouldn't it be easier to simply dance with him?"

By the look on Hannah's face, Priscilla may have suggested she dance with a pirate. "Absolutely not. Because then he will want another dance, and then I'll want another dance, and then I may do something I'll very much regret."

"Bop him on the head with a vase?" Priscilla guessed.

"Kidnap him?" Sophia hazarded.

"Introduce him to an alligator? Just to scare him of course."

The ladies turned to *another* newcomer. "Emma!" They took turns embracing the beauty, then smiled widely at the Earl of Peyton, Emma's husband.

"How was the wedding trip?" Sophia took her friend's arm. "Was Scotland fantastic?"

"It was beautiful." Emma beamed as only a woman in love could. "The land was gorgeous, the weather was perfect and there were endless diversions. We would have stayed forever, but duty calls." She grinned at her husband, who portrayed matching adoration. A hidden message passed between the two, yet it disappeared in an instant. Emma slid a sly look to Sophia. "I heard something else from Scotland has been lurking about."

Sophia opened her mouth to concoct some sort of excuse, when Peyton touched his wife's arm. "I believe I am needed," he murmured. "If you will excuse me."

Strangely, Emma didn't seem the least bit upset by her husband's abrupt departure. "You were saying?"

This time Hannah saved her. "Crawford is heading this way." Her gaze darkened. "Or not. Why is he dancing with Lady Ruby? She's the most mean-spirited lady in the ton."

This time, no one managed to hide their smiles.

"I'm afraid Sophia will have to tell me her news later." Emma linked arms with Hannah. "Didn't you say you wanted somewhere to hide? I know the perfect place to get into a little trouble."

As they stepped in the direction of the ladies' retiring room, neither Hannah nor Crawford took their eyes off each other. Perhaps she wasn't the only one concealing secrets.

Speaking of secrets... She smiled at her sister-in-law. "I've discovered how I can further our cause. I'd like to show ladies their own power."

"Their own power?" Priscilla's brow crinkled. "What do you mean?"

Sophia flexed her fingers. "I can teach ladies how to protect themselves. I learned much about self-defense during my... holiday." She choked lightly. "I'd like to teach women the basics of resisting an attack. It could be my contribution to the guild."

Priscilla blinked, then a slow, wide smile curved her lips. "Quite a contribution it will be."

"You can teach ladies to defend themselves?"

Sophia and Priscilla turned, and the newcomer turned as pale as the pure white gown that hung off her slight frame. "I'm sorry for interrupting." Lady Julia's voice was low and stilting. "I was wondering if you had a minute to talk." She ducked her head.

Sophia's smile faltered, as the debutante all but cowered before them. She appeared to be wearing some sort of powder...

She swallowed a gasp. A blackened eye peeked out from limp curls.

"Are you all right?" The words escaped before she could stop them, thankfully low enough only the three heard.

Julia's eyes darted between the two of them, as her lower lip quivered. "I don't think so," she whispered.

Priscilla stood as stiff as a debutante's corset. "Can I assume your betrothed is the source of this problem?"

A sharp intake of breath revealed the obvious answer. The

entire ton knew about the baron's affinity for the bottle, and his violent temper. A moment passed, then a halting whisper, "There's nothing to be done. We are to be married the week after next."

"There is much that can be done. All will be well, I promise." Priscilla reached towards the younger woman, yet she lurched back. Surreptitious glances turned their way as Julia barely regained her balance.

Do not yell.

Do not cry.

Do something instead.

Priscilla's eyes blazed fury. "My husband knows your father well. I'm certain he can address the situation."

"Thank you." Julia took a shuddering breath. "Did you mean what you said before, Sophia, about teaching ladies to protect themselves?"

Sophia started to reach out, stilled and retreated. "I learned some defensive skills, which can help prevent an attack."

Ever-so-slightly, Julia straightened. "I shall like to be your first student."

Those who claimed women were the weaker sex never saw an abused woman lift herself up and dare to fight. It would not make everything better, yet perhaps it could give her some of the confidence every woman deserved. "I will teach you all that I know."

"Thank you," Julia whispered.

Sophia waved her hand. "It is nothing."

"No. It is something." A spark, tiny and yet filled with feminine strength, flickered in Julia's eyes. "Both of you do so much to help people, changing lives for the better. In a world in which we must hide all emotion, your actions show your true self."

Sophia's breath hitched.

Her mind swirled as Priscilla and Julia embraced lightly, as they said their goodbyes and departed arm in arm. Her thoughts churned as the people danced around her, peddling a hundred dreams and a thousand falsehoods. She remained in place as the words repeated again and again:

Your actions show your true self.

Kenneth had sentenced himself to life without love, afraid to risk his mother's fate. Yet had he truly been successful? What he hadn't said with words, he had shown in so many ways:

His fear when he pulled her from the river's clutches.

His delight when they laughed together.

His kindness as he taught her everything she asked.

The adoration he could never quite hide.

How did she truly feel? For once, she explored without hesitation or fear, recrimination or regret. Forbidden emotions burst forth, an explosion of color painting a gray world brilliant. Happiness and joy, delight and adoration, yet one emotion burned bright above them all:

Love.

She loved Kenneth. Had loved him for so very long. He was honorable and kind, considerate and noble, and he brought her joy as no one ever before. She relished their moments together, wanted nothing more than to remain by his side.

She wanted a lifetime.

She moved swiftly now, propelled by hope, sacrificing but a minute to glance at her chaperones. Her mother had returned the previous night and was busy catching up on a month's worth of gossip. Edmund and Priscilla were deep in conversation, regarding Julia no doubt. Kenneth wasn't visible, yet overheard conversations revealed he'd entered the garden. None of her family members noticed as she slipped through a narrow door, stepping into her future.

The moon cast long shadows on manicured paths, scented with the fruity aroma of Lady Rawling's orangery. Low conversation drifted from behind leafy barriers, natural hiding spots for secret lovers. She slipped past them, delving further and further into the lush grounds. Even as good sense urged her to retreat, she continued on the moist grass.

She stepped through the moonlit trail, amidst memories of another party a month and a lifetime ago. That garden may have been different, the night as well, and most certainly *her*, yet so much seemed the same as she traveled as far as she dared, and beyond.

The voices of the party faded into the background, as she neared the edge of the property with no sign of the duke. Unbidden disappointment traced through her, replaced quickly by determination. She would find him and demand an audience.

If necessary, she would kidnap him.

She pivoted, just as the line of carriages peeked out from behind a copse of trees. The coachmen were not on their perches, but grouped together in lively discussion, paying no attention to their vehicles. Slowly, she slunk towards the luxurious Foxworth carriage. As she neared, it rocked.

She smiled. Her instincts had been correct.

In seconds she reached the carriage. The door opened, and her smile froze.

"Good evening, my lady." The man's smile was chilling and cold, filled with unmistakable malice. Of course, the last time she'd seen him he was kidnapping Edmund.

She turned to flee...

Someone grabbed her.

KENNETH HAD BEEN wrong.

So very wrong.

Bradenton was not the monster he perceived. The evidence had seemed undeniable, the truth irrefutable, with his father's journal and the man of business' claims. Yet an elementary investigation revealed the associate had been stealing from his father for years, and had set up Bradenton to divert attention from his crimes. As for the journal, it was as much fiction as the romantic tales his sister read. He'd asked multiple people, and every single account differed from his father's renderings.

He hadn't been able to ascertain any additional information

about the duel, yet after all he'd learned, his father's account was clearly prejudiced. Tonight, he would ask Bradenton for an explanation.

Before he offered for Sophia.

He would try the traditional method one last time, armed not with anger and revenge, but logic and reason. For he now knew why he ignored the evidence, shunned further investigation. The kidnapping was never truly about Bradenton.

It was always about Sophia.

She'd ensnared him the moment she poked him in the chest, challenging a man twice her size to protect her brother. She captivated him as she defended those she loved, championing justice. She was intelligent and brave, caring and giving.

How he loved her.

When he finally shattered the wall guarding his heart, the emotions had been tremendous, breathtaking, all-encompassing. She was beautiful, not only on the outside, but on the inside as well. She was unconditional kindness, quiet grace, fierce cleverness, feminine strength – he loved all of her, with all that he was.

Tonight he would reveal the truth of his feelings. For the first time, he would share his true emotions, allow himself to be vulnerable. He would do it for no other.

For Sophia, he would do anything.

Hopefully Bradenton would accept his offer. More likely, he would attempt to run him through with his sword. Would he really blame him? After all, he had wronged Bradenton, not the other way around.

He would make it right, or at least he would try. And if it didn't work…

He could always kidnap her.

Before he revealed the truth, he had to destroy the danger that stalked him. It was why he roamed the garden, setting himself as bait for his would-be attackers. This time he would not be caught unaware.

He was also not alone. All night, someone had watched him. Adam's contacts, he presumed, who would take the criminals into custody.

Unfortunately his search had proved fruitless. He'd even traveled to the street, strode up and down the empty pathways, yet there was no sight of the tenacious criminals. He returned to the line of carriages, when he heard a noise next to his carriage.

His lips curved into a slow smile. It had to be the criminals, poised to ambush him. He touched the smooth handle of his gun as he stepped silently over a dip. He reached for the door.

He yanked it open, aimed his gun, yet only darkness and shadows greeted him, with no telltale breathing of hidden criminals. He stepped into the carriage.

The door slammed shut behind him.

He pivoted, but it was too late. He pushed and pulled, but the door was secured from the outside. He slammed his whole body against it...

The carriage sprang into motion.

Kenneth grabbed the seat to keep from falling. Fury came, yet not fear; undoubtedly Adam's friends would capture them within seconds. Yet as the seconds and then minutes passed, it became ever-increasingly clear he was on his own.

Time to fight back.

He evaluated his surroundings, the carriage he'd reinforced to avoid a break in, not knowing he would need to break out. His gaze caught on the window. It was too small to fit through. Unless...

He grasped the curved metal frame. With brute strength, he pushed the sharp edges, harder as a heavy creak sounded. The metal gave under his hands, twisting and turning, slicing into his palms. He sucked in a breath of humid air streaming through the now open window.

They were rolling through a darkened alley, a location bustling during the day, now quiet with darkness' ascension. The horses' hooves beat against the ground in a steady rhythm, with a more measured gait than before. They were slowing.

Time was up. Grasping the twisted metal frame, he pulled his upper body through the window. A single cloaked figure sat at the top, clutching the reins. The others were likely at their destination, which, by the ever-slowing pace of the carriage, was imminent.

He did not hesitate. Did not wait for the carriage to stop. He grabbed both sides of the window, pulled the rest of his body out...

And leapt.

He landed in the seat above, next to the villain who would dare kidnap a duke. A voluminous black cloak completely covered the rogue, a low slung hat hiding all facial features. Kenneth grasped the reins with one hand and his captor with the other. The man was far smaller than he first appeared, as he easily contained his struggles.

He stopped the horses and pivoted to the criminal. He swept back the hood.

The world tilted.

"Sophia?"

CHAPTER TWENTY-TWO

Journal of the Duke of Foxworth:

It is time...
To reveal the truth.
To bring everything into the light.
To retrieve what belongs to me.
It is time to claim my duchess, once and for all.

"YOU KIDNAPPED ME."

The words rumbled on the wind, filled with unmistakable power and unyielding authority. His expression was thunderous, this warrior who captured her. He wasn't letting go.

Yet she had her own power. "Yes, I did."

"I thought you were the criminal." His eyes blazed. "I could have hurt you."

Anger sizzled in his eyes, yet eclipsed by even stronger emotions: Apprehension. Agitation. Fear.

Something unreadable.

He pulled her close. Their chests brushed against each other, pure heat in the cool night. Overloaded senses cried out, shouting conflicting commands: *Move closer. Move back. Embrace. Flee.* She was paralyzed, yet it didn't matter. She couldn't escape.

"It almost sounds like you care," she whispered.

"Of course I care." He edged nearer, shrinking the ever-tightening seat. "From now on, you are my responsibility. I am kidnapping you."

Her breath hitched. "You can't kidnap me. I'm kidnapping

you."

"Not anymore."

She glared at him. "You will not steal my kidnapping again."

"How are you going to stop me?"

She pushed against him, yet it was like trying to move a wall of iron. Her throat dried like the summer desert. She was well and truly captured.

And a traitorous part of her didn't mind at all.

She took a deep breath of courage. Before she revealed the truth, she would explain what occurred. "You no longer need to worry about your father's business associates. I dealt with them."

Emerald eyes narrowed. "What do you mean you dealt with them?"

She shrugged breezily, yet in truth, she'd been scared half to death when Kenneth's "business associate" accosted her from behind, capturing her in his beefy arms. Her training had instinctively surfaced, and she'd kicked in just the right place with just the right amount of pressure.

He went down like a rock.

"One of the criminals attacked me. I dispatched him."

Kenneth stared.

"Unfortunately that was when his friends arrived. I screamed for help, at which point your friends arrived, or at least they appeared to be friends, which was to say they swiftly incapacitated the ruffians. They were disguised in all black, sort of like that mysterious man who saves people. They said the men would get lawful justice."

She left out a single detail. Someone had watched the men from the shadows, observing the scene with undisguised interest. No one noticed Lady Catherine, Lord Peyton's sister, hiding in the darkness, and she appeared ignorant of Sophia's scrutiny. Once the men left, she disappeared into the evening.

"Adam arranged for the assistance," Kenneth admitted. "I must have been searching the street when they arrived. I suspected they may show up today." His voice softened. "I'm sorry I wasn't there to protect you. I promise it will be the last time."

He gave her a speculative look. "You truly took down one of the ruffians?"

"Are you surprised?"

"I'm impressed." He shook his head. "Horrified, but impressed."

She grinned.

"Why did you kidnap me?" He rubbed her cheek with the pad of his finger. She closed her eyes at the feather-soft touch. "Or *attempt* to kidnap me?"

Her eyes snapped open. "I most certainly did kidnap you. I'm still kidnapping you." She bit her lower lip. "I wanted to talk."

"We have much to discuss," he agreed. "Although this is not what I planned for tonight."

She exhaled lowly. What *did* he have planned? "Have you truly schemed to kidnap me again?"

"That remains to be seen."

She gulped a breath of air scented with amber, bergamot and pure male power. Was he going to steal her?

Would he give her back this time?

He picked up her hat and reached for her. "We need to return to the ball."

The ball. She'd been so caught up with the kidnapping, she'd forgotten all about it. If Edmund realized she was missing again, he would tear London apart in a minute. "Before we return, I need to tell you something. I–"

"No." He held up his hand. "There's something I need to do first."

She shook her head. "Ken–"

He silenced her with a kiss.

Passion shattered reality, as she pressed against the man of her dreams, yielded to his unrelenting strength. She surrendered even as she demanded, kissing, caressing, seizing.

How she loved this man.

She could kiss him forever, lost in a world crafted only for them. Yet he pulled back far short of forever, even as desire surged anew. "I need to speak with your brother."

Unease tempered desire, with a dash of fear. "What could you possibly have to say to Edmund?"

He kissed the top of her head. "You shall have to wait to see." He said nothing more as he helped her off the seat and brought her to the door, which was still locked from the outside. She stared at the damaged frame, but didn't remark as he undid the latch and led her into the carriage.

"I suppose you aren't really kidnapping me then."

Would he detect the disappointment she couldn't quite hide?

"Don't worry, lass." He leaned down, his strength and power overwhelming in a second. "One way or another, you are mine."

His voice held all the certainty in the world.

THE PARTY WAS exactly as before. Revelers still twirled and spun, eating and laughing with carefree abandon. Countless candles still burned up above, as guests indulged in fresh meats and sweets, and most especially spirits.

Sophia padded stoically through the crush, her expression one to deter conversation, fierce enough it worked. She was completely and not at all alone, Kenneth so close, and yet so far. Despite what may happen, appearing together would invite questions she'd rather not answer. She could avoid all but a single person.

Edmund.

The expression on her normally unflappable brother's face revealed the truth within seconds. Agitation and apprehension before he saw her, stark relief when he did. When he looked behind her... pure fury.

There was no need to ask if he knew she left.

Or with whom.

He strode directly to her, clearly fighting for a neutral expression, as he grasped her arm. "We are leaving." Then he was walking towards the exit, with her firmly in hand.

She pushed back as hard as she dared on the ton's stage. "We cannot leave," she hissed.

"You do not have a choice." He moved another step, then another and another. "I made arrangements for Mother and Priscilla to return home separately."

Why did every man in her life steal her choices – and *her*? Already the whispers swirled around them, louder with every step. If he didn't stop, her reluctance would become clear for all the ton to see. "Unless you wish to carry me out of here, you will listen to what I have to say."

Kenneth strode closer to them. By the gleam in his eyes, he looked half a second away from seizing her himself.

She held her breath. Surely, Edmund wouldn't actually whisk her away. Although Priscilla once claimed...

"All right."

Relief loosened tight muscles, even as her brother grasped her firmer, continuing to lead. Yet he changed direction, heading for one of the private rooms instead of the exit. Heavy footsteps behind them proved Kenneth never left. Just like he'd promised.

They entered a gold and green room furnished with jacquard-covered chairs, emerald settees and oversized mahogany furniture. A crackling fireplace provided warmth and heat, its smoky scent mingling with the aroma of leather and wood.

She walked in side by side with her brother, then Edmund released her, stepping between her and Kenneth. Was he going to slam the door in the duke's face? That very intention blazed in his eyes, yet after a moment's hesitation, he held it open instead, unwavering as the duke strode through. He shut it in deliberate slowness, undoubtedly a performance for the riveted crowd, then travelled to the sideboard and poured two splashes of brandy into cut crystal glasses. He took a generous gulp of his own, and handed the other to Kenneth.

Her heart swelled with love for the big brother who, while not perfect, always *tried*.

Edmund's question was immediate. "Where were you?"

She bit her lip, took a deep breath. "I kidnapped him." She looked upward. "Actually, if you want the truth, I kidnapped him the first time, as well."

Edmund stared. "I don't know what he's done to confuse you, but *you* were kidnapped. I received the note."

"First I kidnapped him." She cringed at his stupefied expression. "Perhaps we could call it a mutual kidnapping."

"You don't understand the definition of kidnapping," Edmund growled, as he turned to Bradenton. "Do you deny your wrongdoing?"

"No." Kenneth stood tall. "I take responsibility for everything."

What?

Edmund opened his mouth. Hesitated. "You admit your culpability?"

Kenneth nodded firmly, as he stepped forward. All anger had vanished, the candlelight reflecting only earnestness, honesty and *guilt?* "In the past day I did what I should have done so long ago – investigated. My father wrote a work of fiction, disguised as a journal, implicating you in horrible crimes. He accused you of ruining him, destroying everything and anything he cared about."

Breathing deeply, he continued, "The last entry was about a duel, which appeared to lead to his murder. I corroborated my father's accounts with multiple people, and all countered my father's claims. In addition, I discovered the man of business who accused you was lying to cover his own thievery."

For a moment Edmund stayed silent, regarding the Scotsman. "The journal was not entirely incorrect. There was a duel."

With a gasp, Sophia gripped Kenneth's arm. Edmund tracked the movement, yet made no move to intercede.

"Explain," Kenneth said simply.

Edmund gazed upward, his eyes turning unfocused. "Your father thought I ruined his life, but in truth I merely stopped him from ruining others. He was always attempting one scheme or another, such as when he tried to swindle an elderly woman out of her home, or the time he chased a young debutante with dishonorable intentions. My only goal was protecting others." He turned back to Kenneth. "I never intended to fight him that day. I was going to shoot high and scare him. When he pointed the gun the wrong way, I tried to warn him..." His voice trailed off, as his eyes shuttered.

Sophia put a hand to her lips, as Foxworth stepped back, his face arrested in horror. "He shot himself."

Edmund gave a barely perceptible nod. "It was an accident. He'd been drinking all night. I should have known–" He shook his head. "I took him to the best doctor in London, but it was too late. The best I could do for your family was pretend it was natural causes, and make all the arrangements. I didn't want to cause further scandal." He drowned the rest of his glass, and set it on the table. "I truly am sorry."

Kenneth stood as still and straight as a mountain, his fists clenched, his back straight. He said nothing, as a million emotions sparked in his eyes.

She gently squeezed his arm. "I'm sorry," she whispered.

"You do not need to apologize." He turned to Edmund. "And neither do you. My father created his own troubles, and I..." He tightened. "I am to blame for yours. I should have investigated sooner, yet in the end, the kidnapping was never about revenge." He turned to her. "It was always about Sophia."

"About me? I don't understa–"

"I love you."

"What?" she breathed.

"What?" Edmund breathed.

I knew it all along, her heart breathed.

"I love Sophia." Even as he spoke to Edmund, his gaze never left hers. "When I offered marriage, I spoke of revenge, yet nothing could be further from the truth. It was an excuse – the kidnapping, my anger, everything. I lied about my motives, not just to you, but to myself." Raw honesty burned in his eyes. "I could have avenged my father a thousand ways. Yet I didn't, because of you."

He looked back to Edmund. "I'm sorry for the pain I caused, but I cannot regret my time with Sophia. You'd never allow me to court her, and I simply couldn't walk away. My greatest desire is to care for her, protect her." His voice deepened. "Love her."

She blinked, her vision blurring with liquid emotion. "You've always done that." She stepped closer to the man she adored, unable to stay away any longer. "With your patience, your kindness, your sacrifice. You taught me everything I wanted to learn, brought me endless joy and laughter. My goodness, you jumped into a raging river to save me."

"What?" Edmund gaped in horror.

"It was my fault," she admitted. "I never should have delved into danger, yet every time I did, Kenneth was there to save me."

"And I always will be." Now Kenneth turned to Edmund. "I am also a brother, and I understand the pain I caused. I wish I did this differently, but I cannot change the past. I can only apologize, and hope you will reconsider my offer."

He took her hands. They were so large, so strong, engulfing hers entirely. "I wish I had the words to tell you how much I love you. How I dream of you every night, think of you when you are not with me. I am overprotective because I cannot imagine my life without you. I want to spend every day bringing you happiness, every night making your dreams come true. I may have kidnapped you, but you stole my heart."

Her eyes flooded with joy. And there was only one thing left to say.

"I love you, too."

Kenneth's eyes widened. "You do?"

He hadn't known.

He was sharing his love, risking himself, and he hadn't even realized the truth of her feelings. "Of course I do. I haven't been able to get you out of my mind since you kidnapped me." She grinned wryly. "You're a good man, Kenneth. You do so much for people, without expecting anything in return. You may hide your feelings behind your strength, but I see the man you truly are." She beamed all the love in her heart. "I want to spend forever with you."

His eyes reflected pure happiness, as he brushed a kiss on her wrist. Her heart swelled.

Edmund stepped up to them, and a frisson of unease rose. Her brother cleared his throat. "I have one question for you, Foxworth. What will you do if I say no?"

She bit back a gasp as her future quivered. Was her brother going to deny her the love match she'd always wanted?

Not. In. This. Lifetime.

"I'll simply kidnap her."

She gasped, as she stared at the two men. Did Kenneth want Edmund to call for seconds this very night? Yet instead of demanding satisfaction, Edmund's expression was level, tranquil even. "You love her that much?"

The truth shone in Kenneth's eyes. "I do."

Edmund turned to her. "And this is what you want, Sophia?"

She stood up tall. "It is."

He regarded them a moment more. "Foxworth, you are not the only one who conducted an investigation. I know about your charitable projects and the upstanding way you deal with your tenets, your sister and those under your care. And although you erred, I understand your father's death changed your life. You took a responsibility you didn't want to serve others. Most importantly, I believe you truly love my sister."

"With my every breath." Kenneth squeezed her hand.

Edmund stood taller, straightened his cravat. "I cannot stand in the way of true love. As long as Sophia agrees, you have my blessing. And…" He held out my hand. "My friendship."

His eyes shining, Kenneth grasped Edmund's hand. Then he turned to her, and asked one simple question.

"Lady Sophia, will you do me the honor of becoming my wife?"

She held her fingers over her mouth, and nodded the only answer destiny would allow. "Yes."

He opened his arms, and she jumped into them. Perhaps it was a surrender, but her heart would be safe. Just as his was with her.

"It's time we settle this," she whispered. "We kidnapped each other."

"Precisely." His eyes shined. "Because I'm never letting you go."

And he never did.

EPILOGUE

The Private Diary of Sophia Hawkins, six months later

How to kidnap a duke:

1. *Send him to the carriage to retrieve something you supposedly forgot.*
2. *Lock him in said carriage.*
3. *Drive him to an undisclosed location.*
4. *Release him, yet keep him under your power.*
5. *Whisper in his ear…*

"HAS ANYONE TOLD you kidnapping is not polite?"

"That advice is not valid when it comes from you." Sophia tapped the bare chest of her *husband*. He gave a sharp intake of breath, then retaliated by raining kisses down her neck. She closed her eyes, exhaling ecstasy as she *almost* forgot why she'd kidnapped him.

He shifted, and the carriage rocked.

"Be careful," she breathed, gasping as his lips found a very interesting spot. She shifted to give him better access to more interesting spots. "What will people say if they discover us here?"

Here was the brand new Foxworth Carriage, grand and plush, for all the times she liked to kidnap him.

Of course, he kidnapped her just as much.

The kidnappings were numerous during a whirlwind six months that were the most enchanting of her life. She never imagined the splendor of a love match, the happiness, the pure joy. She had settled into Kenneth's townhome, where his family welcomed her with unconstrained kindness. Of course, they spent a good part of their time in Scotland, where she met an entirely new family that was just as beautiful, who loved Kenneth deeply, and her by extension. They also returned to the small town, where they watched Molly marry her love. Even Julia was flourishing, back with her family in the country after Edmund had gotten her out of the ill-fated betrothal.

Kenneth had accepted *all* of her. He had not been exactly pleased when she told him about the *Distinguished Ladies of Purpose*, and he was most assuredly displeased when she shared the risks she took on its behalf. Yet he supported the cause, and helped her set up a school to teach women defensive maneuvers. He even helped with instruction.

Indeed life was grand. Yet it was about to get grander, if a little more untamed...

"They'll say the Untamed Duchess is at it again." Kenneth brushed his lips against her ear. "They'll say she has bewitched her husband." He kissed her forehead. "What is it that you have to tell me, Your Grace?" He gave a soft kiss upon her cheek.

"Indeed, Your Grace..." She leaned closer. "I wanted you to know..." Closer still. "The Untamed Duke is to be a father."

She had never seen a man smile so wide.

Now that was a love match.

Author's Note

Enjoy the other books in the series The Secret Crusaders:
Priscilla and Edmund tangle in Escaping the Duke.
http://bit.ly/EscapingTheDuke
Emma and Philip chase their love in Captured by the Earl.

Thank you for reading The Untamed Duke. I hope you enjoyed it as much as I loved writing it. For exclusive news, giveaways and surprises, subscribe to my newsletter at www.MelanieRoseClarke.com.

The Secret Crusaders: Melanie Rose Clarke's Romance Readers is my Facebook group for everything romance. Join at facebook.com/groups/1159564541120841.

I love connecting with readers on social media. You can find me at:
Bookbub – bookbub.com/profile/melanie-rose-clarke
Facebook – facebook.com/MelanieRoseClarke
Twitter – twitter.com/MelanieS_Clarke
Instagram – instagram.com/melanieroseclarke

And a special thank you to my agent and *friend*, Nicole Resciniti.

Best wishes always, Melanie Rose Clarke

About the Author

Melanie Rose Clarke has wanted to be a writer since she was a little girl. Sixteen years ago, she married her own hero, and now she creates compelling stories with strong heroines, powerful males and, of course, happily every afters. She writes historical (regency) romance, contemporary romance, paranormal romance, romantic suspense and women's fiction.

Melanie is a three-time Golden Heart® finalist. Her manuscripts have earned numerous awards in writing competitions, including several first place showings. With over two decades of professional writing experience, Melanie has written thousands of pieces for businesses and individual clients. She has worked in advertising and marketing, and her freelance articles on the web have garnered hundreds of thousands of views.

She writes amidst her five beautiful children, her dream come true. Besides writing, she loves to read, exercise and spend time outdoors. She is a member of Mensa.

I love to connect with readers! For exclusive news and goodies, sign up for my newsletter at www.MelanieRoseClarke.com.

You can also find me on social media:
Facebook – facebook.com/MelanieRoseClarke
Twitter – twitter.com/MelanieS_Clarke
Bookbub – bookbub.com/profile/melanie-rose-clarke
Instagram – instagram.com/melanieroseclarke